Praise for *Down]*

"Satire works best when it's funny, and
I also think it's the best New Zealand
it ought to be a best-seller, bought in droves. This is a book anyone can
read and take pleasure in recognising codes of conduct in 2022.... *Down
from Upland* touches that sweet spot between literary fiction (intellectually
satisfying) and commercial fiction (a page-turner)." *Newsroom*

"Just as the content of the novel revolves around maturity, how teenagers
seek it and Millennial parents shirk it, Down from Upland feels like a
confident stride towards a new, fully-fledged form for Murdoch Stephens."
Landfall Review

"*Down from Upland* is a wonderful satirical tale of modern life set in a
modern-day Wellington; the book is biting in places, often wryly funny
with many layers of meaning woven in." *Wellington City Libraries*

"Wellington's fictional middle classes are at it again. What an entertaining
bunch they are" *North & South*

"*Down from Upland* asks us to reconsider our moderation and our
monogamy - and it asks this with a wry and sardonic wit" *NZ Listener*

Praise for *Rat King Landlord*

"Stephens takes us on a thrilling, surreal, often hilarious ride through
a series of staccato chapters each snowballing into the next as mayhem
descends upon (or is it rises up from?) the capital, culminating in a heart-
thudding climax." *Newsroom*

"Last year's surprise literary hit." *Stuff*

"*Rat King Landlord* is written for us, the undergraduate renter. The
conditions and possibilities of full land ownership reform are only one rat
sentience away." *The Spinoff*

"I find your rat sympathetic." Elizabeth Knox

```
        U
        P
        L       U
        A       P
DOWN    N       L       U
        DOWN    A       P
                N       L       U
                DOWN    A       P
                        N       L
                        DOWN    A
                                N
                                D
```

Lawrence & Gibson Publishing Collective
www.lawrenceandgibson.co.nz

Down from Upland
First edition published in Aotearoa/New Zealand by
Lawrence & Gibson.
Copyright © Murdoch Stephens, 2022

Printed and bound at Rebel Press, Trades Hall, Te Aro, Wellington

Down from Upland / Murdoch Stephens
ISBN 978-0-473-61731-8

Cover image: Alan Ibell
Cover and page design: Lawrence & Gibson
Design consultant: Paul Neason
Copy editor: Johanna Knox

Published with the assistance of a grant from

This is a work of fiction. Any resemblance to actual persons, living or dead, or actual events is purely coincidental.

Printed on ECO100 115gsm
Bound with Technomelt 3635

```
U
P
L
A        U
DOWN     P
         L       U
         A       P
         DOWN    L       U
                 A       P
                 DOWN    L
                         A
                         N
                         D
```

a novel

FROM

Murdoch Stephens

"Nympha pudica Deum vidit, et erubuit.
(the conscious water saw its Lord and blushed.)"
- Richard Crashaw
Epigrammaticum Sacrorum Liber (1634)

PART 1

The Best Night of His Life

"Beer?" asked Pete.

"No question," said Axle as he entered Pete's home and stowed his jacket in the foyer. He could hear the beginnings of the party through the hall, but it was small enough that it hadn't spilled out to every nook of the house.

Pete passed a can to Axle. "Mum says I should only have cans. They're more environmental than bottles cos they're lighter. I like bottles, myself. Glass has a better feel. Girls are on the vodka, though... you could have one if you prefer? There's two full bottles in the freezer. We'll do shots in a bit. Anyway, let me show you around."

Axle had never drunk alcohol at a party before. He'd never been to a proper party. He'd had a bottle of beer with his parents on his fifteenth birthday, but never at a party.

He'd assumed the guys from his previous school liked to get drunk. They'd boasted about it enough, but he'd never been part of it. He also knew that every high school had its cautionary tale of one kid who passed out – images of their comatose limbs beside puddles of puke shared around the school. The video, made all the more grotesque by the bolt of flash photography and snickering commentary, would worm its way across the school, then to the principal and parents. Hardly fair that the drunk kid gets the punishment rather than the Judas who shares the footage. But, Axle surmised, that's the guts of high school.

It was Axle's first time seeing these people out of school since moving to Wellington High from Wellington College. It doesn't sound like much, but the difference between the schools was extreme. It wasn't only that one school was co-ed and the other was all boys. It was much more.

It had only been two days ago that Pete had messaged Axle the invitation. He'd underplayed the whole thing.

Small party at mine Friday night
No big deal, a few friends. Keen?

The boys had met in English and hung out over successive lunchtimes. What had brought them together? It wasn't a love of sport, music or cars. Simply an ease. Pete had other friends, but irrespective of that, they'd recognised something as yet unspoken in each other.

Some parties are too big. These are the ones that make the news. All the right people are at these parties, but they're soon overrun by goons. Bugs attracted to the light. People bulge into backyards and onto the street. Then the police show up and, if you're unlucky, someone's been recording and this becomes a night your parents will never let you forget. The news doesn't even ask permission to share the recording; they just put it on their page and make money out of some kid's misery.

Other parties are too small. Only half your friends are there, and they aren't enough. Axle had been to a couple of these hang outs at Col. New guests turn up and you can see them thinking about what else they could be doing. Everyone wonders if an actual party is happening somewhere else. People stay out of loyalty.

Pete's party was just right, Axle thought. Everyone felt lucky to be there and knew it was the place to be on this Friday night.

"Parents away?" Axle asked.

"Yeah, no shit bro," Pete laughed.

Axle flinched, then forced a smile.

"I mean, yeah. No shit, right?" said Axle.

"Martinborough or Marlborough. Some place with lots of red wine."

Axle knew what Pete meant. His own parents went for trips out of the city too, or they used to, staying in a hotel for a couple of nights to get away from it all. He didn't ask or even wonder why. None of the kids did. The answers would be gross or boring and maybe not even true.

Axle had first thought that Pete's "party" might be like one of those lame hang out nights at Col. No alcohol, no girls, and rugby – or, worse, Premier League replays on the wide screen. Parents in some back room and half the guys itching to get home to play computer games instead of more boring talk with people who weren't even proper friends.

Pete gestured to other doors, behind which were amenities that Axle may need. Toilet here, backyard there.

Everywhere Axle looked were the people he'd seen at school who he wanted to talk to. The promised bottle of vodka was half full on a coffee table surrounded by five cross-legged girls. A deck of cards was strewn across the table, but the game seemed to have been abandoned. People he recognised gave him half-smiles and he nodded in response. Year Eleven had begun three weeks before, but the mood of summer held.

"You guys met Axle?" Pete asked. "He started at High this year. Yep? Axle this is Bex, Tanasi, Beth, Rata and... Michella?"

"If you don't know..." Michella said, "you could ask. Anyway, we're girls, not guys."

"Uh, yeah... I was asking? And yeah, whatever, sorry?" Pete said.

"Well, nice to meet you Axle. I think we're in English together. I am Michella, so your friend was right. It's fine. But, you know, it never hurts to ask. It's polite, even."

"Yeah, right. Got it." Pete shook his head and pulled Axle back to the kitchen. Michella laughed after them. It was a mocking laugh, but also a friendly one. If it had been in public, it would have been cruel, but in the heart of Pete's home it was balanced enough.

Pete slid into a group with Jarvis and Keevan. Axle followed in his slipstream. He recognised them from Statistics, but the introduction from Pete was the endorsement he needed to speak with them as equals. They listed off the people yet to come to the party and guessed as to how long the alcohol would hold. There was some animosity about someone's cousin visiting from Auckland called Sylvester who'd been a bit forward with the girls. Keevan asked after Reggie. Axle had heard of this classmate but couldn't put a face to the name. He had a family thing on, according to Pete. Jarvis was dubious.

Axle studied the group, keeping his mouth shut except for an 'aww' and 'nah, really?' when required. He didn't know much about Keevan, but had heard that Jarvis's family was loaded and his father was tied up in politics. Apparently, Jarvis's dad donated at least five figures to all the local politicians, not just those he agreed with, and was on a few boards. Everyone knew this – it was the first thing people brought up when they learned Jarvis' last name. Still, they spoke of it in whispers, as if they feared being caught up in gossip.

Axle imagined that having a notorious dad was the reason Jarvis was a bit quiet and a bit hurt seeming. He was the kind of kid who looked like he could, and probably would piss away half his life, but still land on his feet. It didn't make Axle at all envious. He would make his own way. He was looking forward to it.

"Your mum's a cop, eh? She going to come round and break up the party?" Jarvis asked, turning to Axle.

Axle felt a rush of shame and turned his eyes to the floor. "Nah, man. My mum's not a cop. She works at the police national headquarters. Boring shit. Admin. Non-commissioned."

Axle risked a glance at Jarvis who met his eye. Like, he thought, what would one cop matter compared to the people like Jarvis's dad who ran things behind the scenes?

"Anyway, fair's fair," Pete said, "we're not responsible for the stupid things our parents do. That's them and their generation. I wouldn't want someone giving me shit for whatever silly things my parents get up to. We're different. Right?"

Pete raised his beer to toast. Axle drank his back, setting the can on the kitchen bench. He guessed that it was Pete who'd told Jarvis about his mum working for the Police. It all evened out, anyway, because Pete had made the toast and defended him. Axle rinsed a glass from the kitchen bench and filled it with ice.

Dropping into a break in their conversation, he pointed to the lounge, and asked "mind if I go get some vodka?"

Pete grinned, said nothing, but nodded. All were aware of the split at the party. The boys didn't want to only be with the boys, and the girls didn't want to only be with the girls. But that was how the night had started. They all knew it would change, but someone had to make the first move.

Michella saw Axle coming. She shuffled to one side, offering a spot between herself and Beth. Axle sat, copying their cross-legged pose. He placed his glass of ice on the coffee table but as he reached for the bottle, Beth pounced on it. He pulled back. She tilted it in his direction and he nodded. She poured and kept pouring until the vodka was near to the rim.

"You didn't say stop," said Beth.

He hadn't known he had to say stop.

The five young women were looking at him, waiting. He felt the burn of their attention and the enmity of a few of the guys who wished they had his place. There were thirty, maybe forty, people at the party. Axle was not about to do anything stupid. Stupid would have been bravado – showing off by drinking deeply. He offered a little performance instead. He drew in a breath, then took a little sip, tasting the vodka, running it over his lips and around his mouth before placing the glass back on the table. He offered no words, just a little shrug and a nod. The party ambled into new diversions.

Axle settled into his place with the girls, these young women. He answered any questions politely but treated the moment like life in a foreign country where his words might not be easily understood. He memorised a name when one was mentioned and made sure to make eye contact but then immediately drop it. Be friendly, not creepy. Agreeable, not overwrought. He wasn't following a script so much as avoiding one. He'd seen how poorly the guys at Col had behaved around women and he was determined to not be like them.

Axle had no sisters (or brothers) and hadn't spent much time with young women. He'd made friends with girls in primary school. But when the confusion of intermediate struck, he retreated to the safety of boys. When he was fourteen, his father had an emphatic conversation with him about women. Sometimes the ambition of his dad's talks reminded him of a video he'd seen of a pelican trying to eat a pigeon – or one called '15ft Snake Eats Whole Cow'.

The most recent talk had been in keeping with his father's instructive spirit, but it had also been twice as serious as any of the others. It had been full of 'not-that-nor-that-but-this' style advice. Find the middle road, his father insisted. The middle ground. Communicate it. The middle way.

The heaviness of that talk contrasted with his mother's offhand advice before he'd left for the party: "Those young women are no different from you, so just have fun!"

They *were* different from him, though. These young-girl-woman things. They were different and that wasn't even accounting for the ones like Tanasi.

He'd memorised her name in the first Chemistry class of the year. He knew exactly how to say it. Ten-ahsi, emphasis on the Ten, which was her nickname. Sometimes – late at night, alone on a street – he whispered it to himself. Their Chemistry teacher was an American and called her Ta-*nah*-see, saying it like 'tenacious'. Tanasi appeared to be okay with it. She sat front left; Axle back centre. They weren't assigned places, but they went back to the same ones each week. He liked having her in his periphery.

Axle had become comfortable in the cross-legged group when he recalled his father's other piece of advice: "Don't stare and don't hide, but be interested." So, Axle did look at the young women a couple of times. And when he looked at Tanasi, she looked back at him. And when she looked back at him a second time, he felt all of his body looking back at her. The hairs on the back of his neck tingled, his skin prickled red, even his toes curled in their shoes.

When she caught him looking a third time, it was over. He stood, grabbed his glass and announced that he needed ice. As he had stood back, Sylvester nabbed his space. Axle pulled himself to the kitchen. He wanted to look back to see if Tanasi was watching him, but he had enough self-control, or vanquished pride, to keep walking.

In the kitchen, Keevan had pulled a bottle of vodka from the freezer and was pouring shots. Axle could have used the icy glass against his cheeks. Jarvis shuffled aside to make space for him. Two new boys stood with them, but the party was well past the time for formal introductions. One of these other boys spoke with admiration for Axle dropping in on the girls. They toasted his courage and drilled him with questions – "can't imagine being at Col with all boys, what's it like?"

The icy vodka went down with a grimace, then a whoop.

Pete strode out the back door for a piss. When he returned, he absolutely insisted everyone had to go out back, too. The moon was the biggest and brightest he'd ever seen.

The night was warm and still and the moon was truly full, or near enough. It was cicada season, but there were no mosquitoes and only a few fluttering moths. The boys talked about the speech competition they had to do for English next week, and the hot teacher's aide who was taking them for Phys Ed. Keevan drew Axle on why he'd left Col and what it was like there. Pete asked whether he knew his friend, Mark, from Te Aro Primary and whether he gets called Ax or Axe Man.

"Dad calls me Ax."

"So, which is better? What do you prefer?" Keevan asked.

Pete cracked open the second bottle of vodka from the freezer and poured more shots. By the time it got to Axle, the bottle was half empty.

The night rushed on. Some of the boys floated inside, then were drawn back to the night air. Boys and girls, young men and women, mixed and talked, all exaggeration and superlatives. Some kissed. Others sat, thigh against thigh. Minds reeled and leaped, from the liquor and from their free reign over the summer night.

Axle found himself nestled in the long grass on a steep bank that the family lawnmower had left alone. Pete was beside him pointing out constellations – some Axle had heard of before, others he was sure the party host had invented. Keevan called bullshit and then the harbour lit up with fireworks. No-one could say why, but that didn't lessen them. Michella guessed it was Chinese New Year, but Tanasi said that was two weeks before.

A new bottle of vodka, not one from Pete's provisions, circled from hand to hand, lip to lip. Jarvis howled at the moon, took his shirt off and swung it round his head. When he slipped and fell, Michella and Pete pinned him down and Rata tickled his ribs. He squealed, squirmed and gasped for air while fighting free.

More spirits were drunk and glorious chaos bubbled through. Someone puked in the bathroom sink, glasses were broken, and a couple from another school were ejected from under the duvet in Pete's parents' bedroom. The party ran on and then – at one point – levelled out and stayed even for hours. Finally, a tranche of guests left, sparking others to check the time and follow. The evening would come to an end.

Pete, Keevan and Axle began the clean-up. The biggest problem was what to do with all the empties. A dozen cans were put into the recycling. Pete's parents knew he'd have a couple of friends over so if there was no evidence of alcohol, they might be suspicious. The rest of the empty cans and bottles were boxed up and sent off with the last of the guests. Their job was to slink the bottles into bins, preferably for recycling, that they might find along the way. Pete kept the empty vodka bottles as mementos for his room, rinsing them, scrawling the date on them with a vivid and placing them on a ledge along with a few others.

Axle stumbled home. He was drunk and felt great. He couldn't pinpoint why he felt so fantastic. He hadn't spoken to Tanasi and he hadn't learned any great truth. Nevertheless, he felt the immensity of the evening on his skin, a zing and prickle. Like a sunburn but pleasant. It was as if he wore a coat of electricity, some invisible material hovering above his pores and delighting him as he went. He rubbed his forearm and revelled in the wattage. Everything was excellent – so excellent and so amazing – and it would always be that way.

Unpleasant

He puked once, first thing in the morning. Well, he puked four times, across one convulsing session. By the final heave, he knew that was that, but he still knelt at the toilet, holding a damp flannel over his forehead and eyes. At least the porcelain was cold, he thought. There was nothing left of last night's dinner or the snacks from Pete's place. They were just a rotten slosh somewhere in the pipes that led away from his parents' house.

Acid coated his throat, while he fished out a few loose chunks away from his gums and spat them into the toilet bowl. He was in control again, but not exactly fit to be. He wanted to gargle some water, but he lacked the confidence to leave the cool tiles beside the toilet. Another minute. He rested, kneeling still, but using the bathroom wall as a support. He closed his eyes, rested, then jolted upright. He may have fallen asleep but, also, he may not have. He did feel better. Should he wait another minute? No. Now or never.

He was well enough to lie down again if he could make it back to his bed. Sleep would solve his problems. He stood. He took it slowly, gripping a towel rail while letting his guts adjust. He wondered if Pete was feeling this bad. He tried picturing Tanasi in similar anguish, hiding in her bed. He allowed himself a smile as he considered his reflection in the mirror. His skin looked almost green, but maybe that was his mind playing tricks. He rinsed his mouth, gargling cold water, and spat it through his teeth, before cooling a flannel, folding it twice, and nursing his brow.

Axle slipped back into bed. His sheets were a sweaty tangle. He kicked them away and pulled the duvet close. His head thumped and his guts lurched. He closed his eyes, willing his stomach to settle. He remembered the electric glow from the night before. He had been too deep in sleep, then low with sick, to notice that waning of euphoria. Now all he wanted was peace and darkness.

Creeping across his room was a sharp strip of light from where the curtains didn't quite meet. The light meant him no harm, he knew that, but why wouldn't it soften or leave him be? He shook his head to free it from these useless thoughts, but the harsh strip of light wouldn't leave him alone. He knew that he was being ridiculous for letting the light get to him. His brain had become hostage, complicit even – an outright traitor – to this feeling. He flipped over and groaned into his pillow.

"I am never drinking again," he promised himself, then added, aloud, "if you can make this go away, I'm never drinking again."

He was not coherent enough to register that his earnest promise of future sobriety was a tender cliché, and that his urge to lie down and pass out ought to be preceded with a glass of water.

The Listening

Listening from the kitchen, Axle's parents knew exactly what was happening to their son.

"Our boy's first proper hangover," said Jacqui, while Scott busied himself with grinding coffee and prepping the espresso machine.

"Not quite as monumental as his first steps or first day of school," Scott replied, then paused as the milk frother foamed.

"You'd think with what we paid for that machine it might be quieter," said Jacqui.

"I know," said Scott without needing to note Jacqui had chosen the model. "Still, it's an important coming of age moment for Ax. Let's mark the occasion."

"Take a picture," Jacqui suggested. "Send an email to the whole family?"

The espresso machine gurgled, then went silent. Scott passed Jacqui her cup. He thought that the machine could use a deep clean. He'd do that later in the day, Sunday at a stretch.

The day was sunny and seemed still, so they would drink their coffee on the deck. The perfect start to a Saturday, the whole weekend ahead. A strong northerly had morphed into a light southerly but the deck would be sheltered. They made their way through the kitchen, past the pantry and out the door to the wooden bench in the sun.

Scott dreamed that if he were ever to be sent to war or jail – though he was too old and sensible for either – he'd pass the long hours by touring through the family house in his head. He liked the idea that he was endowed with an uncommon ability to perceive and meditate on detail. He imagined enemies trying to break him with months in solitary confinement and his triumphant emergence, bearded but unphased. With that slim possibility in mind, he trained himself. He paid special attention to the feelings of moving through the house. He absorbed the sound of each door, revelling in the tension of their handles guiding the bolt back and over the strike plate then into the latch. He truly appreciated a door gauged to perfection.

All in all, the home had done a solid job of protecting his family as they grew. That growing up was almost over. Axle would be off to university in a couple of years and they would have to think about changes. For now, though, all was well and even.

"Did you catch the reek of vodka?" Scott asked as Jacqui sat on deck.

"I did! I thought Axle had spilled glass cleaner for a moment. Like he'd tried to clean the windows at 3am or something!"

"Wine is a mocker. Strong drink a brawler," said Scott.

"Where's that saying from?"

"Church-guy-at-work says it. He's always wanting to make subtle references to Bible sayings in our comms. Might not be a bad idea, to be honest."

"I haven't had a night on vodka since Sydney," Jacqui said, shaking the thought of it from her head. "Maybe we should talk to him about drinking and moderation? I mean, again. Hey, but I thought teenagers didn't drink anymore? What's wrong with our one?"

"That's what the studies say," said Scott, dropping into the way he spoke at work. "The evidence is broad, across many countries, pretty much irrefutable. Here, too. People argue why – health, shame, social media, money, education – you know? But none argue the fact that there's been a generational decline."

"There's always the outliers," said Jacqui.

"There's always those."

They sat in contemplation. It was a pleasant morning. A kererū swooped down the valley. Scott could hear a bus, far below and out of sight. The roar of the engine mellowed as it changed gears for the hair pin corner of Glenmore St. He considered his mug and realised that he'd finished his coffee without savouring it. Perhaps it was time for breakfast.

"A talk on moderation, then?" asked Jacqui.

"Yeah, nothing serious," said Scott. "More of a heart to heart. Or less than that, really. More like—"

"Just a talk," said Jacqui, firmly. She sensed Scott was winding up for one of his long spiels on parenting techniques. She couldn't be bothered with it. She just wanted to enjoy the morning sun. Perhaps an English Muffin.

Scott hesitated and Jacqui wondered if she had been too aloof. Heck, she thought, maybe another of Scott's talks *would* help Axle in the long run. Who knew what worked and in what quantities when it came to young men? She was sceptical about claims made in the name of neuroscience, but she'd heard enough about the perils of drugs and alcohol for those under twenty that she thought there might be some hard evidence to back up the scare stories. The one thing she was sure of was that Scott would take it on himself to arrange the talk, and that he'd likely already strategised how to go about it in his head.

"That's what I was thinking. A talk. Probably best to start out by —"

"How about you do it on Sunday night when I'm out with Kaye? Or we could do it as a check-in before that parent-teacher meeting, midweek?"

"Yeah, I was thinking Sunday might be the best approach. Let's keep it separate from anything to do with school. Low key and casual. As if you and I never talked it through. Start it as something natural. Something that just comes up."

Sunday

On Sunday, around 9am, Axle rose from his bed. An acrid smell reminded him of his sweaty, disturbed Saturday. He made a mental note to swap out his pillowcase and sheets. He shook his head, ran a hand through his hair and assessed. He didn't feel a thing. Perfect! The hangover had become a bad memory. His parents had already left for their coffee-and-bagel walk. He wasn't sure if that *was* what they ordered, and he didn't care, but that's what they called it. He was more interested in if they'd bring back something sweet – maybe a pastry dusted with powdered sugar – or whether they'd punish his drinking by withholding the treat. His parents may not have realised how messed up he'd gotten. There hadn't been much talk over lunch or dinner and he'd spent the rest of the day in his room.

    He wrenched his curtains open and greeted the morning, then he unplugged his phone, strode to the lounge, lay on the couch and scrolled through accumulated notifications. He'd registered Saturday's messages but had been in no state to reply, even to Pete and Jarvis, who'd checked in on him, or, more accurately, enthused about how awesome the night had been.

    He scrolled to his photos and saw he'd taken video of the fireworks and of a group posing with the vodka bottles. He'd be dead if his dad saw these, but Tanasi was in them so he decided he'd keep them. Despite Saturday being lost to his hangover, he felt a splendid satisfaction. Pete. Jarvis and Keevan. Tanasi. When he thought of them, a little of Friday night's electric glow returned.

    He replayed the highlights in his head: arriving, sitting opposite Tanasi, fleeing the lounge and venturing into the backyard. A light wind had chilled them at one point, but Pete had wheeled out the two massive gas heaters that his dad had got at a closing down sale. They'd stood under them as the heat radiated down. His memory juddered a little at this point. He knew the boys had lain in the grass and listened to the night and laughed. Had Tanasi and Beth joined them? They'd gone back to the heaters and then, after a couple of hours in the group, he'd gone inside and the party was still perfect. He remembered being inside where there was a small table of people playing never-have-I-ever and sinking shots of beer. More vodka from the freezer. A third bottle or a fourth? No parents had turned up. No cops. No-one who didn't belong. And best of all, no-one blinked at the new kid. He remembered the end, the cleaning up and the euphoric feeling as he'd started his walk home.

    Axle tuned back to the silence of his parents' house. He imagined hosting a small party of these new friends. He could, he thought. Maybe. His parents wouldn't let it be like Pete's. Twenty people at most – they would make sure of it, somehow. They'd not trust him to host it alone. They would linger downstairs, not understanding how their presence could still be felt even if they weren't in the same room.

    He opened the fridge and swigged from a bottle of orange juice. His mum insisted on using a glass, but he didn't think much of the rule so ignored it when she wasn't around. He savoured the emptiness of the house and the pulp across his tongue. But, while he liked being alone, he realised that he also liked being with people. The sweet with the acidic. He wasn't a loner as he had imagined at Col. He corrected himself: he liked being with the right people.

    The latch on the front gate clicked and he dashed back to his room. He wasn't ready for a conversation with his parents.

    He heard their feet across the entranceway and then their kitchen conversation. He couldn't hear exactly what was being said, but he understood the implication. His father imploring and his mother asserting. His father spoke more, but his mother spoke with greater certainty. Sometimes he wondered why they were even together. He heard footsteps coming to his door, a faint knock then his father's voice: "little treat for you out here, Ax. In your own time."

Axle listened for the steps away from the door. There they went. And then, "Oh and I'm cooking tonight – let's have a wee chat. A catch up, I mean. Nothing serious. Hope you're feeling better today."

Kaye's house

Kaye and Robert lived on the top of the hill – views of Mākara peak and the harbour – while Jacqui and Scott were slightly down from Upland Road. Both homes got good midday sun, but the one that was down from Upland didn't enjoy sunrises and sunsets like Kaye's. On a map, the two homes might not look very far apart, but Kelburn was draped over a series of ridges and valleys. Walking required intimate knowledge of secret stairways and hidden paths. Driving required knowledge beyond the bird's eye view of maps.

Jacqui and Kaye had met in Sydney almost twenty years before, at the café where Jacqui worked. Before Sydney, Jacqui had bounced around the country. She had grown up in a succession of small North Island towns and spent the second half of her high school years in Matamata. She'd moved to Wellington at seventeen, enrolled and then dropped out of university, before enduring a year-long tourism diploma at polytech and a year working as a travel agent. She still knew how to get a good deal on flights and accommodation, but the family hadn't travelled internationally since a rather dull excursion to the Gold Coast in 2012.

Kaye was a year older than Jacqui. She'd grown up in Khandallah, then completed an art history and international relations double degree at Vic but wanted some fun before her career took over. Perhaps, if Jacqui hadn't dropped out of her own degree, the two would have been friends before they met in Australia.

Leaving Wellington for Sydney offered them both the illusion of decisiveness and a clean break from the people who claimed to be their friends. Both had, independently, suspected that their inability to find a tight-knit friend group reflected more on their own shortcomings than those of the people they had known.

Across the café counter, where Jacqui was serving short blacks to already-frazzled office workers, they recognised these shared tendencies and their mutual unmooring. They'd never talked, not at the start nor since, about that. But their twelve months in Sydney passed in tandem and the friendship had endured, even though they saw each other only once every six months.

Jacqui had already known Scott when she'd moved to Sydney but had explicitly avoided any obligations to him. Kaye had known Robert too, but he'd been in Central America doing environmental engineering for an NGO. At least that is what Robert said he'd been doing, but Kaye knew he was prone to exaggeration. Both women had been as free as they would ever be, and this surplus spawned an expansive attitude towards one another. And yet, the undefinable thing that they recognised in each other kept their tether strong by combining respect and fascination. Robert had once called this shared aspect "a mercenary independence". He was being mean, Jacqui had thought, and she initially rejected the idea. But then, she had conceded, even the most mercenary must corral loyalties.

"Jacqui! Great to catch you before we're off," Robert said as he greeted her at the door. "I hope you'll pop over for a visit once we're settled in. The embassy apartments usually have a spare room so... if you and Scott, or you alone, were to pass through then you have to stop by. Lots of planes are routed through Istanbul these days and I could possibly even meet you there. Chaperone you back to Ankara. Take a few days. Take a week."

Ankara! Jacqui had a sense of how cosmopolitan Turkey could be from how people talked about Istanbul, but she imagined Ankara to be somewhat drearier. Like Canberra, but with better food and sweet black tea on tap. Her only real knowledge of Turkey came from an ANZAC appreciation of valour at Gallipoli and her assumptions about the staff, who may or may not have been Turkish, at the Straits of Bosporus kebab shop on Molesworth Street.

Robert lent in for a hug. He always smelled so good, she thought – much better than her husband. Scott had such a neutral odour, smelling of laundry or nothing at all. Despite his smell, Jacqui had never been much attracted to Robert, and she sensed the disinterest was mutual. Maybe she would have tried to charm him if he'd been a Robbie or a Bert.

More small talk followed as Robert led her through the entrance, past the vestibule, through the house and to the top of the stairs, where they paused. She tuned him out as she took in the view. The house faced east to the harbour and hills beyond. She wasn't a tramper, but when she saw that landscape all she could think of was what it would be like to traipse over them.

Jacqui turned back to Robert, who was deep into an explanation of the lira crisis, the opportunities it afforded New Zealand businesses and the risks that could arise. His was the easy patter of diplomatic circles. She wondered if the Ministry of Foreign Affairs held night classes on elocution and comportment. Over the years, she'd learned to ignore the content of what he said, but to appreciate the way he said it. Stock standard affability. Luxurious at best, systematic at worst. And she never sensed that he was flirting with her. She found his type to be utterly bland, despite their good looks and grooming. The easy abyss of those personalities made her glad to have settled with Scott. Her husband might have been overly anxious, but at least he was human.

Robert had stopped talking. He gestured for her to leave him. Jacqui had paused, too, and wasn't sure if that was mirroring her host's behaviour or because she had some well wishes she wanted to add. It felt to her as if the stairway was a threshold between his part of the house and Kaye's. She wondered if they slept in different rooms.

She gripped the wooden rail, enjoying the way the curve felt in her hand and made her way down to where Kaye was waiting.

It was remarkable how typical the house looked from the outside, while the inside was so much more carefully laid out than your normal three-bedroom villa. There were rugs lining the polished floors, vases on plinths and paintings of stormy landscapes. Jacqui wondered if she and Scott could redecorate like this once Axle left for university. Well, she thought, like this but without the vases.

Jacqui knocked on the door where she expected Kaye would be holed up, heard a muffled, "Ah. yes?" and entered.

"Jacqui! Shut the door if you would," Kaye said by way of a greeting. "Confidentiality will be required."

"Congratulations on the move! Ankara! It's all come around so fast."

She used to hate how their speech mimicked courtesans of yore, and how they always fell into the safety of a knowing irony. She'd grown to accept that it was just how they spoke to one another. Still, she was unsure whether the speech was an affectation for Kaye or if she was even aware they were performing a caricature.

"Look at this guy," Kaye said, passing her phone to Jacqui and pouring her friend a glass of wine. The screen showed a young man, topless, clambering up a cliff in a forest that was probably in New Zealand. She couldn't see his face, only clumps of muscle running from his arms and across his back. He was fully stretched, everything in him reaching up and out to an unlikely crag. Jacqui was impressed but sensed she was missing something.

"And? I mean, he's an athlete, but... what? You took this photo?" Jacqui guessed.

"I did."

"And?"

"And nothing. He's yours."

Jacqui knew to be simple or silent when Kaye was in a mood like this. It was the only way she could have some power when Kaye was so intent on leading her around like a puppy.

"Okay, don't bite. So, his name is João. He's Brazilian. He's here on a working holiday. You probably heard about Robert's thing with Tracey?"

"I had not. No."

"Well, this is what I got after he had his little, I won't call it an affair. His slip up. His fun, Jacqui: he had his fun. I can't believe we haven't talked since then. Well, so what? Fair's fair."

Jacqui checked the bottle of wine. It was nearly full. She checked both sides of Kaye's armchair to see if there was an empty bottle lying about. There wasn't.

Kaye flicked to another photo of the same young man, but this time his face was turned to the camera.

"OK then, and how is it that he's mine?" She had an inkling of what Kaye might mean. In Sydney, they'd kept a few men in common. Both had curiosity, then inclinations, towards the Italians, Greeks and Lebanese. João fit the mould.

"Well, he's yours now, if you want him. Clearly, Robert and I are leaving Friday week and João won't fit in carry on. I've already said my goodbyes and I told him all about you, that you and I were going to talk tonight. Want me to call him? I told him to be on standby."

Jacqui glowered and Kaye relented, topping up both of their wines though Jacqui had only sipped at hers.

"I would, of course," said Jacqui. "But my situation is different. As far as I know, Scott has been wholly loyal. Not to make myself into Cinderella, but the shoe just doesn't fit."

"You can make the shoe fit if you want. Be inventive. What did the sisters do in the original, unsanitised version? Cut off some toes, hack off the heel?" said Kaye.

"I suppose. And necessity is the mother of invention," said Jacqui, "but I just don't need him. And I'm old enough to be his mother. Anyway, work is hectic and, like I said, there's no need to rock the boat with Scott."

"My god, Jacqui, just meet him. I can hear you wavering. Meet him one time. He's the best. Truly. I first met him at that park near New World. In town. I was taking Carlos for a walk and I sat down to watch these young guys kicking a football around. He was one of them. They're all over here working in cafés, bars and kitchens... the lifeblood of our service industry. It's an untapped seam of gold. The ball came my way, and he did too, and I sort of flung my boot at it. He invited me to play. So I did. I tied Carlos to a tree and went for it. Anyway, long story short... I'm a convert. No more of this mumbling

Anglo stock and their drunken clutching. I know it sounds like a stereotype, but these men are brilliant. He barely even drinks. I mean, he'd never replace Robert, but the way I see it, it's our duty to teach these boys a thing or two."

"And how old is he?"

Kaye didn't have any kids so didn't have that awkward fear about being attracted to men who might, even obliquely, remind her of her son. "Oh, I don't know. Twenty-five at least. No more than thirty. Certainly not young enough to be your son. I haven't asked. Definitely not thirty. Like I said. He's perfect."

Jacqui scanned the room. The house was usually so clean but now books and papers were piled haphazardly on a table, while a wine box brimmed with clutter that might or might not be of use in Ankara.

"There's no obligation, Jacqui. He understands perfectly. It's like their football. No competition, just fun. Imagine. What's the worst that could happen? Just be open, be honest."

"But, you know. Actually, you might not know?"

"Know what? That you haven't slept with anyone since your husband?"

Kaye never said Scott's name. The two had no interest in each other. Scott felt Kaye was an overly stark reminder of Sydney – a year of untold debauchery, at least in his mind – and while Kaye respected Scott as Jacqui's partner, she never understood Jacqui's attraction to him.

"I haven't. No. Not that, though. I mean. After Axle. Having a kid. Things change. Since then, well, I don't know if a younger man would be... if he... if..."

"What? You don't know if he'd be attracted to you? Relax. I swear. Meet him. It'll all work out. I promise."

Dinner

Scott was searching through his archive of policy documents and using the dinner table as his personal desk. Since Jacqui wasn't joining them for dinner, he stacked them neatly down her end of the table as he set out knives and forks, placemats and various condiments. There were three hours before Jacqui had said she'd return from Kaye's and then the three of them were scheduled to sit down to the second weekly session of their Sunday-evening Daniel Day-Lewis film watching extravaganza. The actor had been Axle's choice, and that right to choose had been won across a tense final round of rock-paper-scissors with his mother, who'd goaded him with a series of preposterous thematic suggestions for films she would inflict on the family.

"Mean hangover, hey?" said Scott.

"Really?"

"I'm only saying that it was mean. I didn't intend anything else. I used to have hangovers, so don't think I don't know."

Axle was making a show of thumping his palm against the bottom of a bottle of sweet chilli sauce. The gelatinous condiment was defying gravity and refusing to ooze towards his meal. They'd already ventured into another instalment of their long-running argument over whether sweet chilli sauce needed to be kept in the fridge or not. Scott, in turn, dusted his meal with a half-turn of pepper and a half-turn of salt from the elaborate grinders he'd inherited from a great aunt.

"Well, my headache's gone now, if that's what you're asking. And it was a good night so it all evens out."

Scott was into his second decade of employment at the Ministry of Health. He'd begun as a schools educator but had seen promotion after promotion so that he now led campaigns on drinking and drunk driving. None of that made talking to his own son any easier. He knew the literature on how these one-to-one conversations were the most effective, and how family, whānau and friends were the best people to offer advice. But he also knew that until you see your reflection in the scathing eye of your own teenage child, you're nothing but a rank amateur. He'd said those same words a month before – "nothing but a rank amateur" – to a conference of educators from across the lower North Island.

"Let me tell you a story."

"Dad, please."

"No, no. Just listen. It's not an easy story, Ax."

Axle had no choice. He struck his fork through a floret of broccoli and rotated it through the sweet chilli sauce.

"When I was your age, well, in my final year, but kids age quicker these days... Nineteen-ninety... in the late nineties – I went to a party. Seventh form it was. Year Thirteen. Your granddad had bought me a box of beer, maybe twelve of them. They were supposed to be for me and a friend, Mark Michelson. You remember Mark. You met him at my fortieth. Anyway, it was one of these things your granddad occasionally did, I don't know why. Maybe he liked the spontaneity of it. You know, gifts are often better if they come outside of the usual birthday and Christmas cycle. Anyway, Mark had his own beers and so when we got to this party it was really kicking off. I was nervous as hell because this girl – a young woman – was there who I'd had a crush on for at least a year. I got a bit drunk. It's normal. Natural. No shame, you know... no shade. I got drunk. Mark did too."

"Dad, you've told me this one before. You crash the car. Drink driving. You've told it, like, seventy times. And then you don't have a car, and you have to take the bus, and eventually you get into cycling and that's why you're fit now. Or the other story about how that crash was the 'raw material' – yes, that's how you say it, *raw*, like the sound a lion makes – for that play you made once. And how it toured all over the country, South and North islands. And how the arts are the most important thing, even if they don't make much money. And then you say that *this* one *did* make money and it allowed you to live without other work for eighteen months and they were the best months of your life. And then you correct yourself and say that right now is the best time of your life."

"Ax, please. Right, you're right, it was this same night. But that's not all of it. This story is different. Are you going to listen? I promise I haven't told you this one before."

"Yeah, right, go on then."

Scott didn't like his son's tone and he didn't like that phrase, "Go on then." He also knew that if he turned this into a conversation about civility then he would have lost his chance to tell the story.

"Anyway. We were at this party. And we were drunk and this girl I had the crush on – remember? – well, she just comes over and talks to Mark and me. Sits right between me and my friend and I thought, 'God, she's going to hook up with him,' because he was always a bit smoother with the girls than I was. Anyway, she didn't! She turned to me. I offered her a beer – it's not like I was going to drink them all – and she said 'yes,' even though she'd been on the wines. One thing leads to another and I said a stupid thing about going for a walk with her. I don't know if kids, young people, still say this – "let's go for a walk" – but that's what we used to say if we wanted to hook up with someone. Stupid really, but we went ahead and ended up at my car and that's how I lost my virginity."

Axle's eyes ballooned and he went bright red. Scott hadn't meant to be so blunt but he ploughed on.

"Anyway, anyway. It was a really good night. Like your one on Friday was a real good night. Sorry, not the same, of course. And I know we've had the talk about sex and everything, but I wanted to let you know that I understand what alcohol can do. It's not all bad. I mean, it's not all good. But it's not all bad, either. The point of the story is that, even though I went on to drink drive and crash my parents' car, to me it was a pretty good night all up. You see what I'm getting at?"

Axle hesitated. "Um. You're saying that I shouldn't drink and drive? I mean, that's obvious. I don't even have my restricted."

"Well, yes. I mean, more broadly, that moderation is the key. I understand the social validation. Sorry, the peer stigma. The, uh, in layman terms, the need to be able to be seen to be enjoying a beer or two. Just don't let it get carried away. Alcohol is a drug like any other. You know? Of course you do. Like, we both know it can be hard to fit into a new school. That wasn't your fault. But just use your sense, eh?"

Scott stopped. He'd slogged through the story and got to the moral, but looking back, he was not pleased with how it had gone. He'd give himself a six out of ten. Five and a half. Not a pep talk to base a training module on, but not terrible.

Now, he thought, I ought to end this conversation with some action points and bonding. Before he could work out what to do, though, Axle had finished his dinner and paced to the kitchen to wash the pots and pans that wouldn't fit in the dishwasher. Scott was satisfied. It wasn't every teenage boy, he considered, who would wash up unprompted.

Parent teacher

"Welcome, welcome along. Nau mai, haere mai. Welcome back to those parents who have been here before, and welcome along to all the parents for whom this is your first time. I can see a few of you didn't bring your children along. No problem, but that is a point of difference at Wellington High. Your kids are encouraged to attend. We're a bit more democratically minded than some of the regional schools. We pride ourselves on being open and transparent."

Jacqui and Scott hadn't seen anything about kids coming along to the evening. Axle wasn't with them.

"A few ground points: I hope everyone has signed in at the back or scanned the QR code. I don't want to take up too much of your time, but just remember that while you'll be speaking to a half-dozen teachers, they'll be talking to, perhaps, sixty of you. So be kind, introduce yourselves and don't take it personally if you have to jog our memories about your kid. I'm Klap, short for Klappenberg, no need to clap."

The principal paused to encourage the smattering of nervous laughter. All the parents and their high school-aged students were gathered in the hall, ringed by well-worn trestle tables each seating a pair of teachers.

"For those who are new, I'd encourage you to come over to my table, too. We'll sign you up for one of our completely free further education courses on the state of youth – young people, teens – today. Get in quick. But if demand is as high as last year, we'll put on a second set of sessions mid-year. This year we'll pay special attention to the growing influence of climate change radicals on our youth. We will also revisit our popular session on trans teens and what you need to know as a parent. Very popular last year, too. Without further ado, then, let's get into it! Kia ora."

The parent-teacher nights at Axle's old school had been far staider, and that principal certainly wouldn't have been comfortable using te reo to punctuate a sentence. Before Jacqui could check in with her husband, Scott was bounding over to Klap's table. He was probably going to chew the man's ear off about climate change or suggest they take up the oft-offered Ministry curriculum on teen drinking.

The table closest to her had no queue. An A4 print out read, "Mr MacMillan: Art". The man behind the table did look like an art teacher, she thought. His hair was thick and closely cropped – silver but not at all washed out. He wore a royal blue short-sleeved shirt, cut in the safari style, but of a light material somewhere between cotton and linen.

"You teach Axle, yes? Year Eleven Art. Mr MacMillan?"

"Indeed I do. He's new this year? So I wouldn't have met you before," Mr MacMillan said.

Sitting still, he'd appeared young but, as he spoke, Jacqui saw he was closer to her age. He may not have been forty, but he was close. Perhaps he just moisturised and kept out of the sun. She imagined he'd once been the recipient of many crushes, but those days were probably past.

"Jacqui," she said, and extended her hand, which MacMillan shook.

"So, what can I do for you?"

"Sorry. I hadn't thought this far ahead. I hate to line up, so I just came over to the only teacher with no queue. My husband is off somewhere else – signing up with Klap – and my son isn't with us either. Do we need to speak to you together?"

"No, that's okay. Is there anything specific you want to talk about, though? Or would you like me to just preview his report card?"

"One thing comes to mind," Jacqui said. "Axle called us 'boomers' the other day. I was going to correct him, but I thought he'd just ignore me and it would probably be – what do they call it? Confirmation bias?"

"Ah yes. It's just most of the parents here could be mistaken for boomers. Not you, of course: you called it 'Year Eleven' not 'Fifth Form'. Everyone in this city leaves it quite late for kids. I don't mean to be rude, but you must have been quite young when you had him. Early twenties?"

"Mid-twenties, yeah."

"Calling anyone over thirty-five a boomer is actually pretty common now for these kids. Just being honest. For the kids I teach, boomer basically means any middle-aged person. Not that I'm implying you're middle aged. It doesn't even matter that it's the grandparents who are actually the boomers, now, and we're Gen X."

"Scott and I are millennials. I'm forty-one."

"Right. You're the first millennials-with-a-teen that I've come across. I mean, it must be more common in small towns where there's nothing to do but have kids. Probably even got a Gen Z-er with a teenager in some of the small towns! So, onto Axle: he's fitting in well. He's got the art basics down. Sketching, mixing colours. His grades aren't great, not terrible. But it's art, you know? We don't really assess them so much until next year and, even then, it's mostly external and about their portfolio. Do you think he'll keep at it?"

The art teacher was handsome and high-spirited and she was happy to talk with him, but she didn't really care about what he told her. Axle's first year at Wellington College had given them a shock. The next one had been no better. She'd imagined the family gaining freedom when her son entered high school, even with the attendant demons of puberty. The last twelve months had been terrible, though, both for the immediacy of Axle's inward turn as well as for what it may have augured for the rest of his teenage years. At the lowest point, she'd pictured him becoming one of those thwarted young men energised by resentment and guarana.

"I think he'll find his place here," Jacqui said. "Scott and I weren't artists but we had our practices and our hobbies."

"It's all we can ask. We're going to have to move on in a minute, I'm sorry. These things are always a bit half-cocked. Great to meet you though and we'll see you in second semester when maybe there'll be more to say."

Jacqui saw that a line had formed behind her and nodded her thanks to MacMillan. She looked over to her husband and saw that Scott was near the front of the queue to talk with Klap.

The till

Jacqui didn't blame Scott for his fantasies, but she was surprised he was so ready to share them with her. They were the typical dull hopes of so many married men: a succession of mid-twenties colleagues with whom he had dreamed up a stream of increasingly fanciful scenarios. It had been like this for a decade. Why couldn't he keep these thoughts to himself? And, anyway, it was never going to happen.

She'd been waiting for the perfect time to bring up the possibility of João and she'd found it. She joined Scott in bed. He was fidgety. She asked if he had a work crush. He said he did. She said he should indulge, if he got the chance. He said he wouldn't. She said that she would, if she got the chance. He demurred. She insisted. He doubted. She insisted. He relented. She took him in her hand. He tried to thank her. She gripped. He grimaced. She worked through his fantasy for him and the words succeeded. She strode to the bathroom, washed it off her hand and returned to bed.

"But you mean it? In reality. It would be fine if I did? If either of us did?" he asked.

"Sure," she replied, reaching for her vibrator without turning it on, "but keep things discreet. I don't want to know. Oh, and one condition…"

"Yeah?"

This was one of Jacqui's annoying tricks that he always stepped into. She would offer two conditions – in this case discretion and reciprocation – and then leap ahead by saying "on one condition?" And he would be in such a fret that he'd agree to the question and, implicitly, the first two conditions.

"On the condition that you tell Axle. I think we're all old enough to be honest with what we want from our lives."

Jacqui was swifter with her own fantasies. She'd had her share of crushes, but she knew the limits when she included Scott in the game. Speak the scenario; avoid referring to other people by their names. The kink she kept circling back to was to have Scott watch her with another man. For him to see her. She wasn't interested in her husband's humiliation. Or, if she was, she couldn't admit that to herself. She had brought this fantasy up a couple of times and, even by her own standards, she'd been clever in circling around the point until he understood just what she meant. But Scott had no interest in teasing out the scenario. Not even as a little bit of bedroom imagining. So, on the two occasions where she had put the idea into words, she had also back-pedalled. She would soften her wishes to a fairly common threesome fantasy – two men and a woman – rather than the thing that really made her reel.

Could she be blamed for playing her cards close to her chest? They'd spoken about the freedom of their relationship when they first met. That was twenty years ago and those talks were propelled by Jacqui's imminent move to Sydney. Back then, she'd thought that Scott was only into the idea of opening the relationship to disprove that he was conservative, jealous or desperate. Either way, things had been set in motion. He could disapprove of what she had planned but he wouldn't be able to say she hadn't given him fair warning.

Tuesday and João

The Brazilian looked exactly like he had in Kaye's pictures. A curl to his black hair, deep brown eyes that were as uncomplicated as a puppy's, lashes – wow, did the boy have lashes! – and a physique she hadn't properly contemplated since Sydney. Sure, she worked with the police and saw plenty of guys who were monumentally invested in their own bodies, but none of them carried themselves softly like João. It might sound facile, and she would never say it aloud, but the man was carefree. She wondered if his ease carried through to his core or whether it was skin deep. She would be careful. Either way, she whispered a little thanks to Kaye.

João. He helped her with the pronunciation. João. One word; four letters. She was bashful at how her lips moved – first pursing, then accommodating the 'o' – when he talked her through the syllables, and through the heave-ho of the tilde. João. She promised herself to perfect it on the way home.

And her name? He didn't need any help. How he said it was perfect. In his mouth it started with a 'z' and ended sharply, rather than in an all-too-common nasal stutter. *Zha*-ki versus Jack-*keeyey*. It wasn't the warbled afterthought of the masculine Jack. It was definitive.

Their conversation galloped. Forty-five minutes felt like fifteen. She couldn't recall much about it afterwards but she knew it had not lasted long enough. She had begun by talking about Kaye which, when he praised her, rankled. She asked about Brazil. About working in a kitchen. She may have asked him to speak Portuguese – she definitely did – and she cringed at herself for that. She'd also half promised to work with him to find a better job than being a kitchen hand at one of the Little Lucknow restaurants that had sprouted up around the city.

She knew that he understood the purpose of these preliminaries. It was an interview, a test, platonic. He knew she knew. There was no need to mention the impracticalities of their match. Nor did they need to get straight to the point. No 'your place or mine'. Only a coffee, café con leche. Wait. That was Spanish, she thought, not Portuguese. Let's not get ahead of ourselves.

The date ended with him inviting her on a climbing trip, this weekend or next. Perhaps the Wairarapa, if the weather was clear. To the Hutt, if not. The idea of getting out of the city reassured her. Why was that? She played with the question and, in doing so, she acknowledged an unsettling truth. She felt more than a fleeting embarrassment. She felt shame.

In her early twenties she had dealt with the way morality had turned her against her swifter impulses. It was not like her parents had been strict, but she had internalised all the usual mores of prudishness. In turn, when she realised how deeply these thoughts held her, she had made a pact never to live secretively.

What had happened to that promise? Jacqui didn't want to blame anyone other than herself, but the vows of marriage had atrophied her vows to live without shame. She would need to renew her pledge. She would not hide. She would say it – "I will not hide" – a number of times over the coming days. She would say it when she was alone, but that was good enough. She would not be ashamed of being with another man.

One thing had become clear: if she was to live in the open, João would have to be truly comfortable with her husband and child. Not just comfortable with the idea of them but the reality. He would have to meet them, if only once. And what of his life? Could she see herself waiting for him to finish a shift so they could walk hand in hand around the waterfront? She would not insist. He could choose. She would not intrude on his life. He might have a slew of others. She didn't care. She would leave him better than how she had found him.

Best Policy

> Morning Linnea,
>
> Can I loop you in on campaign brainstorming for the weekly ops meeting at 11? Short notice, I know, and all good if not.
>
> Ngā mihi,
> Scott

He felt breezy and confident. She had smiled at him in the lift and nodded at his points in a meeting the previous week. He followed up with a calendar invite, doing a little shuffle dance at his desk as he clicked 'send'.

Linnea was in her second year working at the Ministry of Health. She'd begun in the comms team, not policy, but he saw a lot of promise in her work. Seriously. He could tell that she was strategic. If nothing else, they could work together.

He hoped she would come. He'd checked her schedule. It was normal to do so when arranging a meeting. There were no clashes and her timetable was light this week and next. She'd appreciate being invited to join.

When Scott got off with Linnea in his thoughts, he always pictured her eyes locked on his, a ripple of concentration across her brow. Clinical, decisive. He read an unerring intention from her expression – ambition mixed with lust mixed with good sense – and it was that certainty that would drive him over the edge. He wondered why his fantasies about her always zeroed in on a shared climax and a shared future. His fantasies of Linnea were most intense when he linked his orgasm to her conceiving. Always. He visualised conception as an immediate sunburst, though he knew the real thing was slower, darker and more viscous than any combustion or explosion. He could not escape from astral images of an improbable blooming from hollow space. He didn't want it to be this way and he'd never had such fantasies before. It was all more than a little worrying.

On the plus side, Linnea didn't directly report to him or even to anyone in his team. That meant his fantasies couldn't be interrupted with worries about exploiting a power imbalance. Or, perhaps, elevating that sort of transgression was exactly where his fantasies were heading. But it was still okay, for now at least, as he had no power over her. And, besides, half of all new relationships in the thirty-plus category began in the workplace. Even if someone were to say that it was inappropriate, he was with the majority. Anyway, he was not actually going to do anything about it.

His previous work crush had been in his team. That pitiful confusion had lasted eight months. Thankfully, the young woman had moved to Australia and been replaced by a young man who had little to no appeal. He hadn't told Jacqui about that previous crush – the one now in Melbourne – he'd likely only told her about half the workplace crushes he'd waded through. He knew that his honesty reassured Jacqui. He wanted his wife to see him as a little bit flawed because, well, that's what he was.

It was true that Scott was attracted to young women, but he could also recognise the beauty of his younger male co-workers such as Daniel, from his policy team, and Phillip who was a marketing contractor. This meant he'd escaped at least some of the grim hyper-hetero socialisation of high school. He could acknowledge youthful beauty without it eroding the pillars of who he was. He could hold a thought without having to act on it.

Scott wasn't sure if his wife had meant what she'd said the previous night. He'd have to bring it up again, sober and clothed. Things get said, and the good thing about Jacqui was that she knew that. Things get said, but you've got to check in on them. Linnea reminded him of Jacqui a bit – an unwillingness to be led down the garden path. But, he thought, Linnea also had a sense of justice. He wasn't sure he could say the same about his wife. His computer dinged. Linnea had accepted his invite and sent a message.

Consider me looped in.

Two more dings.

Both his other colleagues rejected the meeting invite. What to do? He strolled to the kitchenette, made a cup of coffee and weighed up the pros and cons of rescheduling. He decided to go ahead with just him and Linnea. He felt fine and it passed the sniff test. There had been no calendar clashes when he sent the invite.

He went back to his desk, checked his emails, then logged out. He grabbed his work phone and notepad and walked towards the meeting room. Linnea was already there. She was early.

He took a moment to study her before she noticed him. He saw a ready poise that said she imagined this job was just a temporary embarrassment and that, in five years, she might be his boss or in a role less dutiful than those of the public sector. Despite that, he thought, she dressed more like an optometrist than a bureaucrat. She wore a trim, slightly faded navy blazer over a cream blouse buttoned above her collar bone. Actually, he thought, her attire was stock standard Lambton Quay. Maybe he was delusional and projecting his own silly thoughts onto her. Or perhaps it was the red trim of her glasses that made her appear somewhat out of place? He shrugged the thoughts off as he reached for the door handle and entered the room.

"Joe's out, I'm afraid, and Cath's apparently on annual leave this week. It wasn't on her schedule but I got the autoreply. Whatever. I thought we might do some brainstorming, anyhow. Light touch. What do they call it now in the new tech lingo? Envisioning?"

"I think they still say brainstorming," she said.

He preferred envisioning but he wasn't going to push it. He kept his head down, pulled up a pen from his shirt pocket and opened his notepad. He flipped past the page of doodles from the zoom meeting with the Australians last week and the rough budget for the three-week family holiday to Japan next year that he'd been thinking about. He found a blank page and set his pen down.

"Cool. A bit of context, then: our policy principal advisor thinks we're coming to the tail of the efficacy of the 'just say no' work. We're thinking to try a less hostile and more mindful/wellbeing sort of thing."

"Yeah. Makes sense," she said.

"It does," he said. Her hair fell in blonde ringlets down to the shoulders of the blazer. He hadn't had sisters growing up and he had no idea if her hair was naturally like this or if she'd spent three hours of her Saturday in a salon. She swallowed and he registered that he'd been staring at the skin of her neck. "Tell me why it makes sense. No problem if it was just a throwaway thing, but I'm curious on your read. From a comms perspective."

"Well, it makes sense to me, strategically," Linnea said. "Our analytics are down, even though our spend is up. I imagine we've either got a platform or messaging problem. Or both. Plus, we haven't refreshed since I've been here and I imagine there are a few other fresh people who'll also be itching to change things up."

"Wise. Any thoughts, then?" He realised he didn't have much to offer. He should have prepared more if he was going to impress her.

"One thing I've been interested in," she began, "is the Finnish experiment."

Linnea had mentioned wanting to work for WHO or the UN as part of her career progression. He'd seen the HR notes at the hiring phase, though he hadn't been on her panel. He thought she had what it took. Good looking people always get what they want.

She checked to see if he registered the great civic minds of Helsinki before clarifying. "They – obviously – moved a significant amount of their advertising budget to R&D on low-alcohol beers, while also crafting tax incentives as a sweetener. I think we can ride on their work and perhaps even push for a regional trial on subsidised light beers. In the Wellington craft beer segment, for example. Unless that would be too parochial?"

Scott only caught the second half of what she had been saying. "Go on."

She looked up at him and their eyes locked. Not good, keep cool. He dropped his eyes. He picked up the pen and wrote "Oslo – R&D; tax sweetener", putting a star beside tax sweetener to remind himself to run it past a contact at Treasury.

"It's not fully fleshed out, but I was thinking of a kind of fully integrated campaign around light beer. Not that zero alcohol stuff. I wasn't around then, but I know about *that* mess. Light beer, then. It ticks the harm minimisation box without fully ticking the nanny state one." She paused for him to agree. He nodded. She continued. "If I were running it, I'd pilot across two markets. Central Wellington or Auckland for ease, somewhere else for the optics, and see if we can strongly influence consumer behaviour. I'm talking double-digit behaviour change. Get the kind of data that would force the Minister to pay attention."

Scott nodded and made some more notes: "double-digit; optics; 0% beer campaign????"

"This sounds great," he said, when he was sure she was finished. "Real good. Hypothetically, what do you think we would need to take this to the next step?"

"For a proposal? I would need to flesh out the fully integrated side of things. I think we need to go where the people are – you know? Influence the opinion leaders and they influence the decision makers. So, from a comms perspective, I'd say we start with the arts. Theatre, specifically. Cath told me about that play you did and it sounds amazing. We haven't tied in with the performing arts in years. I love the idea of immersive approaches to audience building and –"

Scott groaned. It was unintentional and he wished he hadn't.

"Linnea, listen. I love the first part of the idea, I do, but let's not start on theatre. I don't know what Cath told you, but I haven't made theatre in fifteen years. No-one's interested. Certainly not the higher-ups. I'm not even interested. You wouldn't go to someone who'd visited Prague fifteen years ago for advice on where to eat? The same goes for me and theatre. I'm more into painting now. I mean, speaking of metrics, wouldn't one striking image be more powerful than ninety minutes of acting? Anyway, digital is the only way. Spruik a series of short films — two minutes max — and I'm with you. Come on, you know all this!"

"OK. That's fine. I'm sorry. I'll park it for now. I do think, with respect, that we could do both."

"I appreciate it."

"People do say your work back then was so good. I just thought you might be interested in reconnecting. I could do the heavy lifting. No? Apologies. I don't want to rule out the arts, though. Like, they're an authentic connection and the ripple from them can be ten or twenty times what we get from social media spend. An exhibition, a gig, something like that. We've got to consider the long-term metrics, not just the week's cycle. Surely you're not totally opposed?"

"That's fine. It's fine. I like your enthusiasm. You don't even report to me, so I really have no say. I'm just a policy nerd. Keep going. Or better yet, stop and put it down in a one-pager and sort out a rough costing of it. Go heavy on international comparisons and light on the art stuff."

"I can do that," she said as she tapped a note into her laptop. "We've also got the operational side of things. Do you know the Norwegian bar on Brandon St? It's been there a while, but they've quietly been building up their low and non-alcoholic beer stocks. All imported, so a bit of a nightmare carbon-wise."

"I'm not really one to hang out in bars, anymore," said Scott.

"It's set back from the road a bit, hard to spot if you're not looking for it. Anyway, I was going to suggest the team go for a tasting session after work. I've looked at the menu. Food is mostly herring. Kidding. All the low alcohol beers are there. It's worth a bit of research, don't you think?"

Antiques

"Axle, we're off to the antiques shop! See you later!"

It was Saturday morning and Axle was yet to emerge from his room. Jacqui and Scott were hardly OpSec experts but they knew how to keep a sensitive conversation from their son. If it was mid-level sensitive they would turn the music up a little louder or turn on a tap and talk in their en suite. If the issue were top secret, the simplest solution was distance. The "antique shop" was perfect code. There was such a shop. And they did, when their tastes converged, buy antiques from it.

They walked single file along a path, then up some steps to Upland Road. Scott made a mental note to log a request with the council to trim back the shrubs intruding on the path. If he ever got tired of working for the Ministry of Health, he'd join Primary Industries and embark on a gung-ho campaign against agapanthus.

"Would you look at the state of these roads," said Jacqui, pointing to a series of potholes outside Kelburn Normal. She stopped, whipped out her phone and took a picture. "I'm going to post it on the mayor's Facebook page."

Scott knew she'd follow through. Jacqui knew how to get things done – it was another thing he admired about her.

Despite the substandard seal, the road to Kelburn Village was active with Saturday distractions. Small families had been bundled into large vehicles, with kayaks and mountain bikes fixed to the roof and various contraptions protruding from towbars. There was an urgency as they escaped the streets, which – on a weekday – would have delivered them in a transfixed state to their schools and workplaces.

"So," Scott began, "the way I see it is we're not getting any younger. We're solid. I love you and I'm committed to our family. More than ever. That being our baseline, our bedrock, I think you were right the other night about perhaps opening our relationship. A little. I mean, if we're trying to teach Ax about healthy relationships then being honest with each other is a very good start."

"You're right. We're solid. And if we don't try anything different, then what have we got to be honest about?"

"Good. Good, we're agreed" he said, buying time to work out what she meant. He couldn't make the rationale fit, but they were agreeing and that was surely the point. "I was a little worried that the other night was, you know, pillow talk."

"If we're all old enough to be honest," Jacqui said, "then we're old enough to explain exactly what's going on. We don't need to fool him with roundabout talk of healthy relationships. I mean, who are we kidding? It's about pleasure, not health."

"But pleasure is healthy!"

"It may be, but it's a cop out. We don't need to play tricks on him. He sees your commitment to your work, so I'm worried he'd just see you reducing everything to the lens of health. That 'a man with a hammer sees every problem as a nail' kind of thing."

"You're right. You're right. We don't need to hide pleasure. Even if it is healthy, it doesn't need to be said. Maybe I'll have that talk to him this afternoon. Take him out somewhere and have the talk."

They'd reached the line of shops that made up the Village. The shops were of two types. The first were modernised wooden villas. Modernisation entailed the creation of new entranceways with floor-to-ceiling windows. These shops sold clothes and wine, or housed restaurants. Renovations made their businesses appear prosperous, though who knew how they stayed afloat.

The second type of shop appeared to be clinging to existence by the fingernails. They were small stores from yesteryear – butcheries, fish and chip shops and a dairy. The crumbling masonry and rotted flushing of their storefronts were only brightened by glistening signs from Lotto, Coca-Cola and Vodafone. Jacqui wondered if, at this scale, these commercial limpets had become central to structural integrity. Without these signs, she imagined, the stores might be rubble after the next strong southerly. Each of them had a small apartment at the back of the property where the owners, presumably, holed up. Jacqui wondered why these second types didn't sell up and move on, let the cool grace of gentrification wash over the suburb. She didn't will it to happen – she had no emotional stake in Kelburn – but if it were her, she would sell in a minute.

"I've got a confession to make," said Jacqui. "After our talk last weekend, I reached out to a man I know. We're thinking of going on a date this afternoon. Nothing serious, still testing the waters. I'd be back tonight, of course."

"Right," said Scott trying to obscure his shock through ready agreement. "Yup. That'll free me up to go to this work thing. A social thing with a few people from work. With a woman from work. But make sure you're home tonight so Axle isn't home alone. Actually, he's old enough to be home alone. No problem."

"You're telling me that you've got a date? Were you not going to tell me?"

She was elated that the conversation had already turned to him, though she hated to see him flustered. No, she corrected herself, she liked to see him flustered, but not like this.

"Not a date. No. I thought about what we said and thought we needed to have this conversation before being free to open up properly. But I am interested in – I've told you about her, I think? – Linnea?"

"Looks like we're both at fault. A little bit anyway. For me, I'm sorry that I went ahead and began to plan something. It was a bit wrong."

"No, no. You're good. We just need protocol. Some ground rules."

They found themselves standing like mannequins in front of the antique store. Scott turned his attention to the window display. They always had interesting things. He paid attention to them as a way of steadying himself. He wondered where the store got all these trinkets from. Walk ups, certainly, and garage sales, too. The range was so vast that he imagined July trips to Eastern Europe, a container filled with old-world objects and the horrors of paperwork for customs.

Their conversation lulled as an older couple wandered by. Scott peered at various goods and tried to guess where they were made. He always savoured turning each item over in his hand – an iron paperweight in the shape of a rabbit, for example – which he would discover was made in Ireland or East Germany. It was a lot more fun than in a modern shopping mall where everything was from one or two places. He'd thought that today he might spy a suitable gift for Jacqui's birthday. He wouldn't buy it in front of her, of course, but he might earmark it in his mind. Perhaps he would get the shop owner to put it aside if she went next door to get a coffee.

"I'm not going to sleep with him today if that's what you were thinking. I haven't even properly met him yet."

"Wait, so you know him… but you haven't properly met him?"

"It's too soon, Scott. I'm sorry. Can I keep it to myself for now? Let things breathe a bit."

"Yes," he said, thinking that he would do the same. He shouldn't have brought up Linnea.

Jacqui gestured to the coffee shop.

"Order a flat white for me?" he asked. He stayed behind to make a last survey of the shop window and think through what had just happened. There was nothing there that he wanted to get her for her birthday and, anyhow, he had three months before then. He waited until he'd fully regained his calm.

When he entered the coffee shop, his flat white was waiting for him and Jacqui was ensconced in the weekend section of the newspaper.

Later that very same day

Scott was barely out of his cycling gear when Axle called across the house, his voice darting through three rooms, that he was heading to Pete's place.

"Pete's the one who had the party?" Scott walked from the bedroom into the lounge.

"It wasn't really a party. A few friends. Not like Mum showed up with the paddy wagon."

"Yeah, well, okay. She's not a cop, you know, so you shouldn't say that. And paddy wagon is a racist term. Not the worst one, but it is, nonetheless. We've been over that before. Anyway, last time I called it a get-together and you gave me a please-don't-call-it-that look. My Dad – when I was growing up – used to call it a hooley. A hooley! I don't suppose that's come back into fashion?"

"OK, fine. No. It hasn't come into fashion. And, yes, the get-together was at Pete's place."

"Just remember our talk from last weekend, then. No need to go overboard." Scott heard himself and cringed at how dreary and level-headed he had become. He could recall a time when he said reckless things. His job didn't help. Flippancy was a rare treat when it came to public health.

Axle thought back to his dad's talk about losing his virginity. He couldn't recall any lessons. What had they even talked about?

Scott walked back to his room, showered and put on fresh clothes. When he returned to the lounge, Axle was still there, browsing his phone.

"You want a beer?" It was a good peace offering to reset the conversation.

"Nah. Thanks though."

"Haven't sworn off the stuff after last weekend, eh?" Scott laughed, then regretted it. He'd hoped to build a connection with his son, not mock him. Axle didn't look up from his phone.

"Say," said Scott, trying again, "I was thinking I might send you a couple of links to some articles. Short ones. To round out what we talked about last week. Would you read them?"

"Depends on what they are. Do I have to read them?"

"Honesty, eh? No. You don't have to read them. We've never been those kinds of parents. You know that."

Scott thought of another approach. Softly-softly wasn't going to work, so now for the old bait and switch. "Ax. Your mother and I are, we're wanting to... We've had an important talk over the last little while. We're not separating. I want to assure you of that to start with."

The colour had run from his son's face. He pressed on. "You've probably had talks about LGBT stuff – sexuality and inclusion, yeah? Probably at school? I know it's a hot topic now."

"Yeah?"

Oh, god, this was not going well, thought Scott. Now his son was imagining some mid-life coming-out crisis. "Well, in those classes, at least when I was in school, they only showed us how to put a condom on and told us about some things that might affect a person's life. It wasn't what I would call comprehensive education. Relax, relax – it's not a big deal. Let me come at it from another angle. So, remember how we've talked about meditation before, and Buddhism and how that worldview is all about finding the calm, centre path. The third way, right? Remember?"

"Yeah?" Colour had returned to Axle's face, but far too much of it. His son was beetroot red.

"Then you'll know how important it is to find new options, and not accept the only two options presented to you. Always seek out another possibility, preferably the middle path, not an extreme one."

"Yeah, I remember. It's important to avoid binary traps. Is that what this is? I don't have anything new to tell you, if that's what you mean."

Despite the cringe stuff that they said, Axle couldn't help but like his parents. The same as how you can't help but like an old cat that's been with you all your life and can't bear to have it put down even though it dribbles everywhere. Yeah, the vet bills get up, but they've done their years of service and that bedrock of affection isn't going anywhere. He thought he'd like to not like his parents. He'd like to be a bit troubled – not too much, just a bit – like Jarvis or some of the kids at Col, but he couldn't muster it. He had too much of his dad's reasonableness and, despite being fifteen, there was no inkling that he would become an erratic teen.

"I mean technically I think we're all on a spectrum," said Scott, "aren't we? Somewhere in the guts of a bell curve? Maybe a parabola – they still teach algebra? So, in that way I'm as non-binary as you or your mum. See? Even though I identify with the male gender. Not that I'm endorsing... anyway, we talked about this, right? Trying to be a good example. Pronouns are the key these days. I'm getting off track. The thing I wanted to mention is about freedom, consent and, above all, openness. All good things, right?"

"Ri-ight," said Axle, drawing out the word in the way people do when they want to agree but have no idea where the conversation is going.

"We should be being open about relationships and ensuring honesty throughout the process. Now, I don't want you to think we're ahead of you on this. It's like at work, we consult with our stakeholders – Pharmac, the Nurses Union – in the planning stage. You know, genuine consultation. That's why I'm telling you now. Sharing with you. Your mum and I are considering – testing the waters, you know, scoping things out – whether we introduce the possibilities of occasionally opening up our relationship. Just a bit. Something fresh. By adding another person."

Axle's eyes squinted as he tried to parse exactly what his father meant.

Scott realised he'd made it sound like they were trying to get pregnant. For a moment, he resented his wife for absenting herself, rather than backing him up in this conversation. "That sounds like we're trying to have another baby. What I mean is opening up to other adults. What I mean to say is that we don't think it's healthy to pretend people are only attracted to their spouses. It's not right, is it? And the thing about your parents is that this is about strength – we're strong enough to be able to be a bit more open with what we want. You only get one life, right? And we can all be a bit FOMO. That's what we used to say. It's about healthy and, well, it's about honesty and... it's about pleasure, too, I suppose."

Axle turned his attention back to his phone and nodded when his father broke off. Scott waited for his son to speak up but Axle kept quiet.

"Circling back, do you have any questions? About this? I know I haven't been completely clear. Maybe we can talk about it again once you've had a chance to process those other articles about moderation."

The rock

Traffic was light so Jacqui arrived at the Clyde Quay wharf carpark ten minutes early. She double-parked for ninety seconds before easing into a freshly vacated spot. She turned the motor off, reclined the seat and closed her eyes. She could feel the sun filtering through her clothes, the temperature rising in the car. If João was late she'd have to lower a window. As it was, the heat, the spare minutes and her reposed state lulled her into reverie. She pictured João driving, likely in her car because, surely, he didn't own one. He would take her to some wonder of nature; some place resembling the Putangirua Pinnacles. Her car would cross the Remutaka Range and a snug flirtatiousness would build. He would gently mock her music and suggest they stream a folk singer from… no… some rock band from Buenos Aires. The streaming would cut out halfway over the hills. In the quiet she would point out sites of scenic and cultural interest. The actual rock climb would be more of a scramble and would not test either of them. He would take the opportunity to guide her leg to a difficult foothold. She could picture how it would start, a kiss on the scree, or pinned against a rockface. This was a second date after all and, despite herself, some expectations had grown.

She sat up and scanned the marina. There he was, looking like an extra from a Marlon Brando film. Shoulders square, João was a little shorter than her husband, but taller than her. A nice middle ground. She wondered if he'd cut the sleeves off his t-shirt himself, or whether this was the fashion wherever he found his clothes. Rio, or São Paulo or maybe an alley off Cuba St. Best not to mention it.

She tried to lower the window but, with the keys off, the damn thing wouldn't work. She turned the car on, the window chugged down and the wind flew in. An expired parking receipt fluttering across the dash. She drew in a breath to yell his name, but caught herself, imagining the vowels of his name warbling out of her throat. No. She opened the door and strolled towards him. A hug to greet.

"So," said João, "I thought we'd take it easy. Yeah? Maybe do some practice routes at an indoor space. Get your grips rights, get familiar with the ropes and harness. You'll love it. We can hire all the gear out there, easier than going past my place. I've got a friend's car until six, so we better leave now."

On their first date she hadn't fully registered the strength of his English. Going in, she'd been unsure if he'd really be able to communicate with her, despite Kaye's assurances.

She gestured to her car, muddled through the payment system, locked the car and threw her backpack over her shoulder.

João's car was spotless. It felt like a rental. He put on a pair of glasses – "for driving" – and reversed out of the carpark. He looked cute, she thought. She hid her glee, but then thought, "Fuck it, why not?" and openly beamed. His car curved off Wakefield St and onto Jervois Quay, the lights green all the way through Customhouse, Waterloo and Aotea.

"How did you... uh, how did you choose New Zealand? Wellington? Do you like it?" She'd been about to ask about Kaye, but she didn't like how that topic of conversation went at their first meeting. She still wasn't comfortable with the way Kaye had gifted him to her, though perhaps the ends would justify the means. Best not to think about it.

"I'm not used to Kiwi roads," said João after a moment. "How about you talk and I listen. Have you ever climbed before? How's your upper body strength? Tell me everything."

She told him about climbing in high school and abseiling on a holiday with her uncle in Bannockburn. The ropes and a smattering of other gyms. She turned to how her family had moved around the central North Island, checking off whether he'd been to the towns she mentioned. "At school, I was more into art, really. Sports are good but always felt like practice with no end point. I guess I was never really so competitive," she said.

"So, you paint, still? Or photography?"

"Uh, I don't really. With a family there's not so much time. You'll see. One day. Maybe."

Their conversation wasn't awkward, at least not to her, but she had to be careful not to appear like a someone's wife or someone's mother. She wanted to be easy and light.

João pulled off the main road and into a car park. There were six or seven cars but many more empty spots. She'd been so lost in her own head that she hadn't even registered them turning off the state highway.

"Listen Jacqui" – again with the *Zha*-ki " –Kaye was cool. Her husband didn't matter to us but we didn't hide. It's important to me. Let's be cool, too. Okay? Relaxed, calm, easy, yeah?"

"Oh, sorry. Yes. I'm sorry. Was I... no, I understand."

"It's okay. I wanted to say that and to be clear."

She admired his directness and she wanted to know its origins. Maybe men, over there, were just different. All she could think of was how it might have been if she'd met João in Sydney twenty years ago. She'd had a lighter spirit then. She realised he would have been six or seven at the time. With amused detachment, she pictured herself walking along Bondi holding hands with a primary school João – him still leading the way with that confidence that seemed innate.

"You good? You coming?"

She broke with her thoughts. She might not be twenty-two anymore but João was here, and so was she, and it was time to make the most of things.

"Yeah, yes. Of course!" she said, undoing the seat belt, grabbing her bag and pumping pep into the few words she could manage.

Skates

It would take thirty minutes for Axle to walk to Pete's house. But, if he took his skateboard, he could walk up the hill for ten, skate along and down for another ten and be there.

Pete greeted him at the door – "A!" – holding his own board. Pete yelled "goodbye" into the house and joined Axle on the stoop, before opening his backpack to flash a hipflask of rum, three quarters full.

"Leftovers from the party. Someone must've lost it in the grass. Lucky I found it before my parents did."

Pete's parents didn't mind him drinking, but preferred him to have beer or anything, really, other than pure spirits. Somehow, they'd accepted that the empty vodka bottles across the back of his dresser were simply for show – or figured that what was done was done.

The boys walked back up to the ridgeline, before dropping onto their boards. They let a few tailgating cars pass but jumped off ahead of the downhill switchbacks. They cantered down the hill, the adrenaline from the skate strong, before cutting through the university. A few weirdos were still lost in their books and laptops, bathed in white fluorescence like lab rats. A potency lurked in the architecture of these new campus buildings, but neither boy could articulate it. Both of them would end up at this university, just as their parents had supposed, unless something sent them off to specialist schools in a different city.

The cemetery cascaded down a hillside and hadn't admitted a fresh cadaver in at least a hundred years. There would be no grieving widowers to disturb Pete and Axle. There wasn't even a sign of flowers, fresh or otherwise. The only out-of-place object was an abandoned paperback from the city library, pages arched and puffed by rain and dew. Axle didn't dare touch the book or the pages splayed like mushroom gills. Pete booted it to one side for no clear reason.

Every schoolyard should have a little cemetery, Axle thought, to keep the students tethered to what matters in life. Not wishing to disturb the dead, the boys traced their fingers over the gravestone etchings and whispered the few names that were legible. Most were families interred in one plot, death dates separated by decades. Axle couldn't imagine people today digging up one grave to throw a new coffin in. Was that even how it worked? It was all so ancient.

The boys settled into a glade on the lower slope of the cemetery. If they came across anyone it would be campus security, goths or perhaps the monthly meet up of drunk middle-aged corporates rote reciting William Blake. The former was what Axle worried about, the latter were the ones who had surprised Pete and Reggie when they'd hung out here last December. Either way, they could escape by scrambling down a bank, across a path and – if a real pursuit were underway – over a fence to bushwhack through the shrubbery.

The city bubbled out below them, the warm orange twinkling a promise of futures when they might have more control over a night like this. When they were flatting. When they had proper money.

"You know my mum went flatting when she was sixteen?" said Pete. "Dropped out of school. Got some shitty job. That'd be like me leaving home in four months. Wild."

Axle took the hip flask and matched Pete's exaggerated swig. "Rum's not bad, but I prefer vodka," he said. "It's so good. Clean. You can taste Siberia. Icy and pure."

"How hungover were you after the party?" Pete asked. They'd talked about it at school on the Monday – it was almost all they talked about on Monday – but either Pete couldn't remember or he wanted to relive the glory.

"Massively. Shit, man, I puked four times. My dad was freaked. He went into this speech on moderation. I mean, I probably won't drink vodka again for a while so, you know."

"Isn't his job doing something about teen drinking? Like, counselling?"

"Kind of. Ministry of Health. Campaigning not counselling. Anyway, hangovers suck. I was fine. But yeah, it's a real nice taste... clear spirits. We could try white rum next time if you want?"

"Sounds good, man. Brown rum is good though. Tasty. What makes it brown, do you think?" asked Pete.

"Dunno. Maybe the sugar cane?" Axle guessed. "Raw sugar? Might be better for you than processed white stuff? My parents always say that about food – brown rice, wholemeal bread – you know?"

Pete sipped from the bottle and passed it back to Axle. There was still half the hip flask left.

"It's magic, right?" Axle asked. "I don't really believe in magic. But, like, can you explain what happens when we drink? Like, alcohol goes into the blood stream. Obviously. But the feeling is in my brain."

"And the brain is all neurons firing and shit, right? So, what does the blood do?" Pete guessed.

"Blood just delivers it. Maybe it thins the blood? I mean what even is that neurons-firing thing? It's not like we can feel them fire," said Axle.

"I don't know. Just loosens you up," said Pete.

"Yeah, and I can actually talk to girls then, you know. That's the important thing."

"Yeah, we saw. Axle coming on strong to those five all at once."

"Strong? Hardly."

"I know, I know. You were smooth, man. Do you like any of them? I dated Rata in Year Nine. My first proper kiss. We were only kids, though, so it only half counts."

"Nah, there's none I'm really into. I mean, they're all cool, whatever, in their own ways. Best off taking my time."

"Don't hold back. You can tell me! Seriously, I told you," said Pete.

"Oh, you told me about Rata. You kissed her two years ago, big deal," Axle laughed. "And isn't she dating some guy from Col now? What about today? Any that you actually like now?"

"Oh man. I mean Tanasi is so hot, eh. But..." Pete trailed off.

Axle wondered why he'd supposed that his crush was unique. Of course everyone wanted Tanasi. "Yeah, yeah, she is hot. But you said 'but'. But what?"

"But she's with Reggie, duh. I mean, obviously. Has been since last year. That's why Reggie's hardly around with us now. I don't know. Maybe you're too new to notice? He's one of those guys who falls for a girl and then flakes on his friends. He did the same for, like, four months at the start of Year Nine. Hell, he even did it at primary school. It's cool. Whatever. And now, well, I asked him to hang with us tonight and he doesn't even get back to me. He'll probably text tomorrow with a 'hey-sorry-bro'."

Axle had been enjoying his secret crush but, as the new guy, he also knew that his priority was to not tread on anyone's toes. He walked over to look at the book that Pete had kicked away. A novel by some New Zealand author he'd never heard of.

The boys chatted away, the night blew on, and the cemetery sheltered the fledgling intimacy of their conversation. They talked of nothing in particular – gossip, plans for the future, bullshit, what they'd do if they won ten million dollars. They finished the rum then rose from the grass and the graves, patting off some leaves and twigs.

"I'm definitely – definitely! – getting cremated," Pete said. "I don't want to be buried."

"Wouldn't it be cool, though, to imagine some drunk kids like us dancing round the cemetery while your bones are down there?"

"I don't know, man. They can throw my ashes wherever. Whatever. Death sucks. When my grandma died, it was real sad. I mean, duh. It was the middle of winter and everything was so cold. Every time I think of it, I think of the waterlogged soil and that feeling in your feet when they're cold all the way through. What a way to go. I'd rather the extreme hot of cremation to being a cold corpse stuck in the dirt. Fire is the answer. That'd get it done."

"You don't believe in the afterlife?" Axle asked. It wasn't that he did, but Axle was curious as to what Pete would say.

"Hell no, man. No. Seriously? I believe in here and now!"
A torch shone across the graves and an adult voice called out.
"Let's go!" Pete hissed.

Axle was already up. They dashed. The escape flooded their chests with adrenaline and, when it eased, they couldn't quite find their way back to their drunken high. The empty rum bottle had been left behind – neither buried nor cremated – but they'd grabbed their skateboards on the way. Pete yawned and Axle laughed at him, called him "nana", then said he should head off, too.

"Hey, there's an all-ages show in a few weeks. At the old war bunkers up in Brooklyn. Jarvis, Keevan and I are going. Want to come?"

They paused at a set of stairs. It was quicker for Axle to carry on along the road to get home, rather than climb the hills to Pete's then go back.

"I don't need you to walk me home, bro," said Pete. "It's Kelburn. What's the worst that could happen? I get bored to death?"

Rice noodles for two

> I'm heading out to that Norwegian bar tonight to test how the Scandos do light beer. Keen?

He'd tried three or four ways of writing the email but he sounded more and more geriatric the more he tried. He wished he could have texted her, but for some reason her email sign off didn't have her number in it and he felt a bit weird searching for it elsewhere. In the end he thought the message was good enough.

Scott had put on some music and started to prepare dinner, keeping one eye on his inbox. As he diced vegetables and turned the rice down to simmer, he heard the bang of the front gate, then the click of the front door.

"Forget something?" he called to Axle. Where he expected to see his son, his wife appeared. She didn't answer.

"Early night?" he asked without much thought. Despite her assurances, he'd assumed her afternoon date would merge into the evening. He'd mentally prepared himself for anything.

"You can wipe that look off your face. I told you it was casual. We went rock climbing, if you must know, and I'm exhausted. Don't say a thing."

"I didn't say anything."

"Right. But you thought it. You cooking for me, too?"

"I can be, yip."

He was about to say he was sorry that her night hadn't gone as planned, but he held his tongue. Better to check the timing for the rice noodles than make small talk. Maybe in an hour or so they could have a proper chat, if Linnea didn't reply.

"Would you turn the music down a little?" she asked.

He obliged. His computer was connected to the kitchen sound system and, while he only needed to tap shift-F11 to reduce the volume, he logged on and also changed the album. A more soothing album was needed, Gurdjieff or something, not music to hype him up. And then there was that familiar ding. One new message.

> Just heading out to something
> else now. But meet me there at 9?
> I have friends in tow, too.
> Feel free to invite others if you
> haven't already.

He caught himself grinning. He didn't end up changing the music. Why pander to his wife? They were both adults. She could ask, if she wanted to change it. He merely turned it down, as requested.

> Nice, nice. See you then.

He regretted the message as soon as it was sent. Bouncy bloke-speak like a divorced dad arranging to pick up a kid for the once-a-month visitation. Too cheery, too task oriented. A wanker. What could he do? The message was sent. It wouldn't matter. The date had been set. Time and location were locked and loaded.

God, he thought, who says "locked and loaded"? Even his inner monologue had been set to doofus.

He whizzed up some peanuts and tahini into a satay sauce then drizzled it over the steamed veggies and noodles. The secret, other than using a medley of colours, was to sprinkle fried shallots on top. He dished up a bowl for himself and then served a bowl to Jacqui in the lounge, who didn't look up from her phone. He placed her favourite chopsticks beside the bowl, as well as a spoon. It was good food, but not like you'd get at a restaurant. He didn't go overboard with salt or sweeteners.

"I'm off to meet some work colleagues tonight, hun. I think I told you this morning, yeah? Didn't think you'd be home. Axle's out but I told him he had to be home well before midnight after that last party at Pete's. He told me it is just him and Pete. Probably meeting up with some girls. And yes, I reminded him of the talk we'd had."

"Yeah, good," said Jacqui.

"I had that other chat with Axle, too."

"Oh yeah?" She put her phone down and picked up the chopsticks and bowl. "Go as planned?"

"I think so. At one point he might have thought I was transitioning – coming out as trans," said Scott, "but we got there in the end."

"I know what transitioning is, *hun*. And no, I'm sure he didn't think you were doing that."

"I know. I was joking. It's just a bit tough figuring out how to get the conversation started on the right foot. It's not like we put together a full strategy with talking points and contingencies. You know? I start out trying to connect with him, but he's on edge because he's not sure if I'm going to be wanting to talk about teen drinking or climate change or sex or some half-assed career advice."

"But it went well?" asked Jacqui.

He sensed she didn't really care, so he responded in a roundabout way. "Well enough, yeah. He knows we're opening up a bit. With other adults. Nothing to be worried about. I think I might need to have that climate change talk, though."

He looked to her for confirmation, but it was not offered. He turned away. He needed to get ready for his date.

Baulk

Scott was on the bus and halfway to the Brandon Street bar when a string of emails came through.

> Hey change of plans, sorry. An old
> friend is having a going away party
> and I really should go. Let's do the
> 'research' Tues or Weds.
> After work ;) not before.

But, shit – what to do? He couldn't go home. Jacqui would love that. He'd been so casual about going out that she must have known something was up. If the evening had meant nothing to him, he would have complained about having to get a bus into town at night. A little inconsequential jealousy, he reasoned, might help refresh her image of him.

To save face, he'd have to go anyway. He logged into his Facebook account and messaged three old friends to see if any were up for a beer, I-know-it's-late-notice-etc. Any time he caught up with these guys it took a month's notice to co-ordinate, and half the time their reunions would be cancelled last minute.

He tagged off the bus, thanked the driver and walked in the direction of the bar, checking his phone every other minute. He'd imagined the bar would be full and bouncing, it being Saturday night and all. But the atmosphere was subdued. Was it too early? Or maybe too late? Maybe there was a rugby game or a concert on?

He positioned himself at the smallest, least intrusive table. He knew hospitality ran on tight margins and if the bar filled, any empty seats would weigh on him.

A waiter glided over with a drinks menu.

"Anything I can get you?"

"I've heard a lot about your range of low-alcohol beers."

"List is at the bottom of the other page."

"Oh, ahh, yes," Scott said, flipping over the menu.

"Just call me over when you're ready."

"Thanks. I'll just be a minute."

He should have asked what the waiter recommended. He went back to his phone. Two of his three messages had been seen, but there had been no response.

The waiter looked his way raising his brow to check if Scott was ready. He wasn't, but waved him over and made a quick decision.

"I'll have the Brewer's Special Alabama Red IPA, please. The 2.8% one." He passed the menu back.

"Certainly," the waiter said, placing a glass of water in front of him and making motions to leave.

"Wait, what do you think of it? It's a decent beer?"

"Yeah, of course. We wouldn't stock it if it wasn't high quality. All depends on what you like."

He thought of chatting to the waiter about his troubles. He'd seen that in movies. Waiters – or was it bar staff? – were paid to listen to people's problems. Maybe he had to sit at the bar for that to happen. Maybe that was only in America. Maybe he had to be a regular.

"Wait, wait," he called after the waiter, "I could use something stronger. And darker. A stout."

"Want to see the menu?"

"No. No. You choose. You know the menu better than me."

That had been the moment for some camaraderie but it had fallen short. There was nothing between them. That was the New Zealand way. Why couldn't he embrace being sullen and solo. He'd just been stood up. It was his right.

Scott's beer arrived and he guzzled half of the pint. He checked his phone again and wrote off the evening. There was always the midweek. Tuesday or Wednesday. He scrolled on his phone some more, liked a handful of posts on Facebook and then unliked them. What was the point?

When Scott got home, Jacqui was still on the couch, her empty dinner bowl in front of her. He didn't want to interrupt, so he poured a glass of water and made his way into their bedroom. Jacqui trailed after him. He would submit to anything ahead of explaining his night and she was kind enough not to bring it up. His obvious failure had thawed her mood. She whispered in his ear. He held his breath. Her lip grazed his lobe. Off with the lights, their socks, and into heightened thoughts of the past and future. They had each other. That was true. There was the whirr of the dishwasher, the green light from the clock-radio and the gentle thump of their mattress against the wall.

Waking from slumber, Scott heard the gate click, then the front door open and close. It was minutes before midnight. Their son made barely a sound as he wove through the house – a gush of plumbing, the gentle clack of a door. It was a sober sound, or near enough.

Scott looked to the glow of the clock.

12:07am.

A new day.

Mostly men

Jacqui had almost gone to the protests against the Police in 2006 – and she never went to protests. She could still remember the line of shaved heads in the courtroom and the anger as details finally became clear.

In hiring Jacqui, the Police had made the classic mistake of curing one ill with another. She was the spider swallowed by Old Bill to cure the fly. She was the cane toad introduced to control a hungry beetle. She was gorse for the lonesome settler.

Her per hour rate had been low for the time. She hadn't known any better. When she found out what some of the men were paid, she was pissed. When her contract was rolled over for a second six-month stint, she negotiated her rate up to a respectable level. Fair was fair. After twelve months they were ready to let her move on to her next project but, they soon realised – she hardly even had to emphasise it – their situation was still too raw to risk letting her loose.

Her income had made life a lot easier for their family. They moved from their first home in Crofton Downs to a much nicer one in Kelburn. They paid a bit more attention to how they looked – dry cleaning, laser hair removal from Scott's back and shoulders, and getting work clothes tailored to fit. Axle had been enrolled in Kelburn Normal.

A decade and a half after joining the Police, Jacqui was still there. She had no plans to leave. She'd outlasted five bosses and was onto her sixth. It wasn't in her nature to be rude, but to deal with these men she'd had to employ a method and manner that was.

Her new boss's name was Rothman. He was smart, clearly – he didn't sign off emails with his rank nor did he brag about the gangs he'd busted back on the beat. He was also self-assured in a way that concerned her. Had he actually been a cop before getting into management? She would have to go back to the email that introduced him to make sure.

At the one meeting she'd sat in with him, he'd barely said a word and may not have even been paying attention. His only contribution was to insist that the report into new international policing techniques included a section on private police forces with a particular focus on post conflict situations.

Jacqui had expected Rothman would set up the same fortnightly meetings that her predecessor had insisted upon. He hadn't. January had become February, then March.

Jacqui got curious. She searched for Rothman online. She hated herself for it, feeling she'd already lost to him through her curiosity being piqued. She couldn't find much; his name was too common. Alan Rothman snagged her an English footballer and an Australian novelist. Alan Theodore Rothman? She found nothing and went home in a foul mood. It was only Monday. Scott didn't stand a chance.

Home

"I'm heading out with João again on Friday. I think you should meet him, too."

It had sounded reasonable in her head, but in speaking she hadn't been able to round off the sharpness in her voice.

"Woah! Slow down. This is the guy from the weekend?" asked Scott.

"Sorry. Yeah. I'm sorry." She took a few seconds and backpedalled. "Work, you know. New boss. Stress. How'd your date go, anyway? Sorry. Work drinks, was it? Paula?"

"Paula doesn't work with us anymore. I got a better offer, elsewhere." He paused to see if she would launch back at him. She didn't. Neither had talked about their dates the day before nor had they enquired about how the other's date had gone. He collected himself and continued, "My night was fine. Actually, she cancelled when I was headed into the city. I had one drink and came home."

"I mean, you didn't seem very riled when you got back, so I assumed."

"I might take her up on the rain check tomorrow or Wednesday, though. The whole thing is a lot of work, to be honest. Not to mention trying to make sure Axle is kept up to speed. I'll check in again with him this week. Or you could? Not much really to report though."

"I'm happy for you to talk with him. Keep the message straight. Maybe wait until after I see João?"

"What kind of name is João, anyway?"

"It's Portuguese. He's from Brazil."

"One of Kaye and Robert's friends, right? Posh diplomat type? You're dating the Brazilian ambassador?"

"Ha! No, nothing like that. He's, well, he's a bit young for that. He'd be more like a cultural attaché or the handsome chauffeur for the High Commissioner. No, no. I think he works in hospo."

And, with that, Scott's mind formed a picture of João. For the first time in at least a decade, he tweaked with jealousy. The only other time he'd been jealous was when Jacqui had held back telling him about how she considered a high school Chemistry teacher to be her first love. She'd kept that from him until five years into their marriage. He'd known when she'd lost her virginity, but, because she wasn't the type to talk about love, he'd imagined that he had been her first and only.

Jacqui had been one of three students in the Chemistry teacher's class. Whenever the teacher had ventured out to check on their equations, the stolid grey matter of her brain shuddered with some technicolour bliss. He'd only touched her once, on the shoulder, through jersey and blouse, but it had been enough to set her off on a prolonged infatuation. The situation peaked when she drafted a letter to him, and her mother found it. Over one long, cold weekend – Queen's Birthday or Labour Day – her parents wrangled the truth from her and forced her to drop out of his class. She'd sworn that their efforts wouldn't keep her from him, but they had. Those with wise advice had been right. She had hated them for it.

Scott knew jealousy was the saddest passion, a chemical instinct shunting evolution forward through possessive impulses. With this young Brazilian, a twinge of the old feeling had returned. He tried to put João out of his mind.

The night eked on, with Jacqui busying herself downstairs and Scott keeping himself out of her way. He helped Axle plod through preparation for an English test, then traipsed up to Upland Road with the glass recycling. He washed the pot and saucepan from dinner, then dried them. Before decamping to their bedroom, he set the dishwasher to start at five minutes past midnight to take advantage of cheaper overnight electricity rates and so as its gargling wouldn't ruin the peace of the evening.

    Scott brushed his teeth and eyed himself in the mirror. There was only one salve for the ulcer of jealousy. Respect. He'd always known she was clever. She was just as strategic as Linnea. Perhaps more so because she had proved herself. Scott had valued her before, of course, but this newer form of respect required he combine that earlier esteem with an unexpected awe drawn from his jealousy. Now, through this João character, he saw how little he knew of his wife. And even what was to come he could not begin to presume or predict. Hence, the awe. Jealousy was an annoying side-effect. He could think his way through it.

Climate for change

The climate strikes had moved from Parliament to Wellington High. Axle and Pete stood back and watched as a handful of teachers tried to talk their way through a line of students. The national leadership had given way to wildcat demos and non-violent direct action.

The previous Monday, the school had lost the first battle with these blockades. Detentions had been assigned to any student who wouldn't leave the protest line. One by one their names were read aloud, then the sentence announced.

"Roberta Mary Eagleton. Detention. Aaron Joseph Benderson. Detention. Kyle B Kazakhski. Detention." And so on, for at least thirty minutes, across the school's tinny intercom system.

Footage of the blockade had bubbled over on social media on the Tuesday and, by the lunch break on Wednesday, hundreds of other students had arrived from other schools.

That same evening, Klappenberg convened the board. Someone had to decide on whether to call the Police. Not likely, said the Chair, whose only son had been one of those given detention. The board asked what the students' demands were. Klap couldn't say. He hadn't thought to ask. The board recommended de-escalation. Divide and dissolve. Get the leaders into the deputy principal's office and let the process begin.

On Friday, the students had delegated three Year Nine students with a list of impossible demands: voting rights for all high schoolers, climate-centric curriculum and the firing of any teachers who would not sign a pledge to personally honour a zero-carbon policy.

On Monday morning, a third period Stats class was blockaded and there were plans to do the same for a class after lunch.

"I heard Col and Girls were onto it last Friday, too," said Reggie, joining Pete and Axle. "It's time we get involved."

Axle wasn't sure. He knew he wasn't in a place to lead things, but nor could he be seen to be a coward. He'd listen to Pete, if Pete had anything to say. But Pete had withdrawn from the conversation, so Axle bounced from foot to foot, hands in his pockets, listening. Reggie edged away from the guys and over to where Tanasi and Beth sat.

"So, what do you think?" Axle asked, once he was alone with Pete.

"Dunno," said Pete.

"Imagine, though, if Reggie and Tanasi were leading it then the whole year might follow. We could win!"

"They're not leading though, are they? See. It's all maybe and might do. Those two have a way of getting through without too many scrapes. Same with the others protesting. See the one yelling at Mr Amis? Aaron Benderson. His mum's a partner at one of the big law firms. The girl beside him? Her grandfather was head of the Reserve Bank. I don't know your parents, but I can tell you're not from one of these old families. You and I need to be more cautious. No point getting expelled."

"So, we just do nothing."

"Nothing as obvious as all this," said Pete.

"So, we just sneak around and... and do what?" asked Axle. He was genuinely perplexed by his friend.

"Nothing. Nothing. All this, though, is for people who are going to be alright whatever happens to them. You and I are borderline. We could go either way. I mean, you probably don't know but Reggie gets a $200 a week allowance."

"Fuck me!" said Axle.

"You wouldn't know by looking at how his family lives, but there's a lot of money there."

"So, we do what then?"

"The same as the powerless always do: subterfuge, sabotage, guerrilla warfare."

"Dude."

"I know, right? I'm serious though. I mean, what else is left to do?"

Linnea on Tuesday

Linnea was ten minutes late and apologetic on two counts.

"Sorry, eh. A bit late. Oh, and sorry that I had that going away thing at the weekend."

"All good," said Scott.

"To be honest, my friends thought it was a bit weird to be meeting a guy from work for a drink on the weekend. They bailed on me and I felt a bit weird. I'm sorry. Is that rude of me to say?"

"No, no. Not at all. If we're being honest, well, I came here on my own anyway. Sat at this exact same table. Had a drink, was thinking of catching up with friends, but they were all tied up. They messaged me the next day saying they'd had early nights or were at the movies with the wife and kids."

"Probably no place for a married man," Linnea laughed.

Was that flirting? Best to assume it wasn't.

"Yeah, maybe," Scott answered, "but maybe things have changed since the 1970s. For the better."

"Like, how?"

"For starters, low alcohol beer. It might not sound very sexy, but moderation is the new cool. Oh, you're laughing, but I'm telling you, it is! And in one way that's really freeing."

"Ah yes, you men and their freedoms! Men have been using that line since the 1960s. 'Come on, baby, relax. Free up a little.'"

"No, no, not like that. I know you're joking, though. You can't imagine... no. You can imagine. What about women though? Like, I read the other day that as many as 25% of young women now identify as bisexual. Isn't that freedom?"

The waiter, a young woman this time, chose her moment to interrupt. Scott was unsure if she'd heard the conversation.

"I'll have the Brewer's Special Alabama Red IPA, please," said Scott, then turned to Linnea.

"I'll have the same? Wait, no. We should try different ones. Is there a tasting tray?"

"Ah, no. Well, yes, but it's only for the tap beers," the waiter said. "The Brewer's Special – all those ones on the menu – are canned."

"Oh, that makes sense. What do you recommend? How about the Ringnes Lettøl?"

"It is very low alcohol. One of our lowest. Just checking that you're fine with that."

"Yes. Completely. We're here to sample a few of them," said Linnea, raising her brow to bring the waiter into her confidence. "Work drinks."

Scott couldn't tell if he was the butt of her joke or if the concept of low-alcohol work drinks was.

"OK, yeah. So more of the ladies are bi," said Linnea. "Twenty-five per cent? Nah. But if so, great. Fine, I mean. What use is that freedom if patriarchy is still on top? Like, it seems a very specific freedom that gels with the fantasies of men. Top up women's pay? Hell, make it transparent so we can negotiate ourselves? Not a chance. But create a spectacle of young women's sexuality, and you're off to a flying start. Even the old boys in the Sensible Family Coalition would mumble in bemused approval."

"I mean, sure, roll all men into the patriarchy. That's fine. Do I look like I'm on top?"

"Guilty until proven innocent," said Linnea.

"I mean, sure, men have a history. Categorically. I don't blame you, but..." he paused while the drinks were delivered. Hers was in a can and his in a bottle. She poured half of the can into a glass, and he followed suit. A rustic little dish of spicy, salted peanuts was placed between them. He took a taste, then poured all of his beer into the glass.

He continued, "... but let me plead my case."

"Your case, or all men's cases? Anyway, sorry, I'm listening."

"Neither really. Or both. Did you mean... anyway, it was a throwaway line. I'm fine with how I do or do not fit into your idea of my gender."

"I mean, patriarchy is more than gender though," she said.

He nodded but didn't really know what she was getting at. He was more concerned that his tone had been too intimate. If he'd been her boss, then certainly. At this moment he felt that they had landed on the banter expected from work colleagues.

"Ok, but this is between us. I wouldn't want others at work knowing. Can we agree?" asked Scott.

"Sure. Why not? Blanket agreement for you to tell me whatever you will. Go."

"I'm serious," Scott said.

"Yeah. I don't doubt it."

He frowned. She did doubt it. She had her own share of presumptions.

"Cool. So, this Friday my wife is going on a date with this handsome, young Brazilian man. He's about your age. I've told her I'm happy to meet him, too. Well, sort of. As I said, this isn't only about men and our freedoms."

"And you're fine with this? You're totally happy with this guy, this suave Latino who we can only assume is some sort of bronzed demigod, seducing your wife?"

"Oh, I think my wife – Jacqui, is her name – would be more than a match for him. And why shouldn't she be? It's about her pleasure, not some one-sided seduction. Why would I be concerned about that?"

"Let me guess. She's only allowed to do it because she caught you having an affair. Her Brazilian fling is what you give to make up for your take."

"Not at all true. In fact, she brought it up."

"She did? Apropos of nothing?"

"Nothing is from nothing. It's true that I've had some close calls. One or two. Not really. Not even close calls. I was honest to her about some things that I wanted. That's normal. But what I really want you to know is that this idea of all men my age, married or otherwise, being creeps is beyond a stereotype. It's a cliché. Caricature. I can handle the prejudice from society, but I also don't think people should be so quick to judge."

Linnea paused, unsure of which claim to challenge.

"So, she really brought it up first?" she asked. All the irony and chiding had been stripped from her voice.

"I mean, I didn't lie when I said that she did. I remember it clearly. Though we've been talking about it for years. On and off. It's not a thing I'd lie about. I was telling her about this fantasy I had about... a woman... an old work colleague. She lives overseas now... and how... I won't go into it."

"Hmm. Do I know her?"

"Probably not. How long you been around? Over a year, right. Paula was her name. But back to the story."

"I don't know her."

"No. Well. Jacqui and I have always tried to be open about sex and desire. We're married after all, it's the end of the road for hedging and brinkmanship. There's no use for charades or pretending we're psychic about each other's needs. A week or so ago she came out with it: how about we try it? For real. I thought she was joking – pillow talk – all that. I mean, what's hot is hot, right? It doesn't mean you have to act on it. We've all got fantasies that might not be a good idea to act on. Nothing weird or gross. Just complex. Of course, if we don't try then how do we know?"

He'd been talking at a pace and, when he stopped, the silence was disorienting. Heavy air. He took a sip from his beer, a little too conscious of his lips against the glass. "And so, I checked in with her the next day and she said we really should try it. Really. You only live once. Where's the harm? I don't know. What do you think?"

Linnea was embarrassed. He may have spoken too loudly. Scott looked around. No-one appeared to be listening. He checked himself and saw that he had been leaning forward and she had pulled back.

He sat back and swilled the beer around his glass. She didn't speak. He took a sip. He knew the journalist and cop trick of being silent to get a person to run their mouths. He'd also read about how to deal with this situation: revisit, clarify and strengthen your key messages.

He began again, quieter this time. "I mean, it's as much about my pleasure as hers, you know? That's the crux. I know men aren't supposed to express their feelings like that in this county. Surely you understand what I mean, though? I mean people say that young people aren't having as much sex anymore... maybe that's our fault for being too successful at minimising alcohol consumption, though I'm not sorry for that... I mean you must have a boyfriend. Or have had one?"

Linnea didn't answer. This was not going well. She didn't look at him. Shit. He could feel beads of sweat roll from his armpit and trickle down his arm.

"Or a girlfriend. Or a someone... maybe? Fuck, you're not an asexual are you? I'm sorry. It doesn't matter to me. Honestly. I'm sorry I brought it up. I'm not saying... you don't have to say. Just forget that last part. I'm sorry."

He tried to think of the point he'd been trying to make at the start of the conversation. It did not return to him. He felt a long way from where they'd started and a longer way from the kind of stable reasoning that was required at the Ministry. He needed her to respond.

Linnea offered a glance over the lip of her glass. The silence pooled, threatening to spill over into whatever lay beyond.

"Uh, I'm sorry," she said. "I have to go. I'm sorry if I crossed a line or said something that implied I was interested or wanted to talk about your problems with your wife. I really don't think we should have had or be having this conversation."

She rose, went to the bar and paid for her beer. Then she was out the door without a goodbye or any more explanation.

Scott sat back, then reached forward and shook her can of beer – 0.3% alcohol and half full. She'd barely drunk from the little she'd poured into the glass. He finished his own beer then looked around the bar, thought, "what the hell," and took a sip from her can. Not bad!

The next day, just after he'd returned from lunch, Scott was messaged by Erving from human resources. The dreaded HR. There was an urgent matter that they needed to discuss. A meeting popped up on his afternoon calendar, seconds before the ding of the alert.

The ropes

Two days had passed since João had introduced Jacqui to the climbing gym. Her biceps still held the ache. This tiredness is good, she told herself, but it does blunt one's mind. All day she'd been thinking of balancing a new focus on her upper body with a commitment to intellectual stimulation. That stimulation took the form of a simple and practical commitment: finishing the history of Antarctica that she'd begun last winter.

She trod downstairs to her study to find the book. It sat on a desk, buried beneath a film festival guide and a credit card statement. She almost picked up a thin volume of poetry instead. No, she told herself, she could have poetry once she was finished with history. She brushed away the dust which clung to the book's cellophane jacket and bounded back up the stairs. She went to the far side of the bed, stretching out on the carpet with her back to the wall. It was her favourite spot for privacy in the house. The sun bobbled above the horizon, and she fought the urge to close her eyes and doze. She drew a pillow down from the bed to rest against, and then another.

She read one page but the words would not come together into meaning. She flicked back to the start of the chapter, but the sun was too bright and the pages were too shiny. She turned away from words to gaze at a photo of a couple standing against, grinning amongst, the glare of anonymous ice. They wore old-fashioned overalls and she tried to work out if it was the photo that had faded or if the dull pastel was the clothes' original colour. Their faces were trimmed with fur linings and their eyes were hidden by goggles. Still, she thought, they seemed happy.

Jacqui recalled some fact about the quantity of condoms supplied each year to Scott Base. It was an improbable number. She couldn't imagine they'd all be used. Condoms were for teenagers, anyway. Adults made other plans against conception. She wondered if João would be one of those men who became petulant when told to wear a condom. Surely not. She should have asked Kaye. She turned back to the book and the picture of the couple. Fucking in Antarctica: one for the bucket list.

She placed the book to one side and closed her eyes. The house was quiet. She tasked her mind with recognising the noises beyond. There was a rumble of a bus in the valley below and, when it had passed, a hum of electricity, perhaps from the substation at the bottom of the hill. The sun became stronger and, as she inhaled, she noticed that beads of sweat had appeared either side of the bridge of her nose. I'll just enjoy the sun, she thought.

Jacqui's mind returned to the climbing gym. She'd been a little discontented ever since. What had not lived up to her expectations? Perhaps it was that the photos she'd seen of João climbing were all in the outdoors. That may have been it. The scene she'd imagined had been the two of them in a fresh expanse. But inside the climbing gym, all the human vigour was trapped and noxious. The smell of gym mats spritzed with droplets of sweat, paired to a cocksure atmosphere that she had not expected. It was competitive, and that was fine, but Jacqui felt like João had also been more focused on the sport than on her. It had been a date, after all.

Jacqui opened her eyes and tapped the pin to unlock her phone. She laughed. João's profile was still open in her browser. She scrolled to the images of him climbing. It was the lighting, she realised. In his pictures, the sun streamed through the trees and across the cliff face. Even the lichen was vibrant. The photos showed his shoulders and arms. His muscles and a mole. There was the harness, and she remembered how it felt being strapped in. At risk but secure.

Despite her coyness with Kaye, Jacqui had wanted to sleep with him ever since she saw his face. She felt a tenderness towards Kaye as she realised how well she'd been set up. If Kaye had delivered him with a ribbon on, it couldn't have been easier. He was a gift offered without that horrid sense of obligation or reciprocity. She should really send a message of thanks to Kaye.

So that was how she began dreaming of what might come, of how it might happen. She pictured him on top, her on top, her on her back, on her stomach. She saw his body looming over hers. She thought of them in the bed in her room, white sheets, his skin contrasting with hers. Then she pulled back from the thoughts. She was with João because he was young and fit, not because of some skin fetish. If he'd been a young white man, she'd have had the same thoughts. She was upset with herself, but she hadn't opened her eyes, nor departed from those thoughts. She settled back in, asking herself what was so wrong about a little exotic role play. People played roles all the time. It was okay and no-one got hurt. Just keep it in your head. Accept the gift. She wasn't so naive. But nor was she self-denying. She opened her eyes and looked back at the pictures of João, flicking through a few until she had what she needed. She closed her eyes, once more, drew her legs up and a pillow close. When she was through, only a little of the shame remained. She picked up her phone, flipped the camera mode to selfie and took a dozen pictures. She chose one where her face was obscured, but a sheen shone from her breasts. She sent it to him, with the lines:

> Loved our climb.
> Let's meet up soon.
> xx

Glum

"Scott, I'm Erving. Senior Advisor. People and Culture. This is Justin, Scott. Yup, alright then? Scott, Justin."

An array of printouts and documents had been carefully arranged across the meeting room table, like viscera in an autopsy. Scott knew the tricks of human resources. He wouldn't let them intimidate him. He picked one up. It appeared to have nothing to do with him. Maybe from a previous meeting? He relaxed a little.

"Gidday, Scott. Great to see you, Erving," said Justin, reaching for his hand. Scott dropped the printout and shook Justin's hand.

Scott had checked out Erving online. He probably should have known him before, should have cultivated a relationship with him over his years at the Ministry. He'd never had a need for friends in HR. It seemed impure. He took pride in being so focused on his work that he wouldn't go out of his way to network with the higher ups. He should have known that, at best, he was seen as a steady pair of hands. To the higher ups he was nothing exceptional or that could not be replaced.

"Nice to meet you, Justin. Erving, quick question: should I have a PSA rep here? Seems like an awful lot of paperwork for an informal meeting." Scott was trying to decipher, from his upside-down view, exactly what the rest of the documents were about. There was no way HR took this much of an interest in him. Some of the documents appeared to be emails. His emails?

Erving shuffled the papers into a single stack. He passed a rather long series of printouts to Justin, tapping the top one with a stubby forefinger, before clearing his throat. "No, no. It's fine, Scott. Trust me. Well, no, trust Justin." Erving turned to Justin. "You can take it from here."

"Thanks, Erv. Appreciate the confidence."

"Best guy we've got," Erving said to Scott, gesturing at Justin, "rest assured. Safe hands."

Scott did not feel assured. Erving left the room and he considered whether it was because the meeting was a trifling matter or because the senior staff always took pains to avoid the dirty work.

"Best guy, huh?" asked Scott.

"Mm, yes," said Justin. Then, looking up from the printouts, he asked, "Mind if I record this meeting? Protocol. As much for you as for me. I've already started, actually. Protocol. Got to get your consent on tape."

"Bit of a catch-22 then, isn't it?" said Scott. It was supposed to be a joke.

"A catch-22," repeated Justin, making a note.

"Doesn't matter. Is this about..." said Scott, but then he stopped. He didn't want to ask.

"About? Something troubling your mind?" asked Justin. It felt like an impromptu visit from a youth pastor.

Scott had heard a little about Justin but not enough to summarily dismiss his worth as a human. Whispers around the office. Women said he was tricky, that he wasn't necessarily on anyone's side. Surely that is the universal truth about HR, Scott had thought at the time, downgrading the whispers to gossip. Apparently, Justin had completed a degree in law before ending up in human resources. Scott wondered at the story behind that. He ought to do some digging.

"No. No. Nothing from my end," said Scott. "Maybe you could tell me what this is about."

"That's fine. Yes." Justin checked his work phone, took down the time and a note. "All standard, nothing to worry about. This will take very little time. Please interrupt me if any of the following doesn't ring true."

"Right," Scott said.

"On Tuesday evening, you had an alcoholic drink with a female colleague outside of work hours. You discussed a range of sexual and marital issues."

"Low-alcohol, to be precise."

"But alcohol, yes?"

"Yes."

"So, a range of sexual and marital issues, then? No objection? And the colleague you drank with has fewer than two years' experience. You have more than ten. She does not report to you, directly. You have asked her to be involved in numerous projects outside of her direct area of expertise. How are we going?"

"Only one project. Well, one and a half."

"A half?" asked Justin.

"Two, then. Not 'numerous'."

Justin made a note.

"What are you writing?" Scott asked.

"I'm writing what you said. Nothing more. And you are correct. Two, if your account is true, does not count as 'numerous'."

"Thank you," said Scott.

"True or otherwise, there is little need for please and thanks. You can make a more general statement of clarification after if you wish. You can also have a support person present, though I'm sure you know that."

"Yes. Fine. Keep going."

"Not much to go. Your colleague expressed discomfort through her body language. You asked numerous questions of the colleague of a sexual or relationship nature that she refused to answer."

"She did not refuse."

"Ah. So, she did answer?"

"She didn't answer. But she did not refuse."

"Refusals come in many forms when there is a power imbalance."

"Fine, but I will clear this up in my statement," said Scott. He eyed the flashing red light on the screen of Justin's phone. He felt pinned down but knew not to speak in anger. The recording was the most important thing now. He'd modulate his tone, shorten his sentences. He should speak to the union. He wondered if his membership might have lapsed. He didn't read their emails anymore. Ah, but if he was getting emails, then he was probably still a member.

"One last fact to check in on," Justin added, pausing for effect.

What a little shit, Scott thought, he's enjoying this! Scott looked at the man. He assessed him from his hair down to his socks. He could be a bank teller. He could have been any anonymous henchman.

"Your colleague left the bar abruptly – not finishing her drink – after you had asserted the high value that you placed on physical pleasure and had enquired into her sexual and relationship status."

Justin cleared his throat and fingered his tie. Time crept on.

"Well?" asked Justin.

"Well?" said Scott.

He was worried that they knew he had drunk from her can. That fact was not incriminating in and of itself, but he imagined that little bit of information would have been enough to seal his fate. He was a pervert. A creep. A sex pest. Justin had nothing extra to add. He kept his eyes levelled at Scott, playing a game that only one of them enjoyed. He wondered if this is what Erving meant when he'd said Justin was the best, or whether he had no idea about the cat and mouse games his subordinate played.

"Alright then," Justin replied, when he saw that Scott would not deny the final statement.

"So, you're complete?" asked Scott. "And you want me to make my statement now?"

"I don't want anything. But now is as good a time as any if you would like to make a statement."

"But I've hardly had time to prepare it."

"What preparation would be needed? Just tell the truth and correct anything that I've said that's incorrect. Procedurally, I should offer five minutes to ensure the chronology is correct. At most, you are permitted seventy-two hours and to file a written report. Any written submission won't be considered a statement of clarification, though.

It – and any subsequent comments, correspondence or infringements – will be considered a post-interview appendix. They may be subject to new, additional or further investigations."

"Fine. So, you're recommending I make a statement now."

"I am not recommending anything. You may like five minutes to consider your response? I am pausing the recorder at the ten minute thirty-three second mark. Recorder paused."

Scott trod out of the room and back to his workstation. He took a long drink from a water bottle on his desk. He could barely think of what Justin had told him and how he should set the record straight without digging himself a deeper hole. He checked his email. Nothing of note had arrived other than the typical noise from one of their peskier stakeholders – a school upset with what one of the trainers had or hadn't done. People expect so much of us, he thought. He took a few deep breaths, jotted down three clarifying points about the previous evening with Linnea before returning to the room.

"Before we get back into recording," Justin said, "I should let you know where we currently sit if, for example, you choose to make a statement or not to. Let's imagine I put the recorder back on and you decide not to challenge our statement of facts. Okay?"

"Go on," said Scott.

"In that case, if you do not offer a statement, I would end this process by issuing a formal, written warning for being in breach of our sexual harassment code. Note that this warning is a lesser offense than being adjudged to have actually sexually harassed a co-worker. It's a breaching of code, but not of practice, you see? It is a breach against the company, not an employee. Seems minor, but legally it's very significant. You would be required to repeat the online learning module on sexual harassment. You would also be entitled to free, independent advice on the matter and to make a final statement, which would be appended to your file. That option would make my job a lot easier and yours more tenable. I apologise if that's blunt."

Scott eyed Justin's phone. It didn't appear to be recording, but he was cautious.

"And if I do dispute the so-called facts?"

"If you dispute the statement of facts, we will need to go through an additional disciplinary procedure of clarifying and contextualising the events. Due process, establishing substantives, et cetera. I'm telling you now that it's not worth it. The disciplinary procedure involves lengthy recorded interviews with colleagues, the complainant, yourself and other witnesses – the bar staff for example. You can see why one might suggest you avoid this. Some people find that procedure to be more of a punishment than the code breach. I'm not officially advising you either way, however. This is simply letting you know how these things tend to go."

Scott had nothing else to say. Justin swiped back to the recorder app.

"Second part of the Scott Andrews disciplinary session. Scott, after having five minutes, would you like to make a statement in response to our statement of facts?"

He felt sick at the idea of his words recorded. On reflection he knew that he had overstepped a line with Linnea. He knew he was getting away lightly. He hated that he'd left her with no option but to complain about him. He knew he couldn't explain it to her because that would just compound the mess. He had no option.

"I have no statement, no."

"Then, given due consideration I am formally notifying you that you have breached our code of standards and will be required to..."

Scott stopped listening. It was going exactly as Justin had said. Was he getting special treatment? Had management already discussed the matter and felt Scott was, against his original assessment, actually too valuable to lose? He imagined Linnea's response. She might feel forced into quitting, moving on to another job or another city. That would be the worst. But what could he do? He was now complicit in an old boys' network. Who knew what favours they might ask of him now?

His guts felt rough, all at sea. His chest was tight and his eyes moistened. Would he cry? Would he faint? Would he merely crumple?

They were all such theatrical responses. This wasn't about him. That was all he had to remember.

Justin was waiting for him to say something. Scott mumbled back to him the last few words Justin had said, "and you'll email me the official notice."

Justin reached out to his phone, turned the recorder off and winked at Scott. Before Scott could react, Justin scooped up the papers, dropped the phone into his pocket and said he'd be in touch.

The wink was a horror that would stay with Scott all day, all week, and would be remembered into his old age.

Scott sent an email to his boss saying he needed a half day of annual leave and rode his bicycle home. He bowled inside and wandered listlessly from bedroom to kitchen to his study. Even after he'd forced himself to throw up, even after a shower, their horrid little connivance stuck to him.

High

Lunch break at Wellington College had been the loneliest time for Axle. The friendships of the other students had solidified into fortresses around the second month of their first year. He searched for some people to welcome him in, but soon realised, like the loser in musical chairs, that if there had been a spot for him, there no longer was. He'd spent two years on the peripheries of the in-groups. In practice, the periphery meant sitting at one of the hexagonal benches next to students his own age, but never partaking in their conversations. This was the worst of both worlds. He was not close enough to bask in the warm solidarity of a clique, but nor was he free with the devil-may-care spirit of genuine outcasts. Where he had tried to wedge himself into a group through bravado or flattery, he was greeted with silence or jeers. By the end of Year Eleven things weren't getting better, and he realised that he couldn't survive three more years of ostracism.

At High, things were different. For starters, the seating was octagonal. And, through Pete, Axle had gained access to an in-group. He'd only realised he was genuinely accepted on the day when Pete was absent with some illness and Keevan had waved him over. Add Jarvis, and the group was now a solid four. Sometimes Reggie and Tanasi would join them and, sometimes, one or two of Tanasi's friends would also come.

Ever since Pete's party, Axle had been having quiet conversations about how alcohol worked. He knew these conversations could make him look like a weirdo, so he took it slowly. He hadn't had much insight from Keevan and Jarvis, but Tanasi had some good ideas. As the others gossiped about a fight at a party at the weekend, he sidled up to Michella.

"You've been proper drunk before, eh Michella?"

"I mean, yeah. So what?"

"Nothing. It's a kind of magic, though, right? Like can you explain exactly how it works?"

"What do you mean? Booze goes in, I get drunk. What's more to know?" She'd relaxed when she read that he was genuinely interested.

"Just how it works... how that feeling comes on."

"I mean, you were in Biology?"

"I took Chemistry," said Axle.

"It's all the same," said Michella. "It's how everything works: food, medicine, drugs. There's no difference."

"No. I mean. Of course. None of that explains how I feel when I'm drunk, though. Sure, sure, chemicals get released and the brain has lots of shit going on. Alcohol dulls. And that affects how your body moves... but I feel like there's something else –"

"Are you drunk now?"

Reggie and Tanasi had stopped whatever they were doing to listen in to Axle and Michella. Neither of them had an answer, but they did think Michella was right. Axle was acting wasted and only a drunk would ask that kind of question.

"Best we just flow with it," Reggie said. "That's my answer: flow. Maybe it's possible to know. Maybe not? But in the end it doesn't matter once you're in the flow."

Michella was barely suppressing a snicker.

"Hey! Mr MacMillan! Come here, would you? Axle thinks getting drunk is magic. What do you think?" said Michella.

MacMillan was probably the most trusted of the adults at the school, and that made him ripe for the students to take liberties with. He strolled over to the group, a bemused expression on his face to hide his uncertainty over whether the students were mocking him.

"What's that, eh?" MacMillan asked.

"Mr Mac, Axle was wanting to know if getting drunk is magic," said Michella.

"I'm not sure I should tell you about getting drunk given you're all – what? – three years too young to legally get drunk. I can tell you how most so-called magic works, though. But before I do, you've really got to be clear that you do want to know. A little knowledge can be a dangerous thing."

"Oh sure, we don't care," Michella said.

"But seriously, think of it like a sausage – when you figure out how it's made, no-one wants to eat them anymore," said Mr MacMillan.

"I mean, I'm vegetarian so I totally understand," said Michella.

"So, you're saying leave the magic to itself?" Axle asked. "I would kind of expect an educator to have a better answer to that."

"I'm not an educator," said Mr MacMillan, "I'm an art teacher."

"Or do you just not know?" Michella asked.

"Why not both? You know that magic isn't magic, right?" said Mr MacMillan. "It's deception, sleight of hand. Apparently. It's probably best to enjoy the magic instead of ruining it by seeking answers. Course, if it is real, I wouldn't know. Like I said, I'm just an art teacher."

Hints

Axle attended Mandarin lessons every other Wednesday night from seven until eight-thirty. Jacqui and Scott used the same nights, once every six weeks, to talk through a plan of the family's forthcoming needs and to troubleshoot any gnawing issues. Jacqui had read about the technique in *The New Yorker*.

"We can't pull out of an experiment at the first hurdle, Scott. I don't need or want to know what happened with your date. I've told you – we've agreed – a hundred times: don't shit where you eat. My date went well enough, if you want to know. A six out of ten. The date was. I wasn't rating *him*. Seven, even. If you want my honest opinion…"

"I always hated that phrase – what does it even mean? – 'don't shit where you eat'. It's crass. You know I hate it. But go on, go ahead."

"My honest opinion is that you need to think outside of the simple options. Don't try it on with someone you already know. Certainly not girls – women, okay, women – from your work. I'm not here to go through that again. There are tonnes of people out there. Get on the apps if you feel like it. Or even if you don't feel like it. Get outside your comfort zone."

"That's easy for you to say. You didn't have to do anything. Your guy just appeared out of nowhere. Whereas…"

"What?"

"Nothing," he said.

"Are you implying I'd already been seeing João? Before our agreement?"

"Well, no. But if I was…"

"Well, are you or aren't you? Jesus, Scott, at least have the courage to ask."

"I don't care. I trust you and I shouldn't have to ask. This process only works if we volunteer information."

"Okay. Fuck. You're right. Uh, so it might sound weird but, Kaye introduced me to him. She's been sleeping with him either as revenge on Robert for having an affair or, I don't know, as some whim she felt was justified. Anyway, with them off to Turkey…"

"You've swooped in."

"I have," she said.

Scott eyed a bottle of wine on the kitchen bench. There was a rule that they weren't to drink during these conversations – that's what *The New Yorker* had said – but he always hankered after a glass when it was prohibited.

"Do you know what it's like for a middle-aged married man out there?" he asked.

"Please. Men have it far easier than women. Maybe that wasn't true for me, but as a rule it is. You think people are queuing up to date me any more than you?"

"No. I know. I know. A glass of wine would be nice, right? Would you have one if we left off here?" he asked without much conviction.

"Feel free to open it. Let it breathe. And it is okay to feel a bit hōhā about it all. Objectively, I'm doing better right now. But there will be highs and lows. Stick with it. Let me know how I can help. I'm not going to start setting you up on dates or anything but let's keep things open and honest. Volunteer information. I hate the idea that you felt you had to cast a drift net over my life just to learn the basics. Not that you said it. But I felt it. We can make this win-win. Okay?"

Jacqui had that way of saying "okay" as if it were a question. In truth, the word functioned as a spoken form of punctuation that concluded a sentence and insisted that a point not be revisited.

"Okay, good. It's good," said Scott. "Let's check in next meeting on progress. I wanted to put another item forward for the agenda. Axle. He has friends now. Really good ones, it seems. I think we're going to have to confront some bigger questions. Girls. Or boys, you know, whatever. Both. And alcohol."

"Were you this articulate when you talked to Ax about drinking moderately?" said Jacqui.

"Fine. Maybe we can be a bit more proactive. In Finland, they've developed a culture of drinking light beers. Not the low-carb ones, but the low-alcohol ones. It's really on the rise there and we're talking at the Ministry about proposing similar reform here. A nudge, you know. Strip the tax back from anything under 2.2%. I like it, personally, but it looks like there might be problems with progressing it... Anyway, that doesn't matter."

"You're thinking you and I do a little trial on our baby boy? A case study for the Ministry on subsidising light beer for Axle?"

"Well, not subsidise, as such. Listen. Stop joking. We both know how important it is for young people to be accepted by their peers. In some circles you must drink. There's no question about it. And that appears to be where Ax is going. So, yes. I'm saying, let's give Ax a six-pack of light beer a week to take to his friends' place. Anything 2.2% and under; but none of that no-alcohol stuff. He's allowed to get a mild buzz. A light one. It won't do any harm. Brains maintain more plasticity than some of the temperance advocates are willing to admit."

Jacqui wavered. It was an idea. She rarely warmed to Scott's permissive strategies – it felt too much like cowardice wearing the cloak of progressiveness. She was more the trial-and-error, fuck-around-and-find-out kind.

"Okay," she conceded. "Sounds smart. Maybe you could lead on this one? Some father/son time. Can we review it in a couple of months? I'll put it on the agenda now."

"Sounds reasonable."

Reasonable, she thought. Was Scott mocking her? There was nothing in his expression that said he was. She shrugged it off.

"Back when I was his age, we used to drink Waikato Draught," she recalled. "I don't know why. It was 4%, I think. Ten dollars for a twelve pack. That stuff would just make you piss. We moved onto Kristov pretty quickly, but we had to buy it through one of the girls' older boyfriends. Ick. I wonder what we would've done if the beer had been free?"

"And it's good right, because this also solves a lot of the issues with dating. If he's not wasted, I think we can trust him to make good decisions. You know, he was surprisingly relaxed about us seeing other people."

Before Jacqui could formulate a response, the latch on the front gate clicked, announcing Axle's return from class. Scott went to the kitchen and poured a glass of wine for himself. Jacqui said she'd have a tea instead, so he put the jug on.

Axle could always sense when his parents had been having one of these planning and troubleshooting sessions. A conspiratorial odour hung in the air.

"Cup of tea, Ax?" Jacqui asked after he'd flung his schoolbag into his room. "We've just been talking about that climate change adult education that your school is running. You know we signed up for it – two weeks ago? Three? – but haven't heard a thing. You heard anything about it?"

"No. Nothing. Wait. Actually... there was this." He went back to his room and fetched a newsletter that was so scrunched up, it might have been at the bottom of his bag for a week. "Yeah, sorry. The climate thing for parents was this Monday. Sorry."

"Why are we only hearing this now?" Scott called from the kitchen.

"Seriously, Ax," said Jacqui, "your dad had been keen to go along to that. He even signed up on some sheet, but they never emailed him. State schools, eh? You sure you don't want to check out HIBS?"

"Ax, we've talked about this before," said Scott. Jacqui looked to Scott as he looked back. She tuned out of the conversation until Axle asked if he could go to his room. Jacqui checked Scott's expression. He nodded. That was that.

Job joy

Rothman loomed over Jacqui's desk, letting his shadow announce him.

Jacqui ignored him to see if he might just go away. He didn't. He rapped on the partition as if knocking on an office door.

"Jacqui, yeah," he said. "Solid work on equal pay."

"Eh?"

She was taken aback more at his chummy approach than the comment.

"Wage equity across emergency services. You know what I mean. It's a big deal."

She could barely get over how much his name suited him. That was the cigarette company that had sponsored a lot of sport back in the eighties. Before those arrangements were made illegal by someone like her husband. Phased out, as Scott would say. Jacqui looked Rothman over as he took one step forward. He did look like an eighties type. Moreover, he dressed how conservatives dressed in the eighties. That made him a fifties type, and yet there was something reckless about him which could not be pegged to a decade.

"But" Rothman said, "why haven't our figures been updated for three years? It says we ought to update annually."

"Well," said Jacqui, "Primarily because there's been no official update tracking pay equity since, well, almost four years now. Forty-four months. I've been doing rough numbers on the side, if that would help?"

"Great. Let's sharpen up those numbers. What does your week look like? Can you update the old spreadsheet by end of play Friday? Friday week, yeah?"

She fell silent, smooth-brained and shook. There was a trick here, and half a dozen questions. He was positioning her.

"I've got that new report to do for the Minister. The climate change one," said Jacqui. "God knows what he wants from us, but I suppose every Ministry has to put them together. That'll take my whole week. And I've also got the..."

"Right. Good. Of course. I can see you need time. I'll be straight with you. From what I can see, we've undervalued you these last five years or so. I was brought in to manage you into line – those were the words of your former direct report. It doesn't matter. He's retired. No harm in being honest: he was a tosser. Anyway, there's a chance for a sea change here and I'll admit we're not there yet and you've no reason to trust me. There are changes coming and we can either be a part of them or end up like the Australians. Have a think on it. And get those updated figures to me by close of play, Friday week. Prioritise. We can talk then. Schedule half an hour at four, would you?"

"Perfect. Let me check my calendar. Uh, yup. Perfect."

"One last thing. I'm just checking. You ever work in the private sector?"

"Why? No. I mean I worked in hospo overseas for a bit, but I don't think that's what you mean," she said.

"No, no. Just something I ask. I thought you might have. No reason. I'm interested in the range of skills people have, I suppose."

She didn't believe him. Something else was up.

She waited for him to continue.

He waited for her.

"They're not as different as everyone says," she said. "The public and private sectors. From my reading it's overblown."

"Well, that's where you're wrong," said Rothman. "I take the opposite view. To me it's deeper. Risk. Advantage. Brinksmanship. I'm only telling you this because I think you would understand, right?"

"Maybe."

"Maybe?" he asked.

She nodded and he waited for her to clarify. She didn't.

"Until four, then. Schedule it for forty-five minutes, come to think of it," he said, and she realised he expected her to act as if she were his admin. It was a weird power play to have her schedule his meetings. Very 1950s. And then, sending the meeting invite, she wondered whether, if João weren't on the scene, would she be thinking a little more about Rothman?

Slab

"No chance, mate. Your lad can't come in here. Eighteen plus." The bouncer tapped a laminated sign gaffer-taped to the door.

Scott had been on the planning committee that designed that sign.

"When I was sixteen, we had a law that said you were permitted to drink in a bar if you had a parent or guardian with you. I want you to tell me when that law was repealed. If you can't, I'm going to have to speak with the Duty Manager."

Scott was pretty sure the law had been changed when the drinking age dropped to eighteen. He really didn't know. He told himself he was testing the knowledge of the bouncer as much as trying to angle his son in.

"Like I said. No chance, mate."

Scott was about to drill into this non-answer when he saw Axle had turned away from him.

Axle had not warmed to the light beer plan and, on top of that, his father was embarrassing him. "What is even the point of light beer?" he'd asked.

"The point is moderation without social stigma," Scott had answered. "You know. We've had this talk. Don't tell me you enjoyed that hangover? You'd be the first. Anyway, let's go and test the selections. There might be some great options. Just trust me."

"Fine, mate. Thanks" Scott said to the bouncer, then added, "any off license around here?"

"Specialist wholesaler down the road. Probably got the best selection. There or New World Thorndon. They're your best bet."

"Nice guy. Just doing his job," Scott said to his son on the way back to the car. "A little bit of politeness gets rewarded. Would have been as easy for him to repeat 'no chance' but he warmed to us."

At the store, Scott asked the woman behind the counter about light beer. He wasn't the type to avoid asking for help when he needed it. She called for their specialist over the intercom. Scott had thought she'd called "Gary", but when the man appeared, his badge said Cicerone.

"So, Cicerone – cool name. From Cicero, I suppose? Can you help my son and – help me, really – choose a good selection of light beers?"

"Follow me." The specialist led them through the palleted islands of wholesale wine to the fridges of beer.

"There's an article I read that recommends a few – hold on a sec." Scott pawed at his phone and offering it to Cicerone. "Do you have these two in stock?"

"Sure do. You might want your boy to get a trolley."

Axle took his chance to get some distance from his dad, but as he walked back towards him he noticed his father's attention had become fixed on a red-haired woman in a parallel aisle. In the past Axle wouldn't have thought much of it. But now he thought back to how his father had mentioned opening up their relationship. He closed his eyes and shook the thought from his mind. Whatever this parents wanted to do was fine, but he didn't want to see it or hear it or have anything to do with it.

Scott did some rough calculations in his head. Sixty cans would be a good start. Ten six-packs. Two and a half months. Round it up to a dozen, he considered, preferring the symmetry of a dozen half-dozen to that of ten.

"Listen, you're the expert," Scott said when his son got back. "Can we get one six-pack each of these two, and then ten more of whatever you'd recommend. A good range. Anything between 1% and 3%. Preferably in the 1.8% to 2.5% range. Not too much at the 3%. Up to you, though. Go for the local first, assuming the beers are more or less equivalent. Cut our carbon miles, you know? Cans where possible."

Scott watched Cicerone as he worked. Soon the trolley was full. The young man had been true to his word and didn't try to upsell him. Scott respected that. He paid for the beers and stacked them into two cardboard boxes in the boot of the car.

"Hey Dad, how does alcohol really work?" Axle asked as the car edged out of the parking lot. "Like, I know it messes with your brain and all, dehydrates it. But I just don't get how it makes you feel – actually feel – drunk."

"It's pretty simple," said Scott, once he'd made his way into the flow of traffic. "I mean, it's my job to know, right? Chemicals in the brain, like most other things. Alcohol is basically ethanol. It gets absorbed into your bloodstream and thus, gets to your brain. Release of dopamine, suppression of neurotransmitters. Now I didn't study neuroscience, far from it, but my understanding is that this is the combination that makes you feel the way you do. Pleasure from dopamine is heightened by stupefaction from the neurotransmitters. Voilà."

Axle thought about it.

"But I still don't understand how it goes from the chemical to the actual feeling. You know... feeling drunk? How does it make you feel things?"

"Maybe don't think of how it works, but how it's similar to other things. Like, we can't explain how we experience taste, right? I could tell you that salt and vinegar chips activate taste buds and – well, I don't know exactly – but there's still something unexplained and we ultimately accept the explanation as good enough. Right? We can always play the kids' game of asking 'why' in response to any question. And we know that that game always ends in frustration."

"I mean, right? But, maybe, shouldn't we be trying to understand these things?"

"Maybe, but humans have been getting drunk since before written records. Sometimes you must accept that things happen and we can't – or don't – fully understand them. Mystery is one of the great things about life."

"I suppose. I still feel like – I think – there's some big gap we're missing."

"The riddle of consciousness?"

"Nah. Well, maybe."

"I mean, you might be onto something. It's important to stay curious. Maybe we've gone too far into the chemical explanation for life and not spent enough time on... well, on how we feel what we feel. Like jealousy – what's that about? You could tell me the combination of chemicals that cause it, but it would be a pretty unsatisfactory answer to someone feeling it."

The car pulled off Upland Road and parked in its usual shady spot. There was no garage on their house, nor any real access point for a car.

Scott pulled the boxes of beer from the boot. He was pleased that Axle picked one up without asking and they headed back to the main road through Kelburn, and down the steps to the house. There was no space in the kitchen or the pantry for the beer, so Scott rearranged some of the old sports equipment under the stairs.

"You might want to refrigerate them on the afternoon before you go out – though this darker beer is probably good at room temperature," Scott advised. "I'll let you manage them – and we can re-up in a few months. Six beers a week and let me know if you want some for a friend. I'd have to talk to their parents, but I'd be happy to do that. Always better to ask permission than have to apologise."

"Yup. Cool."

Axle seemed neither particularly pleased nor convinced. He mostly seemed relieved their excursion was over. It was probably a side-effect of being a teenager, Scott thought. The Unconvincables. He thought back on their conversation and made a mental note to talk to the addiction team at work about how the chemicals in our brains turn into the impulses that guide us.

Axle went straight to his room, kicked off his shoes and messaged Pete.

> You are not going to believe what bullshit my parents are trying to pull.

Couch

The morning sun lit up the hills opposite their lounge and streamed through the window onto a man who was asleep on the couch. Axle stopped in his tracks. It wasn't his dad on the couch. That had happened once. Nor was the man on the couch a relative or friend of the family. He wasn't anyone Axle knew, and his parents weren't the type to offer unbidden compassion to bedraggled people they met in a park or at a bus stop.

After running through a short list of possibilities, Axle still had no idea. Maybe it was a homeless man who'd found the door unlocked and decided it was as good a place as any to sleep. Axle took a closer look. The man had a mop of thick, black curly hair but it was too clean for someone who would usually sleep rough. Two feet poked out of the bottom of the blanket that covered the man. A pair of dark blue jeans were pooled on the floor where he had stepped out of them. On the back of the couch was a white t-shirt. It was very clean or, at least, relatively new. Axle sniffed at the air. Not a thing. He tiptoed to the kitchen and was about to open the fridge when he saw the note on the family whiteboard.

> João slept over.
> He's my Brazilian friend.
> Introduce yourself if you wake before me.
> Love, Mum.

Weird, he thought, turning to the fridge to get some milk for his cereal. Weird, weird, weird.

There was an empty bottle of wine standing beside two empty cans of his light beer. He hadn't been enthused about the light beer plan, but he still felt a proprietary dismay that his cans had been emptied without his permission.

Axle had never met anyone from Brazil before, but there were a couple of kids in his class who were Colombian. A rustling came from the couch.

Only one thing for it, he thought.

"Hey, good morning," Axle called out. "I'm Axle."

João sat up. He was younger than most of his parents' friends. To Axle, he looked a bit like a snowboarder or a hippie. No, that wasn't quite right. He was too pretty. No pimples. His hair was unruly but his face was serene. There was nothing poised or pre-emptive about him.

"Yeah, I guessed that's who you were," João said. "Your mum told me about you. Hey, sorry that I drank some of your beers. I just didn't want to drink any more wine. I've got to climb today. So, you know, I had to wake up fresh. Sorry if it's weird me being here."

"It's not weird. I mean, it is, but who cares? What did you think of it? Of the beer?"

Axle hadn't drunk any of the light beer, yet. Instead, he'd ferried a dozen cans from under the stairs into a box under his bed, telling his dad the beer was great. He'd even said how he liked the lager more than the IPA. Pete had told him to say that and to make up some story about the brewer going overboard on hops. Instead of drinking the beer, they'd been taking shots of cheap bourbon that a friend of Pete's had bought for him.

"Hey it's okay, you know? Beer's beer."

"Go on. Is it the same in Brazil?"

"Brazil? Yeah. I mean it's the same everywhere. Brazil, USA, China wherever. You Kiwis do get very drunk so there must be something different here. Not you, you know. Just everyone."

"What are people like in Brazil? Maybe that's a dumb question but I think they're not so different? Or are they?"

"Yeah, not so different. Two arms, two legs. Oh man, I love it there. People enjoy life a lot more, so you don't need alcohol as much. Like, you must have heard of Carnival, right?"

"Right."

"Well, people are almost totally sober. Maybe a little pick-me-up, but that could be anything. No-one goes berserk like guys here. People are way looser to start with. More relaxed. For example, think of a Kiwi girl at some party. You want to kiss her, right? So, what does a typical Kiwi guy do?"

Axle nodded because he didn't know the answer.

"Go on, you know," João insisted.

"I don't know. You just ask her?"

"Sure. Maybe. I bet that's what your parents tell you to do. From what I've seen, Kiwis go from nothing to everything like that," – João snapped his fingers – "and so you kiss some girl and you're basically dating, and the next conversation is how many kids you want. In Brazil it's not like that. You go out to Carnival and everyone has a kiss here and a little one there. I remember when I first flew in and went to my first Carnival in Rio – totally amazing. I got four women coming up to me and kissed me like it was nothing. Amazing! You don't get that here."

"Wait... when you first flew in? Where'd you fly from? Are you, like, from the Amazon or somewhere?"

"Yeah. Uh, I meant, when I flew home. When I flew into Rio for the first time..." João hesitated and looked towards the hallway that led to Axle's parents' room. "That's where Carnival is."

"Wow, right? It's not everywhere?"

"It is. But Rio is the best."

"Yeah. Go on. It's so cool. I wish I'd grown up in Brazil."

Axle had taken an immediate liking to João so was a little annoyed when he heard footsteps from his parents' room. He wanted to talk more about Carnival and he knew his parents would just end up plodding through some boring adult conversation. It might even be awkward.

If this email finds you

Jacqui had one of those messages at the bottom of her work emails that told people that if she were emailing out of work hours it was not because she expected people to also reply out of work hours. It seemed Rothman had the same, but that hadn't stopped him emailing her at 2am.

She and Scott had woken at the same time, probably from the sound of João and Axle speaking in the lounge. She'd been about to dash into the lounge to make sure Axle wasn't put out. But Scott suggested they let the conversation continue. So, Jacqui had gone to her phone, scrolled through the notifications from her anonymous Twitter profile and, then, when no fresh horror had presented itself, checked her work email. She told herself clearing her inbox on a Saturday morning was a simple trick to allow herself to relax for the weekend, like making the bed right after getting up. Usually there was nothing other than the end-of-week stats and whatever positive spin senior management had been feeding out.

> How about this for an idea? Stick with me for a second: we currently only have units set up for the crimes that people do commit – arson, murder, sexual assault, organised crime. It makes everyone look only at the negatives. So, what if we set up units for the crimes that don't get committed and then we pump out the stats on the positives. Like, for example, we haven't really had train robberies in a long time? And when was the last time that we prosecuted someone for blasphemy – it's probably

not even a crime anymore, right? Well, why not focus on that, too? Could be a whole school of thought – Positive Policing, call it Popo? Reclaim that word from the public. A bit of that goofy gumshoe stuff that the public laps up. What do you think? Is this mad? Sorry, I just had to email someone. But let me know as soon as you get this. I think it could be just what's needed.

bests, Al

"Coming?" Scott asked. He'd already put his pants and a jersey on and was hovering near the bedroom door.

"No, no. I mean, yes, but give me a minute. I, um, yes. Give me a minute."

"I mean he is your guest," said Scott as he opened the door and left Jacqui to work out what the hell, if anything, to do about Rothman.

Morning, Dad

Scott had made sure he was in bed when Jacqui and João had returned the previous night. Earlier in the day, she'd repeated that she thought it would be good for Scott to meet him, but she'd also said that she wouldn't pressure João into it. Scott had willingly agreed, though afterwards realised that the same deference did not seem to apply to him. As she hadn't called or messaged, he assumed she'd come home alone. He'd imagined Jacqui coming to bed as soon as she got back from her date.

Then Scott had heard another voice in the lounge. So, she had brought him home. Neither voice was loud enough for him to hear the actual words, just the lilt of conversation. Scott's imagination filled in the gaps and as the conversation continued, his mind mistook every little sound for a moan of lust. He had to admit their own sex had improved. He was thankful to João for that, but unsure how long it would last. To him, it felt like the return to good health that the terminally ill often experienced in the final days before a rapid and permanent decline.

Covering his head with the pillow had not worked and he considered going into the lounge to tell them to keep it down. Instead, he pulled back the sheets, strode into the en suite, and took one of Jacqui's Valium. He washed it down with water from the faucet, then glared at himself in the mirror. After plucking an errant nose hair and assessing his physique from front and side on, he returned to bed. Five minutes later the noises from the lounge didn't bother him. Good for her, he thought. Three minutes after that, he was asleep.

"Morning, Dad," said Axle. On a Saturday morning his father would usually have loped around in a dressing gown, but with João in the lounge he wore proper clothes.

"Hey, morning. Good morning, João. Jacqui said you might sleep over. Got everything you need? Probably a bit late for an extra blanket. Comfy sleep, though? Personally, I prefer squabs on the – a squab is a name for the couch cushion, strange name – floor. Anyway, I'm rambling. Coffee?"

"Yeah, hey. Good morning. Great sleep, thanks."

"Listen," Scott replied, "I'm going to jump in the shower, but can I get you a coffee first? Some muesli? I don't know what people have for breakfast in Brazil."

"Kiwi-style is fine. Scott, right? No rush though. A coffee would be good."

"Did I not introduce myself? I didn't, did I? Sorry about that. Yeah, the old coffee machine takes a little to heat up so I'll be back with your brew in just a sec." Scott padded into the kitchen.

A bit jocular but sufficiently chill, Scott thought. There was nothing to it, really. He had to be reasonable, and he had to imagine the shoe on the other foot. It could have been Linnea on the couch. They were all adults. He doubted that João had even slept with his wife yet.

As he filled the espresso machine with cold water, he tried to imagine Linnea waking in the lounge and Axle meeting her. He liked the idea of his son being agog in her presence, even if it discomfited him a little. Scott recognised a craving to have his son be impressed at his father's prowess rather than the mere competence that filled their current lives. The problem was that it was hard to conjure up Linnea's image without it being tainted by the scattered look that had marked the end of their night and the beginning of his run in with HR. He tried to return to another image of her in his mind – the white blouse, the office party – but every time he did, the same panicked look had crept into her eyes.

Scott flicked the switch for the espresso machine. He had two minutes to wait before the next step. Once more, he found himself listening in to the lounge as João and Axle chatted away. He could barely make out who was speaking, let alone the content. He swallowed whatever feelings bubbled up.

Perhaps Jacqui's plan to introduce João to the family was actually a master stroke. Maybe he should trust her. For starters, Axle wasn't as worldly as Scott might have liked. Perhaps having a young Brazilian around would expand his son's horizons? They might look back on this in ten years as the start of something great.

He fed the ground coffee into the portafilter, tamped it down, then wrenched it into place and set up two of the café-style cups beneath it. He could hear his son ask about climbing. How João had gotten into it. What kind of people did it. How much it cost. How good he was. Scott had been holding his breath, his finger hovering over the button that would set the machine to express. He pressed the button. João's answers had been unassuming, deliberate and informative. That was no need to eavesdrop.

The machine beeped. *Fin.* A thin crema floated on top of the black coffee. He waited for the final drips. Success. The machine could be temperamental. He tested one cup, his lips against the scalding liquid, to ensure it was not too bitter.

"How do you take your coffee?" Scott called through to the lounge.

"Short. Black is good. One sugar if you have it."

"Oof, well, it's somewhere between a short black and a long black. I'll bring the sugar bowl and you can add your own," said Scott as he placed the cup, spoon and sugar on a tray, then carried it to the lounge.

João nodded his appreciation, while Axle enthused about the abseiling he'd done in Phys Ed at Col. Scott returned to the kitchen to clean the machine so it would be ready for Jacqui. He could no longer hear the conversation in the lounge. He didn't need to. He liked that he could like João. It made him feel debonair. Cosmopolitan even. All the things that he'd been saying about open relationships being good could genuinely be true. He could relax. It would all work out in the end.

He returned to the lounge with his coffee, leaned against the couch and listened to the two young men. His son and João were about a decade apart. They talked some more about rock climbing and visa problems and, finally, Axle's plans for the party that evening. It must have been thirty minutes before João stood and said they ought to go. Jacqui had joined them by this point, having already showered, explained about Rothman's bizarre message and put together a day pack.

Scott was confused for a minute, but then he realised that Jacqui was going with João. His brow furrowed. Had they talked about this? Before he could recall either way, they had gone. The house was half empty and he had to move his thoughts onto what he would do with his free day.

Halfway

Six days later, Scott's ease was tested. Jacqui arrived home, half an hour past midnight, and had clearly had sex with João. Perhaps a few times, younger men being what they are. When, where, and how was not discussed. Scott knew because Jacqui simply could not hide her good mood. Was he sure? It wasn't that her hair was a tangle or that she smelled of him. It was a look in her eyes, a confidence and a swagger. She was lighter. She had slept with him, he knew, and it had surpassed her expectations.

I am feeling envy, he told himself. As his wife showered, he sat on the bed and caught himself twisting his wedding ring. Such a cliché. He believed that if you could name an emotion, you were halfway towards dealing with it.

I am envious, he told himself, but short of jealous. It was a crucial distinction. He wanted the same for himself as she had had. He did not want to stop her from being with João. That was the crux. Envy not jealousy.

Work was taking a toll on him. That was true. His mind wasn't as sharp as it should have been. He imagined his colleagues whispering about him. He'd had a sleepless night picturing slanderous words about him in the womens' toilet. He had worked late the next night, until everyone else had left the floor, then snuck into the bathroom to check the walls. Even when he found no scribbling, the paranoia remained. They were probably talking about him from locked Twitter accounts or in some sprawling WhatsApp group. Theoretically, he agreed with women supporting each other to protect themselves from men. He just struggled to see himself as that man people should be cautious of.

Scott thought back to the years of his own sexual peak. If he closed his eyes and concentrated, he could find a way back there. He thought of the night when he lost his virginity. That hadn't been great. It had been an event of sorts, but there had been no sensuality to it. Then he remembered: Jacqui had been in Sydney. He'd been visiting Auckland to pitch a half-formed production to the collective that ran a small theatre that used to be off Myers Park. He'd received some strong criticism – potentially useful, but hurtful nonetheless – so went up to St Kevin's Arcade for a drink. One of the people who'd watched his play, a woman in her thirties, maybe forties – he was too young to know – was there. She hadn't said much either way about his play and had come across as distracted and severe. She was sitting with her husband, but he was speaking with other friends. She waved Scott over. They chatted about the play, she admitted her mind was elsewhere. He spoke of the useful criticisms and she told him not to be so demure. The husband's attention returned to his wife. His evening crept from volatile sorrow into bucolic ease. They talked of silly things that were light and summery. It was March, so the evening was warm and, as he became drunk, he got the impression that a bond was forming. When the bar called last drinks they invited him back to their house for one more instead. He removed his socks and shoes at the door. As he followed them down the hall, he was acutely aware of his toes against the pile of the rug and the cool polish of the floorboards. He had that drink, sitting cross-legged on their couch, crushing the ice with his molars as her hand and then his teased its way across his lap. And then he closed his eyes and there was the warmth of the villa, a scent of jasmine and their three bodies crossing and bumping their way across the lounge and into the near black of the bedroom. Then the soft light of dawn interrupting a brief sleep. The couple had left the window open, not just a crack but the sash pulled all the way up. More sounds of morning: sirens from an emergency, then bird song. The day would only grow and he was still drunk. He recalled the dew on the street as he crept out of the house and tied up his shoes on the wooden veranda. He was up even earlier than the dog walkers. But somehow, the sun was already well above the horizon and the temperature felt like it was in the mid-twenties.

The shower stopped. He shook himself back to the present. He was in bed. A smile, not quite a grin, across his face. Jacqui exited the bathroom and climbed into bed. Her eyes met his. He kissed her, she kissed back.

"I hope you had a good night," he said. He meant it. Her mouth pursed for a second, then relaxed. He wanted her to know that he only wanted what was best for her. She kissed him back some more.

"I did have a good night," she said, pulling the sheet up around herself and rolling over.

He found his spot on his side of the bed. He wasn't going to pester her. They drifted off.

Bunker

Axle missed the first band on purpose. Pete had had a last-minute trip to see his grandparents in Paraparaumu and had messaged to say he probably wouldn't be back in time to see the band. The others said they'd probably see Axle there. He didn't want to be first to the show and had been tossing up not going at all. He just needed one of his new friends to cloak his entry.

It was also the first party that he went to with his six-pack of light beers. They were hiding in a backpack, the bombastic marketing of the cans doing no favours to his attempts to blend in. Of course he was worried what people would say. Better to arrive empty handed than with a drink people might mock him for. He knew how nicknames stuck and he was keen for his to be Axle rather than some cruel epithet.

He needn't have worried. Jarvis and Keevan stood at the rim of the bunker. They didn't notice him until he was right upon them, their eyes fixed to the band thrashing around below. When they did spot him, Keevan shuffled aside to make space for him and pointing out Reggie and Tanasi who stood on the opposite side of the bunker, leaning on a wooden railing. By sinking a band into a pit rather than elevating it, there was a sense of the Colosseum and combat, but also of intimacy. His dad had taken him to a Rockquest, but the bands had been so far away and he hadn't been tall enough to see more than their heads.

The bunker was a brilliant venue but he was unsure how it would have worked as a war fortification. The circular concrete pit looked more suitable to ritual sacrifices than the defence of the nation. He'd never been to this spot before and was surprised it existed.

Axle hadn't been to a proper all-ages show before – going to see Rockquest with his dad didn't count – but the mix of people at the bunker was heavily skewed to under-eighteens. There didn't appear to be anyone monitoring who could drink, no-one in a uniform at least, and some people were even smoking. A group of older punks stood down in the bunker, nodding along to the music and rocking on their heels. Closer to the bands, a younger crowd bounced off of each other. If anyone fell, they were picked up again. They may have all been friends. It was hard to know. A song came to an end and the dancers doubled over to catch their breath.

"Thanks! We're Ruth In Asia... and this song is our last song. Thanks! One two three four!"

Axle was mostly into music where you could understand the lyrics but he was open minded and thought that this music was fine, too. Thrash. Seeing them live, he could enjoy the pageantry of it all and not have to really worry about what was being said.

Pete had sent a message to Jarvis but hadn't heard back. When the band finished, the three of them wound their way down the hill, through a tunnel and across a ridge to Pete's place. They knocked on the door and were half-heartedly welcomed in while the family finished an early dinner. There were no seats at the table, so the boys were ushered into the lounge. The family conversation ebbed through the closed door as the boys fidgeted on the settee. It seemed like the problem of the moment was a recent addition to Pete's vodka bottle collection. Grounding was prescribed. Pete protested.

The boys cringed from the other room. Bad, bad move.

"Moderation," Pete's father insisted, "and if you carry on like that, abstinence. Now finish up and go see your friends."

There was the sound of cutlery on a plate, then dishes being stacked. Pete slunk into the lounge rolling his eyes back in their sockets. Jarvis sniggered.

"Hey, I'm going to go," Keevan said, even before Pete had taken a seat.

"Me too," said Jarvis. "Sorry man."

"Good hanging with you, bro," Keevan said to Axle as he and Jarvis slipped from the lounge, through the dining room and out the front door.

Axle followed Pete to his room. Pete sat at his desk, swivelling about on a chair, while Axle assumed a cross-legged spot with his bag in his lap.

"Hey, I was going to ask if I can leave these beers with you? I've already got quite a few six-packs under my bed. Or would that be a problem?"

"Nah, man. It's all good. My parents know not to go snooping around my room. I don't give a toss, anyway."

"Thanks, bro."

"You want to go to a party in the Hutt next week? It'll be big. I can get some of that white rum if you want to split it? Reggie knows the guy hosting the party. Hey, were he and Ten at the gig? Wish I'd been."

"Yeah. Sounds good. Man, what's his deal? Reggie. He seems cool, like, too cool. You know?"

"You mean the bisexual thing?"

"What?"

"Ha! Yeah, I thought you might not know," said Pete. "So, Reggie and Tanasi started dating last year sometime. Like, a month or so before school shut down. Last November in English class someone – I wasn't there, but we all heard about it – was making a dumb gay joke and Reggie told the guy to shut up and said that he was bisexual. The guts of the guy, eh! That's pretty much what the principal meant at assembly last week when he praised individuals who had the courage to stand up for themselves in Pride Week. Then if you think about it, it's really funny."

"Funny?"

"It's comical. He's dating Ten – Tanasi, *the* Tanasi who is like this goddess and all – and at the same time he tells everyone he is into guys, too. Like, what could people do? Most other guys would suffer snide comments, at the very least. But with him it's genius, you know? And so there's this aura around him now. Not only is he a nice guy and dating Tanasi, but he's also, like, twice as sexually advanced as anyone else."

"But has he... you know?"

"Fuck, I don't know. Maybe. Everyone's too scared to ask."

6021

Jacqui parked outside the Newtown library. She was to meet João outside People's Coffee. They knew it would be closed. He wanted to meet there so he could take her somewhere without her knowing exactly where. A surprise. She checked herself in the rear-view mirror. There were five minutes until they were scheduled to meet. João was always punctual, but so was Jacqui. She had started arriving five minutes early so she had time to herself before he arrived.

    She drew two fingers from the edges of her nose across to her cheekbones. She'd read that massaging the face for three minutes should create a sun-kissed look. She didn't believe the sun-kissed part, but the routine was comforting. At the same time, she hummed a meditation to will away the pressure of the workday and to cast the puffiness from her face. She was like a pastor exorcising a demon while also, to be sure, administering a little dose of penicillin. She wondered what degree of religious heresy was tolerated in modern Brazil. Would that claim – god helps those who help themselves – receive scorn or a nodding appreciation?

    Jacqui turned her attention to the library. A familiar figure had caught her eye. She forgot the massage routine and craned her neck forward, squinting. She could only see the man from behind. He wore the same flecked grey wool suit as her boss and had the same cropped grey hair. It suited Rothman. A stack of books and newspapers were piled beside him and he appeared to be working his way through them with a zest. He was a comical sight but she couldn't work out why. Maybe it was the slight stoop as he adjusted to the undersized chairs. Maybe it was the way he flew through the pages of books as if storing them in a photographic memory to be recalled when needed.

There was a tap-tap-tap on the window behind her. João. She spun around. He'd spotted her watching Rothman. She flustered then wound the window down to tell him to wait.

"Relax, babe, relax. We've got a little walk ahead of us. No rush."

When she turned back to the library, the man was still there, unmoved. It was certainly Rothman. And what, she asked herself, was so strange about seeing him here? He uses libraries. So what? She didn't know why it seemed so extraordinary for one public servant to use another public service.

She shook off the thoughts, grabbed her bag, scarf and keys, and joined João on the sidewalk. It was after six, so she ignored the parking limits. She also ignored Rothman and told João to do the same when he asked why she was staring at the man in the library. Work/life balance required absolute work/life separation. Except for her wedding ring and that annual Christmas party. The one where they paid $10 per month and there wasn't even an open bar.

João led her up the street, and she followed. Her mind stayed behind, peeking through the library window, wondering what those books were and what it could all mean. She didn't register that they'd turned one corner and then another and were circling the block.

They were almost back on Riddiford when she realised something was amiss. João led her through a grubby alleyway into the Italian place where she and Scott had dined for their fourteenth wedding anniversary. She'd imagined João would be leading her to a picnic by moonrise, not gnocchi by candlelight. Both were good, she consoled herself, but she had imagined the moon.

A waiter brought over two menus and she ordered a bottle of wine. Just as the waiter left, Rothman walked in.

"You know that man," said João.

"Uh, yes. I do. My boss," she replied.

"Is he a good guy? Fun? I mean, do you want me to invite him to join us? Or would that be bad?"

Rothman had caught her eye. It was strange that she had no problem introducing João to Scott, but she felt shy around Rothman.

"I'm not sure what kind of guy he is, to be honest," said Jacqui. "He's either very modern or very old fashioned. I'm not sure how he'd deal with... He's coming over."

"Jacqui. Great place, isn't it? I used to come here all the time."

"Yeah, I love it," she said. "Alan, this is João. He's a friend of mine. Alan is my boss, João."

"Pleased to meet you," said Rothman.

"Pleasure is mine," said João.

The waiter arrived with the wine and two glasses. "Should I get a third?" he asked.

"No, no," Rothman said, "I don't want to intrude."

"No, no. It's nothing," said Jacqui.

"Be our guest," echoed João.

"Well, okay. Maybe for just one," said Rothman, then turning to the waiter, "yes, one more glass please."

"So, you are a policeman?" João asked.

"Well, senior management, but yes. New to the role," said Rothman as the waiter delivered a glass. "I was a detective, then in the private sector before, so I'm not what you'd call a career man. And you?"

Jacqui watched the two men as they explained their lives to one another. She was happy to sit back and evaluate the non-verbal cues. Kaye had told her that she would love the nonchalance of João and she did. It was admirable. At first, she'd seen João as a measure that outshone New Zealand men. But now that Rothman was there, she was not so sure. They were all different, as was Scott, and they all brought something to the table. She hated equivocating, but it was true.

The waiter returned and asked whether they were ready to order. Jacqui apologised. João turned to the menu.

"Can I get the gnocchi with a side of green beans? I'll eat at my table," said Rothman, getting up from his seat and turning to João. "I eat here all the time, you see. Thanks for the wine, Jacqui. Nice to meet you João. Oh, and I recommend a side of the green beans, they're phenomenally fresh right now. Best thing on the menu."

"I think he is a good guy," said João once Rothman had settled at his own table and was more or less out of earshot. "He's polite, well mannered. He smells good. Knew a bit about Brazilian politics. He's a good guy."

"Maybe. But he's not really my type. You know? I mean, we're from different tribes. Or maybe there's something about him I don't understand. At work it's all different to this. It's not that he's bad, he's just my boss. I have to be careful."

"I can imagine. But he is a person who takes himself seriously. He reminds me of my father and uncles. I can't imagine he would make things difficult for you. For example, he didn't even pry into what you and I were doing together. Some people would."

"You're right. Should we have a look at this menu, then? We'll get the green beans but what else?"

Justin (and that bar on the corner of Willis and Boulcott where the entire public service always goes for a cheeky wee after work drink)

Scott, mate.
Got twenty seconds for a chat?

Scott had kept to himself in the week since the meeting with Justin. No news was good news and everything from Justin was bad news. He'd mulled over his drink with Linnea and decided that, while he had let his libido control him, he hadn't done anything wrong. And he refused to go through life feeling ashamed for something he hadn't done.

Sure thing, Justin. Now suit?

Better to get it over with, he thought. In a few moments, Justin appeared. People were always side-eye watching when human resources turned up on their floor. The open plan hubbub dimmed as colleagues tried to catch the conversation.

Justin cast a disgusted look around the office. Those staring turned their eyes away, but their ears were still tuned in.

"All good, mate? Good weekend?" said Justin and then, just above a whisper, "Let's talk at half four. No need to be so formal this time. Relaxed. We're all good. I've got something else I want to share with you. Just come by my office."

Scott had always wondered why HR was so privileged as to get their own offices while the rest of the public sector were spread out across open plan offices. The official reason was that the offices were simply there, and it was luck of the draw. The unofficial reason, it seemed, was that HR needed to be able to close their doors and deal with difficult cases. Like Scott.

He thought back to that awful wink a week before. At least the devil waited until a person was dead before he claimed their soul. Scott guessed that he was being cosied up to because Justin and HR needed allies. They wanted a snitch. That was the most likely scenario. And who was a better ally for the powers than a man in his current predicament? He felt like a small-time criminal in one of those films where they're forced to rat on their boss and enter an ever-tightening spiral of conspiracy and intrigue.

When half past four rolled around, Justin was nowhere to be found. Scott knew people were watching him. Well, he suspected it. They were talking. It had been like that for the last week, but never so obvious that he could confront them. He returned to his desk and checked his email. There was still productive work to distract him. He should write up the Finnish experiment and seek permission for a local pilot. He was almost certain that Linnea was not going to volunteer to push the pilot along, but it was still a good idea. Then again, perhaps she'd already started the project herself. No-one was telling him anything.

He finished reading emails and began to dream about a new job in a different ministry. Best not to search for new work on the work computer, he thought, then spotted Justin bounding over. He was already in normal clothes, a leather jacket over his white shirt and his tie nowhere to be seen.

"Come on, Scott. Let's have that meeting. Offsite. What are you waiting for? Didn't we say half four?"

Scott logged out of his computer, grabbed his satchel and strode after Justin who was already headed to the lifts. When Scott caught up to him, Justin was holding the door.

"You're alright going for a drink?" Justin asked. "No pressure. I'm buying."

Better than being frog-marched from the premises, Scott thought. Better than a stuffy room with a take-it-or-leave-it offer to snitch.

When they got to the bar, Justin called out to a bartender, "Jug of Monty's Gold, Sid! We'll be out the back." He led the way to a high table with two stools. Justin turned to Scott and, for a second, Scott worried he was going to be dished up the same demanding voice.

Instead, Justin dropped the volume and said, "Reckon we might get two jugs in before happy hour is done."

Scott eyed him. He didn't like Justin. Nor did he hate him. He simply did not like him. It wasn't only the wink. It was how the younger man held himself, his demeanour, a vulture's hunger. While the two men were roughly the same height, Scott was much thinner. Or perhaps it was just that Justin held himself like he was used to being in charge. Scott wondered how Justin ended up working, not only at the Ministry, but in the public sector. Dumb luck? Justin wasn't serving the Ministry or the government of the day. He was serving a process not a people, and that process also served him. There was no right and no wrong, just well or poorly executed functions. There was no way that this man went to work to make the world a better place.

"Scott. I'll level. We've had another complaint. I didn't want to have to tell you with the others watching on. These things snowball, you see? You've been reported to us because your eye has been lingering a bit too long on certain co-workers."

"What? Who?" Scott asked, shifting on his stool, his feet dangling half a foot above the floor. He felt like a schoolboy.

"I can't tell you that. I'm simply informing you. We're not doing anything about it because at this stage it was only an anonymous complaint. But they did say you'd been eyeing people 'sexually'. Their words. It could have come from anyone. This is not a formal warning. Hence the pub. But it is a notification. I'm not asking if it did or didn't happen. I'm just telling you."

A jug of beer arrived and Justin grinned at the waiter, passing her his credit card. "Sort the tab for us, would you? And ring us up one more of these a minute before happy hour ends."

Justin turned his attention to his phone, pulling it out of its rubber casing, and running his palm over the case before popping it back into place. He locked eyes on Scott and gestured for him to pass his phone to Justin. It was odd. The whole situation was. But it was also in keeping with how their first meeting had gone.

Scott took out his phone, turned it off and placed it on the table. Justin took it, along with his own one, and wrapped them in a scarf. He tucked the scarf in his satchel, which he placed on the floor.

"Alright. Listen, mate. You can't be too careful. Pricks sometimes think a recording will save them. I'm not accusing you of anything, so relax. You might have heard about the hullaballoo at MBIE with that personal grievance swung back on HR all because of a taped phone call. That's all that – the phone – was about. I'm a professional. Shit like that simply does not happen to me. Anyway. Someone has got it in for you. Hyenas. That's all I needed to say. Watch out, and document all your interactions. Including the gents. You wouldn't believe how many of them want to do the whole knight-in-shining-armour thing when a woman has been wronged. Fucking prudes."

Justin eyed the room while draining his glass. Scott followed his eyes and drained his own beer. The building had not been designed as a pub – it was probably a home at some point – and the segregation of rooms and general dimness afforded a decent degree of privacy.

"So, who was this anonymous complaint?" Scott asked.

"Mate! For starters, it was anonymous. Genuinely. Even if it wasn't, what good would it do for you to know? You'd probably fuck it up and it would come back on me. Not on purpose, of course. We might be different, but we've got a lot in common."

"Do we?"

"Yeah. Neither of us buy this new workplace culture rubbish going around. Though you wouldn't have said so until recently. And, if you ask me, you did nothing wrong with Linnea. I'd have done the same. I mean, who do you think signed off on her hire in the first place? You might've noticed all the attractive young hires recently? Guys and girls. You've got me to thank for that. You've noticed right?"

Scott nodded.

"Anyway, almost half of new relationships are made in the workplace and how is that supposed to happen if a man can't be a bit bold? You know? Boldness is underrated in our line of work. I'll try anything once."

Justin ran his hand through his hair. He was performing. Trying to convince Scott of their alliance. Get him to loosen up. Scott was nowhere near loose and nor was his tongue. He desperately wanted to know more about these new accusations, but he drank instead of showing his hand.

"I think that she led you on and, even if you made a mess of seducing her, it's hardly your fault. It was bullshit. I laughed when I heard about it. You've been here a decade and made a rookie mistake. Isn't your embarrassment punishment enough without making more work for me? I'm a believer that communities are best when they self-regulate. Just a belief. Whatever. Anyway, my team should be out there finding the right talent for the ministry rather than dealing with petty grievances. We lost four policy guys to consultancies last year and it doesn't help me fill their roles chasing you around telling you how to get laid without offending anyone. I mean, she's gorgeous. But it was a rookie mistake. Don't tell me I'm wrong."

Justin drew deeply from his glass. He poured himself, then Scott, another. They hadn't made much of a dent in the beer but that was because it was one of those super jugs, almost two litres and, while the glasses were tall, they were also thin.

Scott decided it was best not to answer.

"Come on, then?" Justin finally asked. "My phone is in the bag, too. Speak up! It's just you, me and these four walls. Don't tell me I'm wrong."

"I just want to know about the new accusations."

"Eh, they're nothing. Nothing more than a whisper on the wind. It was a one liner from a burner email account. Does goofyshoes92@gmail.com mean anything to you? Nah? Didn't think so."

"And they only said that I'd been staring at women at work?"

"Yeah, sexually though. Something like that. Historical. This kind of shit is much more common than you think. Not at the ministry.

Everywhere. Like I said, it is not important. The matter is not being treated as important. What else can I say? I fielded the email and I concluded that it was not worth putting on record. It is done. And it's not why I brought you here."

Scott took a gulp of beer. He wasn't quite satisfied but there was nothing more to ask.

Justin continued, "The thing is, mate, that I know what you're going through. Not that I've made a mess of it like you. I'm bi, so, let's just say I have a few extra hoops to jump through. Quickly learn how to read the signs and all that. That's all I mean."

Scott knew the polite thing to do was to act as if Justin's comments on his sexuality had barely registered. He could feel Justin scrutinising him and he knew he should have said something, but enough time had passed that he knew it would sound forced.

Justin emptied his glass. Scott finished his own and refilled both glasses.

"No-one taught you how to flirt, did they?" Justin asked. "Listen, I'll be you and you be Linnea."

"I'd prefer if we didn't."

"Fine. I'll be you and you be some random. Relax. So, I've got this cute woman out for a drink and she's probably a little bit into you because, you know, she's having a drink with you. She wouldn't have a drink with anyone, right? She could have just said no. But also, she's not sure. You're older, married, blah blah blah, men are trash. We know, we know. So, the trick is not to approach the mess straight on. You don't do what you did and blurt out all your old man problems."

"I guess not. Not if you don't want to end up like I have."

"Let's imagine you're back at the bar and you've got a second shot at things. What do you do, then?"

"I don't know. I touch her leg? Not hard, of course. But just brush against it a bit?"

"Touching is even worse than a spoken flirt. Do the opposite to that. Do not touch them. She must touch you, first. Scott, Scott, Scott. Are you one of those guys who met his wife at eighteen and never learned to play the field? First rule: never initiate the touch. I mean, between guys it's different..."

"Well, what do I do then?"

"With a guy? Or a girl?"

Scott didn't answer.

"OK. Well, touching isn't the worst thing. It shows intent. There's a lot to do before then, but you've got to be super casual. Tell me how you'd do that. Imagine you and Linnea. Or anyone else who comes to mind," added Justin

"I guess..."

"Would you touch with your palm or the back of your hand?"

Scott tried to think back to the evening with Linnea. Nothing came to him. He thought back to his university days. It was easier then. He recalled one evening at The Lonely Moa during O-week. It hadn't seemed out of reach then, but those bars were packed and bodies were always gliding past one another. Back then you could reach out and test the waters, and if she pulled back then you could joke it off – the booze, don't be so uptight, my mistake.

Scott was not so much lost in his memories, but bringing the memories into the present. Slowly, but surely, his penis responded to his thoughts. He thought of the long, warm nights of summer, weekdays with nothing to do the next day but some lectures. His flat had a back yard with a quiet lawn that was both private and looked over the city. They'd all gone back to their flat from The Lonely Moa but, one by one, people took off – as couples or alone – to their bedrooms. It had left the two of them in the lounge. He'd talked up the backyard, the view, how this night was the perfect night. He'd placed a blanket down, they'd leaned into each other, and this was perhaps the feeling, he realised, that he'd been trying to recapture with Linnea.

"So?" asked Justin.

Scott wondered if he should tell Justin about his realisation. Would it help, or would Justin brush it off? It wasn't the right mood, he decided and then answered, "The first problem is that we're sitting at these damn high tables. It would feel unnatural to reach out. When I was younger, we'd just stand around and it was natural to lean against other people, maybe. We were drunker then, but it seemed the stakes were so much lower."

"Fine. But really, Scott. We're adults now. You shouldn't give up on pleasure just because the game has changed a little. And this is it: you've got to be thinking a lot more strategically before you even choose the bar. I mean did you choose where you and Linnea went to, and if so, what were you thinking?"

"Well, I didn't choose."

"I know. It was in the briefing Erving gave me. That point actually helped save you. I don't mean to speak down to you. I'm just trying to help. This place, for example, if you'd taken her here you'd want to have taken her to this room, or maybe to one of the sit-down dinner places upstairs. A quiet spot."

"Right," said Scott.

"Yeah. So you're on the right track, these tables are a mess. But you've got to work around that. Were you sitting down with Linnea, or at a table like this?"

"A high table like this."

"So how do you get around it?" asked Justin.

When Scott didn't reply, Justin stood and continued, "You get around it, by freeing up your body. So stand up."

Scott stood, adjusting himself through the front of his pants, hoping Justin didn't notice. He'd had nostalgic erections before and was confident it would go away on its own.

"And now what?" asked Justin.

Again, Scott didn't reply.

"So, you're standing. What would you do?"

Scott didn't know. He didn't want to repeat his previous mistake of suggesting he work out how to touch her.

"Let's just forget about it then," said Justin. "If you don't know, maybe there's no helping you. Lesson's over. I don't mean to be an asshole about it. I'll get these beers."

"Hey, no problem," said Scott, returning to his seat, "and thanks."

"But I did also want to get your opinion on another matter, said Justin, reaching into his bag and pulling out a plastic folder. "You probably know about the new comms plan going to senior management? I wanted to get your read…"

Justin edged round to Scott's side of the table and laid the document before him. As he pulled the pages from the plastic envelope, the back of Justin's fingertips brushed against Scott's thigh.

"Page four," said Justin, leaning in to turn the pages, his breast pressing into Scott's rib. Scott felt light, a little dizzy, and couldn't work out if the pulse of heat was coming from Justin's chest, or his own.

"Or page five," said Justin, his voice a lot lower, and his hand resting on Scott's back.

"I… I haven't," muttered Scott as Justin stepped back.

"Relax, man. I'm just showing you how I'd do it. Fake a pretext to be close to her. Pull in closer, but make sure the back and forth is there. Test how she responds to your presence. Does she pull back? No? Then a light touch. How does she respond to that? I mean, fuck, people say we need civics education in high schools. I think we should be taught how to properly flirt before we get into how local government works. But that's just me."

"I can't believe I fell for that," said Scott. "I couldn't have done that with Linnea. Like you said, with guys it's different."

"It's not different. Not really. Some unimportant things are, but not the basics."

"The basics."

"Yeah," said Justin. "They're easy. Tell a story. Favour the hypothetical. Make them the centre of attention. Do a little role play. Draw them in. Ask open-ended questions. Be confident, relaxed. Take the lead. It's a dance, right? Don't make the first move. None of that pick-up-artist nonsense. I mean, make them work for it."

Scott thought for a moment. "Isn't that exactly what I did? Before? With Linnea. That's exactly what I did with her. Why didn't that work?"

Justin thought for a moment. In one way, Scott was right. He'd done things by the book. Even so, he had somehow made a mess of it.

"Yeah, you weren't totally wrong. I'll give you that. And you're a handsome guy. Counts for a lot. Get this: everything you failed to do, I've been doing successfully for the last ten minutes. We've talked about sex. Check. I've let you know I'm bi. Check."

"Here's that second jug, guys," a new waiter announced as she placed the beer on the table and the payment terminal beside it. "Can I get anyone a food menu, or are you guys good?"

"Nah, I think we're good," Justin replied, hovering his card above the device. The machine beeped and produced a receipt.

Justin finished the last of the first jug and stood.

"I think I'd rather have a glass of wine," said Justin. "Somewhere with less of this noise. My place is just around the corner if you want to join?"

Scott weighed the words. He nodded, seized the strap of his satchel and trailed Justin from the bar.

Hutt party

Axle would typically check in with his parents if he was leaving central Wellington. They would want to know. One day they might have to come and get him. Ahead of going to the Hutt party, he didn't check in — for the simple reason that he didn't feel like it. Explaining his intentions took the fun out of the night. Plus, neither his mum nor his dad were home. So, they were partially to blame.

The party was just as promised. Guests — and plenty who weren't invited — spilled out the back of the house into a deep backyard. Faces turned to Axle, Pete, Jarvis and Reggie, then turned back to their huddles. The crowd stretched as far as the night would allow. There were two young men for every young woman. This was a party for kids from school, but also for dropouts and those who'd recently graduated. Most of all, the party was for the kind of people who had pushed Axle out of Col. They were there and they recognised him.

Axle corralled his friends and drew them inside and away from the worst of the Col boys, but three of them followed their group and lurked around the back doorway at the opposite end of the lounge. One of the Col boys eyeballed Axle across the room. It only took one. Each was hyping the other up to approach the small group from High.

Axle had hoped they would have accepted their victory in driving him from their school. But that's not how it works. Yes, he'd left. It wasn't enough. Leaving their school had made him even more unpopular than before. He didn't know that Scott had sent a scathing letter to the board of trustees that had led to a school-wide dressing down, accompanied by an unsubtle reference to a student forced to move to High. His old year level had been subjected to a full day of insufferable anti-bullying coaching. Axle hadn't been named in the Principal's address or the coaching sessions, but his name was soon being shared as the single cause for their collective punishment.

Pete, Jarvis and Reggie hadn't seen the Col boys approach. The three boys muscled up to Axle, accusing him of "running away from the real world back to Poofter High." Axle's friends only clicked to what was happening when puffed up chests tried to pry into the group. Whether by instinct or by luck, Axle had his back to a wall, and the Col boys had to get past his friends to get to him. There were another half dozen High boys who heard the slander and knew that one of their own was under attack. Axle hated it. He felt himself slipping. He'd spent months pretending to be easy and carefree, while avoiding the real reasons for shifting schools. He didn't want to fight. He didn't want to be there at all. For a few moments, he was fifty-fifty on even existing.

Axle fled, slipping behind Jarvis, stepping through the doorway and dashing down a hall, out of the house and onto the street. He hadn't played rugby since he was eleven, but he made use of a spry sidestep to weave out and away from the crowd.

"Run boy, run. Go! Go hard!" some oaf yelled after him.

Axle burst through the stillness of the evening. Mist hung in the air like a damp towel, but he barely noticed as he ran down one street, then across another. Only at that point did he look back to see if there was a chase. There was not. He didn't stop. He wasn't running from real people who might be after him anymore, but to put distance between what had happened and the present moment. He jogged down another block, then one more across, before pulling up and resting on the lip of a curb. He sat under the bough of a plum tree. The bulk of the tree shaded Axle from the streetlights as, in the day, it would have shaded him from the sun. The tree had long lost its summer fruit and most of its leaves.

After some moments, long seconds or a short minute, he lifted his head to see if anyone had followed. They had not. He buried his head between his knees, his brow on his crossed arms, and cried. He looked up to see if anyone was watching. They weren't.

Axle hadn't wept since he'd started at his new school, but here he was, as before, trapped back in a world of idiot bullies. They were sure to be telling lies to the High kids about him. They'd put wretched stories out there, even if they weren't true. Especially if they weren't true. They weren't there to defend him or search for the truth, but to tear him down. He imagined his friends listening, slowly being won over to this new idea of Axle as a loser outcast. He picked up a browned leaf and twirled it by its stem, before crumbling it between his fingers. With no friends he had no way to get home. That was the immediate problem he should focus on.

Before they could be seen, he heard their calls. "Axle! Ax! Ax!" His friends rounded the corner, running down the road towards him before pulling up around him. Jarvis had a busted lip. Blood had spilled over his shirt, which was ripped. Pete was puffing, searching for his inhaler having trailed behind the rest. Reggie looked as relaxed as ever.

Axle did his best to cover up his tears. It was dark. Maybe they wouldn't notice.

"Fuck those guys," said Pete, pulling in air.

"Seriously. Fuck. Those. Guys," said Jarvis. "You should have seen it. Reggie knocked one of them down. Boom, loser! It was awesome."

"Yeah, man, no problem. It's all good. I'm sure the guy will be fine," said Reggie.

"Those fucking idiots," said Pete, still catching his breath. "Leave them in the stone ages."

Jarvis chimed in, "You're with us now. Forget about that shit. We're taking the eighty-three back into town. I swiped a bottle of whiskey from their kitchen so we can finish that and the vodka off above the Ellice Street quarry. Maybe finish the vodka on the bus. Fuck that party. You all good?"

"Yeah, no. I'm great. Thanks for coming after me. Fuck those guys. Let's get out of here."

Convene

There had had been a minor disagreement on the way over the Remutaka Hill. Jacqui had brought up Rothman, that ineffable quality that she still wasn't sure about. João had joked that if Kaye hadn't introduced them, then maybe it would be Rothman on the romantic weekend away with Jacqui. She'd snapped at him. He'd taken it as confirmation. She'd become sullen and silent. He'd shrugged.

They checked in, then he went for a walk around the small town, telling her he'd get a beer at the pub downstairs from five and she was welcome to join.

Jacqui showered, then went downstairs with her Antarctica book. It was four-thirty. She ordered a coffee and did her best to get lost in the book, but the bar was noisy with chatter as locals watched the last minutes of a game of provincial rugby. She should have brought a novel. From where she was sitting, the game was already well and truly decided. When it finished, many of those who'd been watching left. The bar fell into a lull. Only a few hard-bitten locals remained.

A young man brought her coffee over. It wasn't terrible. He asked about her plans. Where she was from.

"Wellington," she said.

He told her he knew that and he was just trying to draw her out.

The pub door opened and João entered. The waiter asked if he'd like a coffee, too.

"A beer," he said. "Whatever is on tap."

The waiter nodded.

"Much to see out there?" Jacqui asked.

"Not as much as in here. I wish you'd come. I'm sorry about before. Can we put it down to a cultural misunderstanding?" he said.

She scanned his face. She hadn't experienced his deadpan humour before.

"A cultural misunderstanding," she agreed.

"I was thinking, as I was walking, that there's no point in us taking anything too seriously. We both know that this is something that works for us now, but in one year, two years maximum, it'll be a pleasant memory. Neither of us thinks anything else, right?"

"Right," she said.

João's beer arrived and the waiter made some more conversation. It must be entertaining for the bar staff, Jacqui thought, to mess around with the city folk. Was João also from Wellington? Was it their first time in the hotel? Would they stay a few nights or just the one?

Jacqui asked for a white wine – as much to send the waiter off on another errand as to have something cool to drink.

"I thought he was going to ask if you were my son or my lover," she said. João's lips smiled, but not his eyes. The wine arrived at the same time as an early dinner group. The waiter had to take care of them. By the time the waiter returned, both drinks were finished and Jacqui was ready to settle up.

"Another drink for your room?" asked the waiter.

"We have one of our own," said João.

Upstairs, they took their time. They each drank a glass of wine and took off their shoes. They sat on the bed and talked about their respective primary schools. João pulled the curtains closed and Jacqui slid out of her jeans. The day's little antagonisms were worked through. She dug her nails into his back, then drew them across his shoulders. He turned her onto her stomach and gripped both of her wrists so that he held her down with one hand. She fought, not because she was resisting, but to test if she could. She was pinned. She wrenched to one side. She had one wrist free when she paused.

She could see another couple. On a bed. In the mirror. On the wall. By the door.

It had taken more than a moment for her to realise the couple were her and João, her hair mostly obscuring her face and his torso somehow looming larger than without the reflection.

She looked at the couple as João kissed her neck. He tore a condom open and she watched as he placed it at the end of his penis, then rolled it down the length. He caught her eye in the mirror and held it while he lined himself up with her. He reached for a small bottle of lubricant and smeared it across the latex and, more gently, across the folds of her labia. She kept watching him in the mirror as he entered her. There was no mirror in her and Scott's room at home. Watching herself made her more aware of being in her body. She liked it. She could see and feel. She became swept up in it. There had been some distance between them, but that was gone. She reached back, pulling him down and twisting to kiss him over her shoulder. It was uncomfortable but she held him there. He tried to pull back, but she wouldn't let him. When he gave up, she set him free. Then she set the pace. It was twice as good as before, she thought, three times as good. And so it went until it stopped. He pulled himself off her, whispered something in Portuguese, held her close and fell into his sleep. She looked back at the mirror. They were still there.

PART 2

Deus ex Naturae

The Quay had a quickening pulse, as if arterial routes really were pumping blood to a pistoning heart.

"You heard? You heard?" Scott gasped, through a mighty hug. "Carbon Neutral by 2025! The whole public service. Not 2030, not 2040. In our life... this is... in this decade... it's... my god, I'm actually shaking a bit."

All around them people scattered and converged, skidded hither and yonder, frolicked upside and down. Awestruck public servants swirled as boysenberry through vanilla citizenry. The overawed huddled at bus stops in shock, not coming or going, just pausing to regroup. A few doubled over, gasping for oxygen and peace. Others sunk to the pavement, adrift. More still – and this was the majority reaction – hooted, high-fived and let out guttural screams that the role of government administrator had long trained them to suppress. None went unmoved. All were brought to life by the provocation.

Scott had seen nothing like this in all his years in the Wellington bureaucracy. He imagined that this was what it would have been like when World War Two had ended. He hadn't been alive then, of course, and nor had his parents. In his life, nothing was comparable. No world historical event had united him with his people in such a singular manner.

He'd been scheduled to meet Jacqui in Midland Park for their weekly lunch date when the news broke. The lunch was one of twelve techniques recommended by a *Guardian* columnist to keep a marriage fresh.

"I mean, that includes MBIE, it includes SOEs?" asked Scott, but Jacqui was one of the quiet ones, trying to maintain herself among the crowd. "Does it include Crown entities, SOEs? It must, surely – MFAT, think of MFAT! Hats off to DPMC, one hundred per cent. MPI – far out, MPI! – how will that go down? God, what's the mood like in Police?"

"Yes! Well... well, not as much enthusiasm on my floor as with you ministry people. A few of the junior staff were ecstatic, though. But great. Reined in a bit when the more senior members of the administration noted how much extra reporting it would require. Raining on their parade. They were still ecstatic, you know, but it was tamped down."

A cheer erupted from Stout Street, followed by a chant.

Scott upped his voice to be heard. "Health was enraptured! En-rap-tured. God, think of MOD! Their whole job is flying planes and blowing things up! Finally, someone will force them to be peaceful, beautiful even. Imagine! Half the country protests a war and there's not one staffing cut. But this? It will lead to total reform! It has to! Do you get it?"

"I'm optimistic. Cautious but optimistic. Got to see the details, remember."

Scott didn't need to see the details. There was no wriggle room in the announcement. It was strident and all encompassing. Nothing could dull his jubilation.

"Not us! We're rapt. Our whole team have got the rest of the day off to do some deep-level thinking. 'Esprit de corps!' my boss said. 'Capture the vitality of the moment.' Can you take the day off?"

A young woman dashed past, crazed. Seconds later, a young man emerged from the crowd, scanning for her, looking to Scott and Jacqui for direction. Before they could decide whether to point after her or not, he clambered on top of a parked car, stood tall and shouted, "I work for the Ministry. The Ministry for the Environment. You heard it – *for*, we're *for*! We're not ashamed to say it! *For* the environment. For, for, for! We're not ashamed. Death to political neutrality! Long live carbon neutrality!"

The last two utterances were taken up by the crowd. *Death to political neutrality! Long live carbon neutrality!* Jacqui wondered if this kind of overflowing is how year one of a carnival began. Perhaps they would make this day a public holiday?

"The day off? God, no," she said. "The mood's not quite the same on our side of the road."

"I just came from a meeting on the Terrace. People are euphoric. I mean, honestly, this is a big fucking deal, right?"

Jacqui had gone back to her phone for the latest news, but also to keep an eye on the time. She had ten minutes before she had to make her way back to work. There were five breaking news notifications about the carbon neutral announcement. A live blog on *The Biz* had photos from the office towers above the park where they sat. The celebrations had filled the streets. The only other thing to come close was the School Strikes for Climate.

"Look, Scott! It's here! It's us!"

She clicked on the picture and zoomed in. There they sat, on a lip of concrete with the city erupting around them. This was their D-Day moment. She planted a kiss against her husband's cheek.

"I'll take the afternoon off, too. You're right. This thing is too big."

Stocktake

Up to much tonight?
Come round?
Don't bring any more of those
beers though. ;)
Too risky.

Pete's parents were out at some theatre show. They'd bought season tickets and felt obliged to go. That had been their plan from the start: to force obligation on their future selves who they knew couldn't be trusted. They'd left a frozen pizza on the bench with instructions to cook it according to the instructions on the wrapper. They'd be back by ten, at the latest.

Pete offered the last two slices of pizza to Axle, who drew one onto his palm, careful not to let the toppings spill. Pete grabbed the last.

"Mum found the vodka bottle from after that Hutt party. I was stupid enough to put it in the recycling. I mean, I was recycling, right? Way to reward good behaviour, guys. Next time I'll just bin it or chuck it in a bush."

"My parents would definitely notice if there was a vodka bottle in our recycling. They have, like, one bottle of wine per week. Two, maximum."

"Yeah, but I buried it, you know. Hid it at the very bottom of the bin. Anyway. Mum found it somehow and I got the blame. And even though I denied it – 'I found it on the footpath, Mum, I swear' – she still suspects me. All I'm saying is we should probably be more careful taking booze in and out of the house."

"Yeah, but light beer? That shit can't even get you proper drunk."

"I know, but do they? It's not zero-alcohol beer – 2.2% isn't nothing. Okay, we wouldn't get smashed, but I bet we could get a mild buzz if we tried hard enough."

"Give it a go?"

The boys raced to Pete's bedroom, then to the freezer. They placed two six packs inside, surrounded by packs of frozen peas and made rudimentary calculations. The beer had thirty minutes to cool and then they'd have one hour to drink as much as their gullets could take. If the beer would get them buzzed, then it'd have to be done quick. That was the secret.

Their first cans went down quick. Three minutes. Lager, lager, lager. The boys finished at the same time. Not bad for a couple of cans that, just an hour before, had been hidden like drums of nuclear waste. They prised back the pull tab and cracked into their second cans.

"Pete. Peter. Petrovich. Petey, c'mon, man! C'mon, scull it!"

While their plan was immaculate, their results were inadequate. Axle had to go to the toilet at two cans and then again at three. The beer was bloating them. At four cans in, their confidence had subsided. Pete stretched out on the couch with uncontrollable burps. He had a light buzz, but felt so groggy that he refused any more beer. They'd only been going half an hour.

Axle waved a fresh beer under his nose, half trolling, half testing if his friend could be drawn to the challenge. The sight of the beer made his burps intensify. Nausea rose. He pulled himself up and fled to the bathroom.

Axle took Pete's place on the couch. He was onto his fifth beer. Ten minutes remained of the challenge. The race to finish a six pack had hyped him up and he'd barely considered whether he was drunk or not. He took a deep breath and thought about it.

Yeah, he concluded, a mild buzz, but nothing so special.

It took Pete ten minutes to come back from the bathroom and he didn't look great.

"You puke?"

"Nah, nah. Got the bloats. Almost, though. Gross. Sometimes I think it's better to have puked and be done with it, ya know? Did you finish?"

"Nah, man. Five down. Four and a half, to be honest. I'm out, though. And time is basically up."

Pete wanted to sit down and rest, but Axle didn't want Pete's parents to catch them with all the cans. He'd overheard what those conversations were like and he didn't know if he could handle being told off by Pete's dad. Axle collected the cans and moved them to the kitchen, then emptied the rest of his beer into the sink. He flipped the water on and rinsed the cans before crushing them under his heel.

"Next time," said Pete as he removed the remaining beers from the freezer, "we start with empty stomachs and we give ourselves more than an hour. I know we can get more than a mild buzz from this stuff."

In time

"You always knew I wasn't exactly one hundred per cent straight. Who is? I mean, maybe your cousin Ed. Anyway, there was that time in Auckland I told you about. You were in Sydney, remember? I was with the theatre people. I wrote to you about it. And we agree – right? – it's a continuum."

Scott had arrived home, sweaty from the cycle, but certain it was time to talk. Axle was off to Pete's, and Jacqui had been dicing vegetables for a Nasi Goreng. He'd begun with a string of confessions. He'd described his feeling of isolation, problems at work, then more on the Linnea situation.

Jacqui had kept with her chopping until his explanation of the work situation had morphed into his descriptions of his rendezvous with Justin. Then she'd paused.

"Wait, wait, wait," Jacqui said, "this is the same guy – Justin? – who did that awful wink?"

"Well, yes."

"So why are you sleeping with him?"

Scott wondered that himself. He tried out a few answers. "Because it's easy. I don't have to choose or anything. He leads. I follow. Makes it sound like a waltz. I'm... well... let's just say I'm not in love. He's no João. Not that I think you're in love with João. Just that Justin's kind of an asshole."

He hoped Jacqui might offer some words to clarify the situation. When she didn't, Scott continued, "Or maybe I'm not wanting to miss out. I mean, the sex is good, if that's what you're asking. And that's probably enough. I don't know. Maybe he's not such an asshole. Maybe I'm overly sensitive because of everything at work. Maybe it's more of a why-not question. I mean, why not?"

"You poor pup. I can't believe you didn't tell me. Anyway, I think it's good. I think it's funny. Amusing, perhaps. But good. Everyone is letting off steam since the announcement. We're all a bit heightened."

"I suppose. Yeah... but what's amusing about it?"

"Nothing. Nothing. Just how you got played. Hunter becomes the hunted. You know. I'm not saying it's hilarious. Or even fun. It sounds horrible. I mean fine, it's up to you but... yeah, sorry... it is a little amusing. From a wife's perspective."

"I'm thinking of having him over next weekend. He could sleep in my study or on the couch. It might be good for Axle to meet him if we're playing the whole honesty card."

"You think this asshole from HR wants to meet your son? Your words, Scott, not mine. I mean, fine, but give Ax some runway. He might not want to meet Justin."

"Like you gave him runway?" he asked, then took a breath. "No, no. You're right. It's not the same. Like I said, Justin is no João. Though I'm not sure I'd want him to be."

"Hell, Scott, just *ask* Ax. See what he wants to do. João and I could go away for the weekend if you want some space."

"Yeah, you're right. I'll ask. I'm going to pop into the shower. Thanks. I mean it. Thanks. By the way, I was also implying that you might want to meet him, too. But maybe I messed it up by calling him an asshole?"

"To be honest, I'm not really interested," she said. "I've got enough on my plate with work and João. I tell you, this Rothman – I can't tell if he's a genius or a child. But if it's important to you, I'll do it. I'll meet him."

"No, no. It's not important."

Scott stripped off his clothes as he made his way through the bedroom and to the shower. He paused in front of the mirror. He was fit. Fit enough. He was slim without being scrawny. His thighs were toned without being muscly.

"Not bad," said Jacqui. He flushed a little and found it strange that her praise still meant so much to him. He turned to face her but she'd already made her way back to the kitchen.

He tested the shower temperature with his hand as the water went from cool to lukewarm to hot. He turned it down a little. He should have known the settings after all these years, but his mind was somewhere else. He stood under the streaming water and replayed their conversation. He'd anticipated that he'd come out of it a little better. His wife hadn't been fazed. He'd hoped that she would be startled by his relationship with Justin and would then come to see it as a valiant protest against the binds of marriage. That wasn't how it had gone at all.

The water stayed steady and warm as he soaped his armpits and groin. He lifted his left foot and soaped the sole and between his toes, then repeated the action with his right foot. The shower drifted on with his thoughts. Maybe, he thought, Jacqui had respected him all along? There may have been an aberration or two, but, fundamentally, she must have kept her faith in him. And yet, he couldn't reconcile her response with his hopes and so, in the face of this indecision, he took the only available course. He turned the shower off.

10-seven

"Jacqui. You free to talk?"

Rothman had phoned her on a Sunday evening. On her private number. She was certain that she hadn't given it to him. Or maybe she had? He probably just searched for it through the personnel files. She was a little pleased by that though, while also being a bit pissed off.

"Hold on," she said, gesturing to João to pull the car over. They'd gone for a walk in the hills above Eastbourne and were driving home along the Petone foreshore. Wellington stretched out in the distance, orange lights through the gloaming.

"Yup. I'm free," she said when the car had stopped.

"Listen. I'm wanting your help on this climate change stuff. I need someone I can trust. I need someone who hasn't come up through the ranks, from outside. You know? Would you be interested?"

Jacqui had never been seconded into a team before. She'd had a few allies, but those were circumstantial. Even when she'd first been contracted in, there were no justifications for why she, in particular, was needed by anyone. At best, her past bosses would say they needed a woman's eye or a woman's touch. Assholes.

"I've been here ten years. I'm hardly an outsider."

"I don't know about that but, either way, would you hear me out? I'm not going to lie. It will be a lot of work. I've been drawn into the senior strategy role for making the Police carbon neutral by 2025. I heard last thing Friday. I've been working on it since, but they set me up with some young grad who has no idea how the organisation works. No understanding of power, influence, you know. Anyway,

I've got permission to bring you on – we can boost your rates – for a six-month operation. And I personally guarantee you'll be back where you were afterwards, if not in a better place. I'll put it in writing. So...?"

"Let me think about it. I need to talk to my husband."

"Jacqui. You know this is a chance to make a big change all at once. Don't keep me waiting. A once-in-a-lifetime opportunity."

"Alan. I said I need to..."

"No, sorry, you're right. Would you do me this favour, though? I need someone in our first meeting with the Police Union tomorrow at 1pm. Can you do that?"

"Why not take your grad if you just need someone?"

"Well, that's the unfortunate part. They were meant to go. But they quit. It was complicated."

It had all been a negotiating tactic. High ball with the job offer, then follow through with the real short-term need. All these managers talk up their long-term games, but when it comes down to it, they can barely see past their next meal. All the same, she wanted to do it. She agreed to attend on the proviso that she could work from home the next morning to prepare.

"Deal," Rothman said.

She ended the call and looked to João. "Maybe I could stay over at your place tonight? I've got the morning off."

"Hey, tonight is no good. My place is a mess. I could come back to yours?"

"Mmm, I don't know. I kind of feel like keeping you to myself, tonight. How about we get a hotel? I'll pay. Drop the car off then spend an evening in the city. It was pretty amazing last time."

Jacqui's phone lit up.

My god, she thought, did I not hang up on Rothman?

It was only a message from him with the location and time of the meeting.

"Yeah," João answered as he switched the ignition back on and the headlights lit up the seashore, "a hotel sounds nice."

Scotty from Policy

"Right team! All round. Trust you've had a good weekend, a blinder. Lots of blue sky."

Scott's boss's boss never led Monday morning meetings and Scott wasn't in the mood to sit through this attempt to build team spirit. He knew he couldn't let his mood show, so he lurked at the back, and kept his face down.

He'd felt a twinge of jealousy the previous evening when Jacqui had messaged him with her plans. Not even a call. Their own family Sunday evening ritual swept to one side for Scott to clean up. He and Axle had persevered through the Daniel Day-Lewis movie marathon. With a lick of spite, Scott insisted they break with chronology to watch *There Will Be Blood*. He hit the red wine hard enough – three glasses, not one – for his son to give a sideways look. On the final glass he'd even messaged Justin on the off chance he wanted to come watch the rest of the film with them, but Justin hadn't even replied. Without context, he asked his son if the kids still called it a 'booty call'. His son didn't reply either.

Finally, his boss's boss got to something that was interesting. Scott looked up from his reverie.

"Team. I'm going around all the floors this morning because we've got a once-in-a-lifetime chance to make good. Climate change is the number one health threat for the middle to long term. It matters. This, quite literally, changes everything. Climate change that is. Changes. Everything. Policy included. Now, team, as you heard the PM say, this is an all-of-government operation. We've got fewer than five years to make ourselves carbon neutral. We simply can't muck around with the usual silos. We're going to have to be agile," – he paused – "efficient, you understand? Fitter! More productive! Hot desks for global warming."

Scott cared about climate change. He probably cared about it even more than his own son did, who would be more affected by it. He definitely cared more than Jacqui, but he could hardly say that carbon emissions were his area of expertise. Above all, Scott valued expertise, precision and the passions that came with it. That said, he didn't feel the same euphoria as the health experts who drew a straight line from climate change to mouldy houses or mosquito-borne disease. In his role, he didn't see how climate change should or could be linked to binge drinking. But he could fake the connection if he had to, bluster on about something if necessary.

Scott risked a glance at his team. There were twenty-two of them working on policy and they should have been excited to finally be taking climate change seriously. But there was something about the overly jovial mood being hawked by his boss's boss that tempered their enthusiasm. They all knew the narrative arcs of management. Start positive, send in the hard news, end with assurances.

"Here's the play. Respiratory, you're our star. Mouldy homes are our go-to play. Warmer, humid weather will double infection rates and treble hospitalisations. Run with it. We'll partner with Kainga Ora to get an early win over the line. You have my utmost support. Direct line of contact."

The Respiratory Health Unit had always resented the alcohol team. They were all good people, but it was only natural. Alcohol and addiction had monopolised funding streams ever since heroin chic. Today's reversal in fortunes must have been a fairy-tale for those focused on the health of the lung.

"Booze. Alcohol. You're on the bench. To be honest, I think we'll all need a bit of a drink over the coming months as we action this plan. Joking, of course. It's rare that I get to say this, but you're a victim of your own success. Teen binge drinking is lower than it has been in decades. Great job! Drink driving convictions are at a record low. Phenomenal! As a team you'll be right-sized for task. I can promise you there'll be no staffing cuts. A few transfers. You have my... well, not my word, but you have my... I promise to do my best."

Scott didn't believe a word of it. He could feel the ground slipping away from under him. There were always staffing cuts, they just weren't as gleeful as in the private sector. Resignations with a gag order and six months' pay. He wasn't going anywhere, though. Not without a fight. They'd have to force him out. He made a note to brush up on whatever new iterations of employment law the current government had eked through. Maybe Justin could help.

Scott's boss's boss wasn't done.

"Now," he said, clearing his throat. "Let me introduce the big guns."

Two men stepped forward. The pair held a confidence that said, "Sorry mate, but business is business." It was the exact kind of look Scott imagined he'd get if one of their Beamers knocked him off his bike. The type to break your ribs and then tell you it wasn't worth complaining because what's done is done. They were the kind of men Justin would be if Justin had been living his best life.

"Clarence and Sibgun. Specialists in climate interventions and public sector accountability. They're being seconded in for a bit so we can get a hoof on. Lads, I'll pass it to you."

"Kia ora, Chief. Thanks. That's right. We're here to pioneer you through this process. It's not going to be easy; it's going to be one hell of a ride and I can assure you..." and at this point Scott tuned out to consider which other ministries might be hiring.

Bottom line

João left the hotel room at eight in the morning with a kiss and a promise to call. She liked that he called her instead of sending a message. Or was the calling what she liked? It might just have been João. She'd have liked a telegram from him, an email to her work account, a note pinned to her front door for the whole world to see. It was definitely João.

While showering, Jacqui's phone beeped and thrummed. After drying off, she saw a series of increasingly deranged messages from Scott. Messages lined up one after the other like a garland of tiresome homilies. She didn't reply. She was preserving her mind for the meeting with the Union. She'd never seen Scott this erratic. He wanted to quit. He wanted to downsize his life. He sent her some links to house listings. They could move to Greymouth or Greytown. He could start a community theatre. She could do whatever. Have another kid or retire young.

She turned her phone off. He wasn't going to interrupt her excellent mood. Anyway, she had to check out and find some breakfast. She dropped the swipe cards at reception and thanked the man behind the counter. He nodded with polite deference. She wondered how long it took to perfect the acquiescence of a hotel receptionist and whether it bled over into other parts of the young man's life.

She lingered on the sidewalk. Where to go? What to do? She dug into her handbag for her phone and dawdled while she waited for it to power on. Scott had sent another message. She half considered blocking his number until the meeting was over. She would just ignore him. She called Rothman.

"Alan, Jacqui here. Yes. Listen, should we meet up before this meeting? Go over the brief?"

"Yup, yup. Sorry, I'm on the move. I could meet you at the office in, say, thirty minutes?"

"Perfect. I'm coming from Lambton so I'll be there in twenty."

"Ah! Me too. Where are you? Wait for me and we can talk as we walk."

"Yeah, good. Meet me at Midland Park. Left of the main entrance. Good?"

"There in five."

Jacqui jaywalked across the Quay, waited on the centre berm for a trifecta of buses to rumble past, then strode to the harbour side of the street. Last time she'd been at this park she'd been with Scott amidst the carbon neutrality announcement. That had only been twelve days ago.

She'd just sat down when Rothman arrived. He carried a satchel in one hand and a mesh bag in the other. The bag carried four pieces of fruit – apple, orange, pear and banana – and one carrot.

"Lunch?" she asked.

"This? Well, yes. I don't often eat lunch. I have one of these every other hour starting at ten, with a coffee at one. Regimented, I know, but it works for me. Keeps me alert."

"Well, it's just gone ten. Which will you eat first?"

"Oh, yeah. You're right." He checked his watch as if he didn't believe her. He chose the Beurre Bosc pear.

"I was thinking about your proposal," said Jacqui. "I'm going to need a bit more clarity before I can agree."

"Yeah?" he mumbled, through the first half-chewed bite of pear. "But you'll still be at today's meeting?"

"I will. But more broadly, I'm having... my family is having some, well, let's call them teething issues."

"Never stops in my experience," said Rothman, and she wondered whether he had children.

"Just times of change. Nothing so serious. No health problems, thankfully. I just need some flexibility."

Her boss finished his mouthful. She wondered if he was thinking of her dinner with João.

"One hundred per cent. Take it as given," he said. "But listen. This meeting today. It is a bit of an opening negotiation of sorts. That's how I'm treating it. The union wasn't happy with not being consulted on this one. Apparently, they're not part of the CTU after all – not even a union apparently, but an association. Figures. Anyway, someone in comms stuffed up and so we're on the back foot. They might be prickly, but stick with me and we'll soon get them on side."

"Good. I'll let you know my decision later this week. If I'm in," she said. Rothman nodded and she continued. "So, then, what are we thinking success looks like? Do we need to know their bottom lines or are we just there to smooth things over?"

"I'm pretty sure I know their bottom lines: they want to keep the souped-up cars. That's the only reason half of them joined the police: social licence to speed like a demon. Personally, I think they're still mourning the loss of their Holden Commodores. Seriously, there's a Facebook page where they swap memories and pics of the old cars. It's very tender."

"The Facebook page or the pear?"

"The Facebook page. Anyway, in terms of bottom lines, they're probably more interested in what we're bringing to the table. To my mind, they're going to think that we want them in electric cars by 2025. That's what they're saying on that page. You should see the horror. The comments! There's even a poll on it. It's funny when you look at it because the electrics are faster, both in absolute terms and in acceleration. But they're cops, you know, and it's all that bullshit about the roar of the engine. Ancient masculinities and shit they don't pay me enough to dig through. Honestly, the force could use a psychoanalyst to dig into the childhood grief that makes half these boys tick. Still, better to have them be a bunch of bogans than the other law-and-order, old school disciplinarian types. Yeesh!"

Rothman took another bite of his pear, then another to finish it off before tossing the core into a rubbish bin. He offered a mumbled apology for eating and talking at the same time. She made some small talk about Skodas to let him finish.

"So," Rothman continued, "our role is to make them think exactly that: we're coming for your cars. Tell them word has come down from DPMC. Not much we can do about it. Put the fear of the ninth floor into them. The aim is to establish pushback on that as their first and only bottom line. In exchange – I'm talking after the meeting – we get them to sign over all other operational decisions. They keep the Skodas, we don't have to worry about employee pushback on our actual plans. If they're particularly petulant, let's offer a review in 2025… 2028 at the latest. If they seem genuinely on side, we can offer them a permanent deal: keep your toys as long as is feasible – 2035 for example – and we'll take care of the serious policy and implementation work."

Jacqui liked it. She didn't care about climate change in the way Scott did, but she hated to be on the wrong side of history, and it was clear where this issue was going. She would take the role Rothman was offering. Not at once, of course, but in two or three days – after he'd started to wonder about it.

After lunch – a Granny Smith apple for Alan; supermarket sushi for Jacqui – they settled into the meeting room with the Police Association. The Association, as Rothman had predicted, started out by talking about the importance of the cars and the losses they'd already suffered. Rothman offered his sympathy, recalled that his first car was a Holden Commodore which he wrote off on some country road. She was pretty sure that story wasn't true, but she kept quiet and offered the odd judicious nod in support of him.

By the end of the meeting, there was a verbal agreement that Rothman would go back to DPMC to see if the Police could keep their cars. No promises. Rothman said as it was unlikely his boss's boss would agree. But he'd give it a go. The Police Association, in turn, had agreed that if that wish could be met then all other operational matters, as they might relate to climate change, would reside with senior management and Rothman. The cops probably thought operational matters meant increased recycling or using LED lighting. Rothman had a somewhat different plan.

Pyramids

The house was empty and airy and, best of all, Axle had it to himself. Jacqui was working and Scott had driven to the Wairarapa to look at a few open homes. The boys were going to meet at Axle's house and then walk to Michella's parents' house in Wadestown for what Reggie had described as "a sweet little soiree". It had sounded cool coming from his lips, but Axle couldn't quite make it stick.

One Thursday, a couple of weeks before, Axle had complained to Jarvis and Keevan about his stockpile of light beer and his first attempt to get drunk from it. Those two were up for the challenge. Every day since, Jarvis had come up with one more tactic that could help them get as drunk as humanly possible from the light beer. Pete played the role of the grizzled veteran. He listened to Jarvis's enthusiasm, occasionally piping up to say they'd already thought of the suggested approach.

Pete arrived first and the two set the ground rules. Shoes off at the door, no food and try not to drink water either. Jarvis said that if they were making those rules then he and Keevan got to make one of their own. That was how the Everest Conquest was born: you can only drink the beers you can reach without knocking the stack over. If you did that, you were out.

"Wait," Jarvis said as the boys made the pyramid of cans on Axle's parents' table and prepared to drink. "Wait!"

He went to his backpack and pulled out a plastic yard glass.

"It can take one litre. My brother used it at his twenty first. Drank like a fucking fish. There's a technique."

"Fish don't drink, dickhead. They just live in water," said Keevan.

"That's not what we learned in advanced Biology," said Pete.

"Ooh, *advanced* Biology. Well, I saw it on the Discovery channel," said Jarvis.

"Discovery channel this," said Pete as he flipped his middle finger at Jarvis.

"Truth is," said Keevan, "that all fish absorb water through their bodies. Saltwater fish drink a bunch of water and process the salt, to hydrate. Freshwater fish are too hydrated so they piss a lot."

"So fucking what," Jarvis said. "I don't care! Let's do this! I'm first."

Jarvis took three cans of beer from the top of the pyramid and poured them into the yard glass. He'd barely got on to the third can, when the foam rose to and over the top of the vessel. Axle sprinted to his room for a towel to mop up the spill. The others cracked open their beers and made exaggerated sounds of enjoyment as Jarvis slurped at the lip of the yard glass.

"Tasty."

"Tangy."

"A marvellous drop!"

This experiment was far more precise than Pete and Axle's first attempt. Everyone was able to go at their own pace. Jarvis finally conquered the foam and filled his brother's yard glass to the top. He began while the others cautiously finished their first can. It did not go well. Although most of the beer went down, it came back up just as fast. While Jarvis was throwing up, the other boys agreed that he was disqualified. He could still drink with them, but it would be like finishing off a game of pool when you'd mistakenly pocketed the black. Keevan added some machismo to the task, focusing on the stronger beers in the Tall Boy 440ml cans. Each of these was still well less than one standard drink per can and Pete and Axle got into giggling fits as Keevan flailed against his sobriety.

After the first hour, Pete and Axle turned their attention away from trying to get proper drunk and into the mechanics of blood alcohol levels. They searched Reddit for some formula about what level of alcohol in a beer would allow someone to get a proper buzz. Pete suggested buying one of those personal breathalysers. None of them had a credit card. Nor did they want to be the one to pay for it. Pete suggested they pool their money, although he wasn't sure he wanted in. "It's the competitive side to drinking I don't like. This is science."

"But we're competing now," said Keevan. "How would a breathalyser change that?"

"We're not really competing," said Pete. "We're doing it together. Or I am. And as soon as that machine puts a number to things, it changes. Too much striving. Not enough... not enough, I don't know. I prefer the amateur spirit."

"Yeah, I get that. I hate try-hards trying to outdo everyone. That's what Col guys are like," said Axle. The light beer had done enough to relax them. They dropped talk of the breathalyser. The three were joined by an almost-recovered Jarvis while Keevan left for the bathroom as his bladder fought back.

"We still thinking of heading to the party at Michella's?" asked Jarvis.

"Why do you think we needed to get a buzz on?" said Pete.

Last time the boys – before Axle's time – had been to Michella's they had been astounded by her parents' mix of carefree values and luxury living. The scene was hard for them to describe to Axle, and whenever the boys would try, they'd lapse back into clichés about words not being able to capture the experience. It was like they were describing some foreign country where the rules and rituals were all turned on their head.

To finally leave the house, it took admissions from each of the three boys that Keevan had won the Everest Conquest – that he'd drunk the most alcohol. It was hard to tell if his belligerence was an overbearing teenage pride or if it was a consequence of the alcohol. Either way, he eased back to a more collegial spirit as the boys walked up to Upland, down a little, then through the Botanic Gardens and onto Glenmore Street, which led to Tinakori Road.

The expedition party made three stops on the way to Michella's house. First, they stopped at a dairy for Jarvis to buy some Juicy Fruit chewing gum. Next, they stopped for a burping contest outside Premier House. Convincing themselves that the Prime Minister's security was after them, they bolted. No-one gave chase.

The final stop was when Axle disappeared. The other boys looked around, and spotted him thirty metres back, peering into the window of a restaurant. Jarvis was agitated that the Prime Minister's security would find them. The boys agreed that Pete was to go back for Axle and the pair would have to catch up with the rest of them, who would keep moving. Worst case scenario: they just meet them at Michella's house. Pete accepted the plan. He remembered the Hutt party and he felt some responsibility for his friend. When Keevan and Jarvis set off, he looked back to Axle but could no longer see him on the street.

Axle had spotted João in the restaurant. There were only a couple of customers waiting. He caught João's eye. It would have been rude to not go in.

"You've got to be the first Brazilian to work in an Indian restaurant," Axle laughed.

"Must be, eh?" laughed João.

"You Brazilian now, João?" said the man behind the cash register with a laugh. "If that's the case we're going to have some work explaining your visa to Immigration. Could always rebrand the samosas as empanadas, I suppose."

"You're not from Brazil?" asked Axle.

"Yeah, right. If he's from Brazil, then I'm the Maharashtra of Mumbai!" laughed the man.

Axle's brow knotted and João asked the man if he could take five minutes. The man neither agreed nor disagreed, just chortled "Brazil!" while João led Axle out onto the street.

"Okay, listen. I'm not from Brazil. I only tell people that I am because Kiwi women won't give me a chance otherwise. It's just racism. I can trust you, right? I don't let it get me down. History of the world. There's no point. You won't tell anyone?"

"Yeah, sure. Of course."

"I'm actually Indian. I'm from India. I did spend a couple of years in Brazil, though, so I know what I'm talking about. And it is exactly like what I was saying. I wasn't bullshitting you, Ax. I hate it when adults do that to kids. You know. The way they talk down to you."

"So, wait. Really? India... damn. India's cool."

"Ha. I don't know. Maybe the country is cool. There's a billion of us and things have been going sideways since, well... I don't know. People overseas seem to think Kerala is cool. And all those spots in the Himalayan foothills. Anyway, that doesn't matter. I'm not even from those parts. Listen. Here's the deal. I'm not going to bullshit you, kid. I know I lied about where I'm from, but you get enough of that from the adults. So, from now on, no bullshit. Seriously. Ask me anything and I'll tell you the truth."

"Yeah. No, I totally get it," said Axle. "And your secret is good with me."

"The thing is, though, I'm from Diu, which actually was Portuguese until the 1960s. My parents moved there when I was three. My dad grew up with Portuguese as his second language. Catholics, too, so we always felt a connection with the Brazilians. Just a part of the empire. I imagine I'd feel the same connection to people from Angola and Mozambique too, if I ever got the chance to get there or meet one of them."

Axle spotted Pete loitering a little down the road. He'd started towards them when Axle and João first came onto Tinakori Road. As he got closer, he'd seemed to see that there was something uncomfortable about the conversation, and had held back.

"I think you're not totally wrong in doing what you've been doing," said Axle. "I don't know. I mean, it's unfair to be racist about anything and you're not exactly hurting anyone, really. Not directly."

"Oh, one hundred per cent. I don't feel great about it, you know, deception. But what you've said is true. Before – on Tinder – I had a little Indian flag in my profile and I got nothing. Like, almost nothing! Just a bunch of scammers. Some guy behind the screen, probably from India – I know! – trying to get my credit card number. So, I did this experiment. I change one thing – one thing! A flag emoji. And then I get all sorts of attention. People act like they're not racist over here, but I tell you, when it comes to this kind of thing then this country is as bad as anywhere in the world."

"I'm really sorry, man. I won't say anything to Mum. I promise. But maybe you should?"

"Yeah. I'll think about it. Seriously." He glanced back inside. "I've got to get back in. Come by for some food some time. My boss isn't here Tuesdays and Wednesdays, so I can sort you out."

João went inside as Axle jogged down to Pete, who explained that they'd better run to catch up. They spotted the other two boys as the gradient of the street steepened. Axle and Pete dropped their jog to a fast walk, eventually joined the others and wound their way up Wadestown Road towards Michella's house.

"What was that about, Ax?" asked Keevan.

"Nothing, man. Just saw a friend of my parents. No big deal."

"Weird," said Keevan, but let it slide.

Alan or Rothman or Al

"Time is not our friend. Let's get our main strategy down and then we'll take our weekend to drill out the detail, if need be?"

That had been Rothman on Wednesday. He'd made a point of her watching as he cleared his calendar. She did the same to hers.

On Friday, he'd checked if she could work Saturday morning. She said that she would. She hadn't known what was going on, but it was genuinely good to be a part of his team. Things were going great with João, not terrible with Scott, but now there was this connection developing with Rothman. She couldn't tell where that attraction came from and she hated not being able to read his intentions.

She replayed her interactions with Rothman and came to the worst of all possible conclusions. He had actually done nothing out of the ordinary. He'd been professional. If anything, she thought he might be more interested in João, given the friendliness he'd shown him at the Italian restaurant in Newtown. That scenario was something she wasn't totally opposed to. For one afternoon, all she could think of was having both of these men share a bed with her. This time she didn't even think of Scott looking on. She imagined them back in the hotel in Wairarapa, watching in the mirror, and she hated how much she loved the idea.

She made a pact with herself that if she worked past 3pm Saturday, she would book another hotel room for that night and invite João over. João, alone, would be enough. If they met early, she could do something charitable. Help him with his CV perhaps. Then a late dinner and the rest of the night, whatever that might bring.

"What have we got?" asked Rothman, but it was less a question and more a prompt for him to recount their thoughts. "Admin support in place, first. Evaluation of our current status, complete 2022. Good. Feel-good achievables delivered in 2023 – get the team on side. And then 2024 as the year of delivery. We'll need a new name for that, but let's keep it as placeholder."

"Did you get clarification of when in 2025 we're supposed to tip into neutrality?" Jacqui asked.

She wished she'd been in the meetings with senior leadership. She also knew that there were mixed views of her in the upper echelons. At best, she was considered to be a specialist wheeled out for a singular use. At worst, she was considered toxic and a loner.

She checked her phone. It was 3.30pm.

"No word on it. They waffled about it coming down to whatever notes came down from DPMC."

"That was weeks ago! They should have been..."

"To be honest, between us, they're still hoping the government will lose the next election and we'll be able to scrap all this rapid carbon neutrality business. Apparently, the opposition thinktanks have a rival clean carbon proposal that, on the surface, sounds the same, but which strips out all aspirational goals. I'm telling you all this so you know where the ground lies."

"It's useful. Thanks. I'll keep it between us."

"Great. For the sake of argument, let's imagine we have until 31 March, 2025. That way we're either frontrunners – comms always appreciates a PR win – or assiduously on time. And there's in-built slack, too."

"Can't hurt to have in-built slack," she replied as she pulled out her phone to text João.

"Listen, Jacqui: I wanted you on this team because I have a plan that most of the usual team wouldn't be into. Too radical for them, but I know you'll hear me out, right?"

He was asking her to put her phone down. She savoured the conspiratorial manner. She nodded, sent the text and placed her phone face-down on the table.

"Go on," she said.

"I woke up at 4am on Thursday and the idea was in my head. I don't know how. It was so simple and so effective. We've got to play to our core strengths, right? No, that sounds like I'm a simpleton. You tell me. Where does the strength of the police come from?"

She was about to say something about a strong team, but that wasn't right. There were plenty of answers but none were definitive. "The consent of the community that surrounds us? The partner who rides beside us? Fuck, what else do we say? The uniform and all those who've worn it before us – no, that's the All Blacks."

"Nope. Not even close. I'm not trying to be evasive. Think of the Police like a business, Jacqui. What is our real competitive advantage? The steely, physical reality?"

"What? Like... our monopoly on the legal use of violence?"

"Close! But not quite. Take that as read. It is more than that, though. It's our ability to arrest, detain and – especially in this case – to seize assets of criminal gangs. The violence is a fringe benefit for some of the old school thugs, but it's not our bread and butter. Our real core strength is in depriving freedoms, levelling charges and seizing property."

"I mean you're not wrong," she said. "But can we just call it enforcing the law."

"Exactly. Interpreting the law and enforcing the law. Legal language is never as precise as it seeks to be. Let's try it this way: imagine I'm arresting you for disorderly conduct."

"Yes."

"Well, you show me where it says I can do that?" he asked.

"I'm not totally sure. I'm not exactly a commissioned officer. The Crimes Act? Summary Offences Act?"

"Exactly. Yes. No-one in the community knows what 'disorderly conduct' means. Define disorder."

"It's about inciting violence against people or property."

"Right. Now define violence. The Act says inciting also pertains to the present and the future. You can see how much leeway we have to arrest people for disorder?"

"Right," she replied as her phone buzzed. She knew she shouldn't but Rothman was being terse, so she flipped the phone over. João was keen and finished work shortly.

"Listen, Alan. I've got to be somewhere shortly. Can we round this off? What does this have to do with anything?"

"Understood. Understood. Let's think less of our actions and more of the actions of, if you'll excuse the term for a second, climate criminals. This was the thought. Simple. The best solutions always are. We, as the Police, can arrest alleged climate criminals and seize their assets. We have precedent to prevent future bad conduct. We now have the remit to interpret the Zero Carbon Act in a sufficiently ambitious manner. Then we can offset the reduced emissions from shutting climate criminals' businesses down to allow us to keep our cars on the road. Hell, we wouldn't have to change anything about the business except for a few of the simple public-facing tricks everyone is going to be doing. It's beautiful and, better yet, it's simple."

"Simple is beautiful. I get that," said Jacqui, "but let me repeat it so I can fully understand what you mean. You're saying we interpret the Zero Carbon Act – or some related Act – in an aspirational way to allow for aggressive enforcement against climate criminals in the same way we define gangs. Yeah? Then when we arrest these climate criminals, we somehow claim credits for reducing carbon emissions. We take them. And those credits are used to offset our own emissions, making us carbon neutral by 2025?"

"Yes. I mean, best case scenario is that the public loves it and we end up with a massive carbon surplus that we can sell off to the rest of the public sector."

"That's insane, Alan. I'm all for showing the next generation that we didn't drop the ball on climate change. But this isn't practicable. I mean, you're not serious. You're wasting our time."

"Blue sky thinking, Jax, let's keep it blue sky. Aspirational. And practicable, in my opinion."

"Call me Jacqui. Never call me Jax. This is really insane. No-one will let you go through with it."

"Just think this through with me. It's all about the pitch."

"Don't treat me like a simpleton. It's not like you can just give a bit more detail and I'll understand. What is the real plan here? Like, what angle are you running? I'd appreciated being in on your actual strategy. We put this out there as a first negotiation? As a bluff? It's science fiction, for fuck's sake."

"I'm not following."

"Sure you are."

She tried to look at him anew. He was a fantasist. Utterly and thoroughly delusional. Surely this was one of those weird power moves those men in management like to play.

She tried to wait him out, but in the end, she was the next to speak. "This a gambit, then? A feign? We've got them to say their bottom line and then we act like lunatics so that... and this is where I get lost."

"I think you're missing the big picture. This is a crisis, right? The earth is literally dying. You don't fix that with business as usual. That's how we sell it. Don't you see? We actually have to do something different for once, rather than drawing out the same answers from the same old handbook."

"Really? I mean, sure the planet is dying. We're killing it, or we're killing ourselves. I don't know. But if you're not going to include me in whatever your wider plans are, fine. I just don't believe for one second that you think this will fly. And know this: if you're looking for someone to take the fall for your weird-ass climate clusterfuck, it won't be me. That's all I can imagine you're doing with this. Setting me up to take the fall and then bargaining down to something more reasonable."

"Jacqui. I'm serious. The plan would take finesse and a strong communications and PR outlook, but I genuinely think it could work. Genuinely."

"Fine. I'll think about it. I've got to get home. Flexibility, eh? God, it's already five. Sorry. I have to go."

Wade

Michella's house didn't look different from any other from the outside. Sure, there was the million-dollar view, but half the homes in the city had those. If you looked close enough, though, there were discreet signs of wealth. For starters, meticulous shrubs grew from bulbous planters with a symmetry and unity that did not occur by chance. The path to the front door was weed free, delicately lit and swept clean. If their trees shed leaves, it didn't show.

Keevan rang the bell and Reggie answered the door, gesturing to them to take their shoes off. He stepped outside and closed the door as the boys lined up down the steps at the entrance, each tugging at their shoes with most not properly undoing the laces. As the boys strained and struggled, Reggie offered hushed facts about Michella's parents. It was odd to hear anyone their age so keen to defer to status and it didn't sit with how Axle had previously seen Reggie. He half-hoped the near-whisper indicated they were to learn some scandal. It did not. Michella's mother – Faye – was a patron of the arts and was the first daughter of some old family. Her father – Ron – was a partner at some double-barrelled law firm and had once represented the country at the Winter Olympics.

"At bobsledding," said Reggie and the boys smothered their snickering.

Once shoes were off and they'd made their way inside, Reggie paraded the new arrivals in front of Faye and Ron. Ron was perched on a stool in the kitchen, while Faye got up to greet and inspect the young men. To Axle, it felt like something between strutting down a catwalk and being paraded in front of an opposing army's officers as a fresh prisoner of war. Axle could hear the sounds of the young women at the other end of the house but supposed he and his friends had to start with making a good impression on the parents. It was awkward but quick. They were the special guests, apparently. They were most welcome.

Michella's dad mixed cocktails for the group. Light on the rum and heavy on the mixers. It was a rarefied feeling to have an old gent pouring them and passing them, one by one, to the boys. He dropped a sprig of mint on each one and said, "Here you are, Sire," then waited for each boy to sip and tell him how good it was. Axle had never drunk from a martini glass before and he looked to how the others balanced their glasses via the brittle stem.

He wished he'd put more thought into how he'd dressed. His socks were mismatched but at least his shoes had been left outside. There had been slander in Phys Ed that his shoes reeked. He knew that his shoes smelled bad, of course, but all the boys' shoes smelled that way.

With some comment about not keeping their hosts waiting, Reggie led the boys away from the kitchen and into the lounge. Beth, Tanasi, Michella and someone Axle didn't know were waiting. Before they could claim seats and settle in, Michella flashed a vape and offered a tour of the house. Mostly she guided the new arrivals through her room to show off her collection of VHS tapes and records, then to the balcony off her room.

She drew Jarvis to one side, while the rest of the young men contemplated the harbour. There were rumours Michella had a crush on Jarvis. She'd told Tanasi as much, apparently. And, even though they were all still in high school, their friends talked about how they might be considered a good match. Michella passed the vape to Jarvis, who sucked in before handing it to Keevan, and exhaling.

"It's weed, eh?" Keevan asked, gesturing to Michella's vape. She nodded, then shrugged.

The view from the balcony was epic. As the rest of the boys huffed on the vape, Axle stood to one side, surveying the city. He wanted to try weed, but not in this situation. While he was becoming comfortable with his friends, he was also aware that being invited to Michella's was a new test of his compatibility with this wider circle. It wasn't like his parents were poor, but this house was truly opulent.

Any sense that others had been gifted a head start in life was thoroughly offset by Axle's own wild optimism for his future. The last months had built a burgeoning sense of his life's potential to exceed everything that had ever existed before or that he could possibly imagine. He had one word for it: expansive.

The vape had been passed back to Michella. Axle, along with Reggie, Keevan and Pete left their host and Jarvis on the balcony. As they crossed the threshold to the inside of the house, Axle saw Michella tracing a fingertip across Jarvis' split lip before asking if it still hurt. There was insinuation and intention in her question.

Axle caught up to Pete and Reggie as they re-joined the group in the lounge, but, as soon as they were settled, Reggie pulled them back to the kitchen for another round of drinks. Pete groaned, "can't we sit still for a second," and Reggie told him he shouldn't have drunk his cocktail so quick if that was what he wanted. Tanasi offered a conspiratorial shrug and Axle sent a dopey grin back as he and Pete followed Reggie. Keevan stayed behind, gesturing to his still-full glass.

In the kitchen, Michella's mum noted her daughter and Jarvis "getting cosy".

Her father chimed in. "Our parenting philosophy is simple. A tincture of adult supervision, trust in the acumen of our girls, and ankle bracelets for you boys."

"Ankle bracelets?" Axle laughed. "Like the one my aunt brought back from Bali?"

"Home detention," said Ron. "Not some hippie accessory. Don't make me explain the joke."

Axle's face must have registered his fright as Michella's dad pulled him aside.

"Mate. I was just having a joke, there. Seriously, we're about freedom not discipline. It is truly, bloody good to see you kids having such a good time. Bloody good. I haven't seen you here before, I think, but I want to let you know the ground rules. First rule. You lot are safe here. I know some other parents have a lot of rules about what can and can't be done. Faye and I are not like that – get high, get drunk, make out, whatever. Probably best to keep it in your pants until you're a bit older but, if not, wrap it up. Shit. Not appropriate, I know. You lot will do it anyway whether we say you can or not. Main thing is, know you can always do it here without judgement."

Axle looked over to Pete who was humouring Michella's mother while Reggie had been tasked with filling the blender with ice cubes.

Michella's dad had been waiting for some sort of agreement, but Axle asked a question instead. "What's the second rule?"

Ron was distracted and took some time to answer. "Eh?"

"The first rule is that we're safe and without judgement. I don't mean to be rude but I'm curious about the second rule."

Michella's mum had finished making a new round of drinks for those in the lounge. She led the way through and Axle's three friends trailed behind her. He could hear laughter from the other room and, while he was eager to return, he was also curious to hear where Ron's rules would go.

"Yeah, um. I guess a first rule does imply a second. Astute. I like that. Let me think... I guess the second rule is that none of this matters, really. Happiness comes from within. You can't buy it, can you? Your parents? They're not the ones with the winery in Martinborough are they?"

"No. I'm not sure who that is. Jarvis's parents maybe?"

"Oh, right. That's good then. Those were some unhappy people."

"True?" Axle asked.

"Your parents happy, Pete?" asked Ron.

"I'm not Pete. I'm Axle."

Axle felt odd being the only lucid one in the conversation. He felt like a hypnotist must feel when they realise that their subject is firmly in that in-between state.

"Axle, eh? Bloody strange name if you think about it. Teutonic, I'd guess. Maybe Dutch. Either way, how are your parents? They good?"

"I think so. I don't know," Axle replied. "How about you? You two seem good."

"That's what Michella says, eh? Doubt she'd say that! Eh? Nah, we're good. We're all good. Nothing for you to worry about. I mean we're together even through it all. These days divorce is as common as spit. If people have the courage to get married, then they should have the courage to divorce and we shouldn't even blink. No point, really. I don't believe in it, anyway. Divorce. Faye can do what she wants. I do what I want. We're all good. Why get divorced if you're all good?"

Ron was tilting forward on his seat and Axle was concerned he would topple forward. He edged back a little and moved his weight so he could spring to the side if Ron did collapse.

"That's funny," Axle said, "my parents are sort of the same. I mean, they're different but they give each other space, you know? Live their lives."

"I know. Yeah. I know. Hey, you know that my name is Cuban for rum? At least that's what they say in Cuba. Spanish for rum! Not Cuban! Ron that is," he laughed before swaying, slipping and catching the bench. "Sorry for rambling on, mate. You're alright. Let's see what the rest of your lot are up to, eh?"

Vitae

Jacqui had arranged to arrive at the hotel first so she could pay for it without João having to worry. She called him with the room number and, within half an hour, they were sitting in the room together.

"I just can't get over today," said Jacqui. "Rothman. He's mad. I'm not getting paid enough. I'm mad! I swear."

João nodded. Jacqui had expected some sympathy, but he was right to be quiet.

"So what's up with you?" asked Jacqui.

"Nothing. Nothing. I'm fine. Let's just relax," said João.

"Oh, don't tell me to relax. Work has enough of that bullshit."

"Whoa! Hold up," said João. "Yes. I'm sorry."

"Ah shit, sorry," said Jacqui. "I hate being told to relax. It's what people call a trigger. But you're right. I'm not relaxed. It's not about this."

"Hey, I'm not relaxed either," he said, his pursed lips curling into a light smile.

"Work?" Jacqui asked.

"Yeah. The Hustle. Visas. One foot in this world, one foot aimed at home. Half wanting to see things out; half wanting to cut and run."

"From me?"

"It's all tied up in it," he said. "But no. Not from you, precisely. From here. From shitty jobs. Disrespect. From being a ghost."

His presence in her world had been such a boon to her that she was taken aback that he might have troubles.

"Why are you not saying anything?" he asked.

"Just thinking. It's the same for me. No. Nothing. Turn off the lights. Come here."

"Are you sure? It's only seven. I don't want to dwell on it, but it's not the same for you. C'mon, let's go out."

"Okay. You're right. Going out sounds good. Can I take a shower first?"

"Who's stopping you?"

She stepped into the shower and closed her eyes as the water soaked through her hair and ran over her body. She tried a few exercises to shake out the tension of her day. She could hear João cycling through television channels in the bedroom. She dried herself off, combed back her hair and slipped back into her work clothes.

"João?" she asked as she left the bathroom. He was sitting back on the bed. The television was off and his attention was fixed to the ceiling.

"Yeah?"

"Why are you with me? Surely you could have a lot of women? Different women? Younger ones. I don't know. Ones you might have a future with."

"Sure. Yeah. But maybe I'm not like that. Not everyone is looking to trade in or trade up. I'm here with you, now. And it's good. So why think otherwise?"

She scanned his words and surveyed his expression. He was sincere. He was right. "So where should we go?"

Downstairs

When Scott got back from the Wairarapa, Justin was waiting on the footpath of Upland Road. Scott began to apologise, but Justin batted his words away and pulled him in for a kiss. Scott pulled away and shot him a deathly glare. He scanned the path to see if any of their neighbours had seen, before turning back to Justin, who seemed pleased to have put him in that position. As the two men walked down to the house, Justin mocked Scott's prudishness. When Scott tried to rationalise his fears, Justin smacked his ass then grabbed at it.

The house was still. They set up in the lounge and Scott passed a bottle of Malbec and a corkscrew to Justin before turning the heat pump on and upping the temperature to twenty-five. Knowing they were the only ones home, Scott felt exposed. Maybe it was spill-over from how Justin had approached him outside the house, or maybe it was just strange to finally be in their house when all of their time together had been at Justin's.

Scott made an excuse and led Justin downstairs. Jacqui had thought to turn the downstairs rooms into a separate flat and rent them out, but they didn't need the money enough to put up with the hassle of a stranger living there. So, the downstairs rooms remained underused and, whenever Scott went in, he noted how much colder they were than the rest of the house. He half-believed their lack of use was what allowed the chill in.

"What's this?" Justin asked, as Scott closed the door and turned the heater on. He was gesturing to a piece of art on the wall.

"Oh, I spent a good year trying to become a painter. To innovate, if you'd believe me," Scott replied. "Flip it over and you'll see it's kind of a double-sided work. That was ten years ago. I liked the idea of using glass to create what I called a reversible painting. It's the first paint that goes down that matters, and can never be painted over, at least if you look through the glass side. Then, when the final coat is done, you press another sheet of glass down and that protects the final layer. There was a Lebanese painter who pioneered the idea. It's not so original."

Justin flipped the painting over to see the imagery on the reverse.

"I thought there was some sort of symbolism to it," said Scott. "Birth and death. But now it feels about as profound as one of those reversible coats. Two jackets for the price of one. A gimmick. In the end it became more about the process. Maybe that's why I stopped."

"The process, eh," said Justin. "Much interest from buyers?"

Scott shrugged. He'd lost all interest in painting. He busied himself with dimming the lighting, while Justin popped the cork from the bottle and poured two glasses of wine.

"It was bisexual visibility day on Wednesday," said Scott.

"You think I give a fuck?" laughed Justin.

"I was just saying. It's interesting." Scott was not sure why he said this. He was, all at once, trying to be earnest, teasing and get a rise from Justin. But those intentions had no way to co-exist.

"I really don't care about visibility," said Justin.

"Well, I think it's important. Or maybe not. Sorry. I was just messing with you. Payback for you grabbing my ass where the neighbours could see, I guess. Visibility, eh! I knew you wouldn't care."

The room was heating up, but it was still damp. Scott had led the conversation into a petty squabble in which he had no interest. He was bored by the prospect of an evening talking with Justin, and Justin wasn't interested in that either. Scott ventured another line of conversation, then stopped. He half-heartedly gestured at nothing in particular and then gave it up before realising that this awkward back and forth was precisely the prelude that Justin wanted.

"You're only overthinking things," Justin told him, filling the silence. "It's okay. But you need to realise that if you keep up with this conversation, you'll ruin tonight for me as well as for yourself. I'm not responsible for your mood. I don't know how Jacqui puts up with it, to be frank."

Justin was right. Scott thought up a couple of apologies, but none of them would halt the drift. He couldn't work out if he was being expertly played or whether he was fucking with his own mind. He needed to take control again but as soon as he opened his mouth, Justin smirked, grabbed him by the wrist, spun him around and pulled him closer.

"Slowly, now," said Justin, though Scott was in no position to direct their movement. It was easiest when their roles in the bedroom mirrored their roles at work.

"Sorry. Just a second," apologised Scott, pulling away and switching the lamps off. As his eyes adjusted to the dark, he traced the few steps back to Justin. He knew Justin would use the moment to retake control. He had anticipated what would come. One hand curled around the back of his neck and the other gripped his shoulder. He could just make out the outline of Justin's face. All in all, it was dark enough that he felt transported back to where they'd left off the previous time. Scott reached back to Justin's waist. Though he couldn't see a thing, he registered the leather of the belt and the metal of the clasp, before releasing it.

Days later, trying to recount the evening to Jacqui, he struggled to explain what their sex was like: it was warm, gruff, and there was that strip of light under the door that meant he could only see in faint outlines. But those were all observations he'd made in the moments after it had darkened. He tried to tell her of Justin's expertise, about how moments slowed down, and how Justin's tenderness made him wonder whether he'd been wildly awry in his judgment of this man's character. The only thing that felt definitive, however, was when he told Jacqui he didn't have the words for how he felt. He changed tack, focusing on a chronology of the night and how there was just this other body and his. How Justin had pulled two squabs onto the floor, but how he only recalled how the carpet felt against his body where the cushions couldn't reach.

"Guess you had to be there," he said.
"Maybe next time," she said, feigning a leer.
"You bring João, I'll bring Justin."
The words hung in the air a little too long.
"I was joking," she said.
"I know. Me too."
It was a draw.

Bloom

Got time for a chat? x

The message lit up Jacqui's phone but the number was unknown. She had to Google the area code. Turkey!

Give me five? I'll just log on.

Jacqui skipped downstairs, plugged in her headphones and settled into her armchair. The app chimed its melancholy tone as the call arrived. She saw that Kaye didn't have her video on, so she kept hers off too.

"Kaye! Can you hear me okay?"

"Yeah. Perfect. You?"

"Great! How is it? Is Robert there?"

"No, no. He's at work. Always. It's just me. How are you?"

"You know. Nothing changes here. Work is strange. New boss. He'd be your type. A little weird for me – no, not weird, not even eccentric. Energetic. Like Robert, but without the elocution and finishing school. Weather's been good. You?"

"Oh, I'm great. Crossing things from my lists. I hadn't really prepared for being here aside from a few language courses for spouses. Is this new boss single? Have you… you know?"

"No, I haven't. I don't know if he's single. He's sort of aloof."

"Confirmed bachelor?" asked Kaye

"Yeah. I really don't know," said Jacqui. "I don't think so. So, there's no new João on your end?"

"No. I mean, there are only so many hours in a day," said Kaye.

"Are things okay? You're not calling for anything specifically? I've been seeing what's going on over there on the news. Sounds tense. Especially in Istanbul. Ankara coping?"

"It is a little tense, yeah. But we're fine. Ankara hasn't really experienced the same unrest. That's what Robert's crowd call it: unrest! Single figure casualties are an incident; double digits are unrest; triple digits are probably a bit of a tizz. No real reason for calling. Checking in. Making sure things are good."

"With João?" Jacqui pressed.

"Or anything. Just curious. Missing home, I suppose," said Kaye.

"Well, João is good. He's still floating around a bit. Me too. Not sure when I'll come back to earth, it's complicated," said Jacqui.

"Good. Good to hear. Sex can be confusing. Stratospheric but untethered. Like that scene in that movie where the astronaut is drifting away from the spacecraft and you're not sure if they'll find a way back or not. I was wondering if... Listen, I'm coming back over in spring to see my parents. Would you mind if I saw João while I'm there? I've been missing him."

"See him?"

"Yeah," said Kaye.

"You're asking permission?"

"Well, I suppose," said Kaye.

"It's not for me to give. Ask him for permission. I've got nothing to do with it," said Jacqui.

"Come on. What? Are you angry at me?" asked Kaye.

"No. Not angry," said Jacqui.

"But you're not exactly pleased. You know he'll probably want to have us both at once. À trois. Has he been hectoring you about that? He's lovely, but he's just a boy, you know? Incapable of guile."

Jacqui could tell her friend wanted to lighten the mood and, in doing so, she'd be granting herself the right to repossess João. Jacqui could imagine how their conversation would go afterwards. Kaye would defend herself by referring to this talk. Jacqui would say that no agreement had been reached. Kaye would say that might be so, but she had at least broached the issue. It would end with Kaye getting what she wanted and offering a milquetoast apology.

"You know, perhaps I don't see João the same way," said Jacqui after some moments. She'd considered just hanging up on the call and pleading technological interference but decided against it. It would be worse having Kaye chase her by Messenger.

"I'm serious, Jacqui. Don't get too involved with him. It's a honeymoon phase for a reason. It doesn't last. Nothing to ruin your marriage over. How is Scott?"

"He's fine, and I think you're projecting your own problems onto me."

There was a blip of static, then Kaye spoke. "So, you're fine with me and him doing whatever we want?"

"I don't know why you're acting like this. I said it was none of my business," said Jacqui.

"Listen, let's step back a bit. I don't know why this conversation has gone the way it has, but let's talk about it when I'm home."

"Fine," said Jacqui. "But I think you know exactly why the conversation has gone this way."

"Oh, come on, it's not like you're in love with him. You almost sound like those men who think the marriage should be open for them but not their wives. How about this, then: you send me a picture of this hot new boss. A video if there's something online. And set me up on a date with him. And if that goes well, I won't even let João know I'm back in the country."

"I'm not going to do that," said Jacqui.

"Jesus, Jacqui. What have you got your head mixed up in? Men are plentiful and low value. That used to be what we said. You need to relax."

"Don't tell me to relax," said Jacqui.

"OK. You do what you want."

"Fine."

"Fine, what?" asked Kaye.

Jacqui couldn't believe her friend was still pushing it. She let the silence take hold.

Kaye didn't care. "Fine, you'll introduce me to your boss? Or fine, I can see João and you won't get upset?"

"There'll be some unrest, but I'm sure you'll figure it out. I've got to go," said Jacqui.

Jacqui had already pulled the headset off and was closing the app as she faintly heard Kaye say, "Right, Hoşçakal." She closed the laptop, chewed at her lip for a second and, her mind still on the call, strode back upstairs.

Climate High feat. BoT and the kids

Axle couldn't isolate the one moment that made him feel at peace in the world, but there he was. At home, at school, with his gang of friends. Then, outside of that, an optimistic ripple had spread over his life. He'd started looking forward to school. The change was so profound he even looked forward to being alone.

The school bell rang. Art was over. Lunch was about to start.

"Did you hear?" Pete asked, as Axle joined the group sitting on the lawn above the tennis court. "Mad shit. Total war."

"Yeah," Keevan said. "Time for a reckoning, they're saying."

"What's this?" Jarvis asked.

"The seniors," said Pete. "They've gone to the media. They're trying to force the Minister of Education to fire our Board of Trustees. It was on *The Biz* this morning."

"Yeah, but the media will publish anything," said Jarvis.

"Nah, but it's true," said Pete. "Didn't you see the climate pledge going around? *I, the signed, pledge to enforce the school's existential commitment* – like, a life-or-death commitment – *to Wellington High being carbon neutral by 2025*. Didn't you guys get one of those in your locker?"

"Shit, I still don't have a locker," said Axle.

"Me neither," Pete added.

"What's this about the Board, though?" Axle asked.

"Just what I said," said Pete. "No more news yet, but apparently there are a group of kids who are trying to get the board fired for not taking the Carbon Neutral thing seriously. I mean, I'm up for a ruckus, but I'm amazed at the guts of the seniors. I guess they're graduating – if they'll let them – at the end of the year, so now's the time to kick on."

Reggie and Tanasi joined the group. Axle hadn't seen them together since Michella's party. He'd half hoped maybe they had broken up.

Tanasi whispered in Reggie's ear. He grinned. She kissed him on the neck, more of a lick really, and jogged off.

"You grace us with your presence," said Jarvis.

"No shit, bro," said Reggie. "Now what's this I hear about you guys experimenting with getting wrecked on light beer without me?"

Domestic lager

"How are those beers holding up?" asked Scott. "Too soon to re-up? Any favourites? Perhaps we should crack into one this afternoon?"

"What does re-up even mean? You're such a boomer, Dad. No offence."

"C'mon, Ax. Why you gotta play me like that, son?"

"Dad. That's cultural appropriation. And it's not even fresh. Stop."

"Good to know the kids are saying fresh again."

"Sure. The beers are good. I don't want to drink every weekend, anyhow. I might head out tonight, though, if that's okay?"

Jacqui hadn't said whether she was going to be home, but he suspected not. She'd be off to work with Rothman or to play with João or some combination of the two.

"Sure thing. I might have a friend around, too, then."

"Cool, cool."

Scott was relieved. Cool still meant cool. Or was his son patronising him? He didn't think so, but it did lead Scott to consider if today's fifteen-year-olds were markedly different from yesteryear. Teens had got taller, he'd read. Growing up quicker, literally, as well as emotionally. They'd said that about his generation too. It might be true. In his job, he'd become particularly sensitive to intergenerational moral panics and their soothsayer ambulance-chasers.

As the afternoon waned, so did his feelings of being left alone. The pleasures of his new life fell back into focus and he messaged Justin to see if he'd come round to watch a film or to hang out. The flirting made him feel young and he savoured even the smallest drop of this reckless energy. With this new lover, and his alienation from his workplace, he felt that he'd been unchained from a Sisyphean life.

He pictured Justin arriving before Axle went out. If he did, Scott would have to tell him. Or he wouldn't. His son was old enough to figure it out. What would pre-empting it matter? His son had unflinchingly accepted João. But, of course, that was different. Everyone could like João. Justin wasn't likable. Scott still wasn't even sure if he liked him. And, while Axle must have sensed his dad's life had changed, there were plenty of other factors to which that could be attributed.

His worries ended when Axle took off at 4pm, and Justin hadn't even replied to his message. A quiet night in, he thought.

Scott ate dinner, washed the wok, and was about to get in the shower, when his phone buzzed. He hesitated. One buzz was a message. Any more was a call. There were more buzzes.

"Still keen?" Justin asked. "I'm heading out to a bar. You should come."

"Ah, I was just getting settled in," Scott said.

"Let me stop by. I'll drive you."

"I've got the house to myself..." said Scott.

"I'll come by then. But we're going to the bar. After."

"Yeah. Cool. Why not? We'll see."

"We won't see. We're going. See you in twenty."

Scott knew that twenty was a minimum. He returned to the shower, taking the time to soap himself and wash his hair. He'd go to the bar for one drink. See how it went. Get the eleven-twenty bus home. He kicked himself for thinking too much, pre-empting the end of the night. Why couldn't he roll with it?

Justin knocked as Scott threaded his belt through the loops of his jeans. He checked the mirror one last time and yelled that the door was open.

Degrees

"A lot of people think water evaporates only when boiled," Reggie told the boys, who'd gathered around the largest pot in Pete's kitchen. "Not true! If we keep it under seventy-eight degrees, the water still evaporates – slowly – but the alcohol stays."

Reggie had lined up the thermometer, a selection of saucepans and a notepad. His enthusiasm had elevated the boys' game into a real experiment. Jarvis and Keevan were refusing to drink, although they watched on, and Axle sensed the ghost of some grievance.

"It'll taste crap anyway," said Keevan.

Reggie explained that he'd thought through the taste dilemma. He'd chosen the three simplest beers, even sampled them beforehand to make sure the mouthfeel matched the marketing. It was enough, at least, for Pete and Axle.

Jarvis grudgingly accepted being deputised to record the experiment as Reggie set it up. An empty page was ruled into a table with headings and columns. Before they could begin, Reggie took more notes and asked questions about the previous experiments. He wanted the exact details and none of the hype.

Axle understood. They were men of science. Everything should be considered, including the wellbeing of the test subjects. A bathmat had been folded before the toilet in case they had to kneel and vomit. Three glasses of water were lined up on the bathroom vanity.

Reggie volunteered to be first, Pete would be second and Axle was third. Since Jarvis had acquiesced to being the scribe, Keevan volunteered to be a neutral observer.

The beer had lost all of its carbonation as the golden liquid browned in the saucepan. Axle said that it actually smelled quite good and Jarvis made a note of this. Pete said it smelled like a brewery but then Keevan asked if he'd ever been to a brewery. Instead of retracting, Pete insisted. Reggie ladled the liquid into a glass and the arguments ceased.

Reggie puked almost immediately. Jarvis led the chant, 'chunder, chunder!'

Pete was next up, but doubtful. He drew in a breath and downed the fluid. It did him no good. He didn't even get to the bathroom. His vomit clogged up the InSinkErator, which then gargled and sputtered as the mess eked down the drain. The scene reminded Axle of a mechanical version of mother bird chewing up a worm then retching it into the baby bird's mouths. The three boys who hadn't been sick were starting to feel as if they might be.

Reggie had recovered just in time to see Pete's effort. As Pete rinsed his mouth, the two looked to Axle. Axle declined his turn. Half-hearted pressure was applied. It did not succeed, so Reggie announced his departure. He was off to hang with Tanasi and her friends. "Boys – men – this isn't over. We may have lost this battle, but we'll win the next. I've got another plan."

Sir

Jacqui hadn't made a presentation to the leadership team in eight years. Back then, she'd been tasked with presenting an overdue report on the internal outcomes of a culture change programme. She'd been combative about the shortcomings. Leadership had not appreciated being told that their six-figure spend on cultural reform hadn't made an iota of difference. She'd been asked a series of stinging questions, escalating in the expertise required to answer. She'd done better than they'd expected but had eventually been put in her place. Only one member of the leadership team, June, remained from that meeting of eight years ago. June had been interim deputy chief executive, but was now head of operations, a sideways step but with more control.

Rothman began when everyone was seated and small talk was dispensed with. "The answer – let's just start with the answer – lies in the private sector and ingenuity. Our presentation comes in three parts. I'll outline the broad plan. Jacqui will discuss the timeline. Then I'll get into the practicalities. I'm happy to take questions at the end, but, as this is a bold plan, I think it's best to wait until the full scale of our ambitions are set out."

There were a few nods around the room, but of the same kind one might expect if he had just announced a new financial model for staggered depreciation.

Rothman continued. "So, the private sector is our model, with suitable engagement for local situations – iwi, etc. I want to put that out there first. Fresh thinking. If we're going carbon neutral – and we are – then there's no model in government anywhere in the world that will show us how to do it."

Perhaps Jacqui should have joined Rothman for a dry run of the presentation. They'd last met on the previous Wednesday. Rothman had outlined his plans. Made her feel guilty for leaving on the Saturday. Said he'd take the reins if she chipped in a quick section on timing.

"Excuse me," June added, "but the Canadian model of carbon-neutral poli –"

"I'm sorry, June. Please. I respect the Canadians. But let's wait for the end. We'll address your concerns – right Jacqui? – I assure you."

"Sorry, yes, Alan. Go ahead," said June.

"The answer. Sorry. I've lost my train of thought."

Rothman poured a glass of water, took a long sip and collected himself. Jacqui was pretty sure that neither of them had considered international models. She considered excusing herself to the bathroom to do a quick search on her phone for the roughest of details on June's Canadian model. No, she decided, it was too late. They would just have to wing it.

"Ah yes," Rothman resumed, "so, our proposal is broad and requires a specialist delegation from accounting, as is the norm. In consulting with the Police Union, we –"

"Association. Police Association," said Jacqui. Rothman glared at her.

"Yes, with the Association. Thank you, Jacqui. Back to business: we know they won't give up their cars. What did they say, Jacqui? I wrote it down. 'The explosive powers of the combustion engine cannot be the competitive advantage of the criminal class.' You see? Cro-Magnons. But we must remember that even these types still have their role in evolution. That is, we think the Police Association have a point and can be used. In short, we've worked out their bottom line. Their only bottom line, as we understand it. They've already signed off all other matters as operational. That's a great win. It gives us carte blanche to rip into this problem."

There was a smattering of nods from the team and an increase in interest. Jacqui poured herself a water and topped up Rothman's glass.

"Our operational competitive advantage is simple and blunt. We can arrest people. We can detain them. And we are empowered to confiscate the proceeds of their criminal activity. In our case, the proposal is simple: the police keep their cars and we use the full force of the law to detain people breaking our new carbon emissions legislation. Climate criminals. We'll workshop the name. This will allow us to ensnare carbon credits and offset our frontline officer's emissions. Jacqui will lead you through the timeline. Jacqui?"

Jacqui kept her head down as she read from the notes of the last meeting she'd had with Rothman. She tried not to apologise too much for her lack of precision. "And, of course," she said, her eyes lifting to scan the room, "we are still waiting – a lack of clarity again from *this* government – to see the cut-off date in 2025 for neutrality to be fully implemented. Based on that, Alan and I decided we need to be seen as fast movers, not first followers. We'll implement the post-pilot, climate criminals policy – we'll workshop the name – from early 2025."

She paused and looked to Rothman. He nodded her onwards, but she hardly knew what else of substance there was to offer.

She continued: "Before then, there is a raft of other public relations initiatives. External stakeholder planning, consultation, as soon as possible but concurrent with Board approval for a pilot. Community testing in 2024... and so on."

Rothman cleared his throat.

"No, that's not quite right," said Rothman. "Earlier. Much earlier. Certainly before 2024. We'll start planning right away and it will be tested in 2023. With that overview, appreciate it Jacqui, let me get into specifics. On the Canadian question..."

Jacqui slumped back into her seat, then righted herself, making sure her face gave away no signs of distress. She felt a teetering anxiety. It had begun in the pit of her stomach and risen to her head. She would do well not to pass out. They were both going to lose their jobs. It was an insane plan. It was a plan that only a teenager in the height of pubescent turmoil could have dreamed up. It lacked precedent and practicality.

She was surprised, then, when Rothman outlined the Canadian model. New Zealand Police were to copy those aspects that resonated with the public the most, regardless of their efficacy and cost/benefit ratio. Solar panels and ambitious rhetoric were in. Reduced open-road speed limits were to be touted, then ruled out.

Rothman called a five-minute break and Jacqui took her chance to flee, decamping to the bathroom. At least she didn't need to look up the Canadian model. No matter how bizarre Alan's proposal was, he'd at least done some basic research.

When her pulse had returned to normal, she made her way back to the board room. She couldn't have been away for more than eight minutes, but when she returned, only Rothman remained. Everything had been cleared and he, too, was also about to leave.

"Victorious, Jacqui. We did it. There were no questions, nothing to answer. They're one hundred per cent on board. The Board is next. In my opinion, there was only one genuine question – who are these climate criminals? I batted it away. Fudged it. It's our work over the coming months to identify and assess the net carbon worth of a range of our worst offenders."

"That... that's great? Is it?"

Of course it was great, she thought, they'd succeeded. But would they really go about arresting climate criminals? It was so out of the ordinary. So exceptional. Maybe Rothman had caught the mood of the times. Maybe an exceptional plan was needed and he'd come up with it?

"It is great," said Rothman.

"No. Yes. It is great. Truly. You did a great job."

Jaggery

When they'd first met, Jacqui had said she was unwilling to love Scott. Unwilling and incapable. Not solely him, though. All people. "Love," she had said, "begins as a joy, but within five years is a farce. It's often worse."

Scott heard out her reasons and, he said at the time, thoroughly agreed with them. He didn't accept the fatalism of her conclusion, but the premises were sound. And he could respect what she thought. His inner voice argued, of course – naively and without hope or ambition – for the power of love to transcend any statement or will.

Jacqui hadn't been Scott's type, at first. And then – tada! – she was. From then on, it had been a lesson in patience and perseverance. Even when Jacqui had announced the move to Sydney, he read it as a test. Love was inevitable. He would wait her out.

Scott had won her over. He'd stayed firm even through the months when she was in Sydney. He didn't say much about it, but just kept a low level of communication with her. He didn't ask for anything in return. He was just present, a subtle hum. She could sense him holding on, of course, doing the basics to keep present in her mind without making demands or appearing to cling. She wasn't too hard on him but nor did she hold back from making the most of her time abroad. And then he sensed his chance. He made a case for himself, for her to return to him. At the same time, she, unrelatedly, lost her job at the café. Did he know her situation? He repeated that he did not. She never really knew if that was true.

Scott thought back to the month in which all of his persistence had paid off. She had let him visit for a weekend. He had paid for a hotel and she had joined him. And then, with Christmas approaching and no new job, she returned to Wellington. He had never pressed her on how she had come to this decision, but he thought that her acquiescence was as much due to her fatalism as to the constancy of his reason. Then, without too many months having passed, Axle announced himself.

Scott tasted the dhal from the serving spoon. He should have never dropped the tamarind in. It needed something sweet to offset the tart. They were out of palm sugar so he crumbled a chunk of jaggery into the saucepan and stirred.

Scott called out to Axle that the table needed setting as he served two portions, then garnished them with a drizzle of lemon, a sprig of coriander and just a little rock salt.

Axle had stopped automatically setting the table for his mother, though Scott still cooked enough for at least three portions. If Jacqui wasn't home by the time the dishes were to be done, the last third would be dolloped into a pottle.

"Have you ever thought of separating?" Axle asked as his father sat down.

Scott dipped his spoon into the dhal. No words immediately came to mind, but he anticipated that the time had come for that the long overdue conversation about Scott and Justin. He hadn't seen Justin in eight days. Not at work, not at Justin's apartment, not at Scott's home. He wasn't sure that he would see him again. He blew across the first spoonful of dhal and placed it into his mouth.

"From Mum, I mean," said Axle.

"Have I thought of it? Ever? Yes, but not seriously. Have we talked about it? Yes, but not seriously. Every serious couple's talked about it at some point. It's not a big deal."

"Really? Not seriously?"

"Honestly, we haven't. We've never talked of it seriously. I can't say what your mum's *thought*."

"I'm not worried if you do split up, you know. I mean, I don't know what it would be like, but you should do what's best for you and not sugar coat it for me."

"I'm not lying, you know. I can't say what your mother's thinking. We're managing the situation. Personally, I think it's working well. For now, at least. Maybe we don't have all the hiccups out of the beast, but it's not like your mum and I are any less in love than we've ever been."

"Yeah. I get that. If it helps, I don't think João is so serious about Mum."

"I don't think it's about who is or isn't serious. Ax? Remember when I said it's about pleasure as much as anything else... But wait, why don't you think he's serious? Because of the age gap? I think you'll find, as you get older, age becomes less of an issue."

"Nah, not that."

"What, then? The language gap? So he misconjugates a few verbs? He seems to have excellent English. Better than a lot of New Zealanders, formally speaking. Anyway, it doesn't matter. That's between them."

"You can't say to anyone, if I tell you."

"Of course."

"Seriously."

"Seriously."

"So, he's not serious because, if he was, he wouldn't be lying about who he is. It's okay. It's just that he's not Brazilian. He's from India. He told me that Kiwi women wouldn't date him, so he changed his dating profile and it all kind of went from there."

Scott tried to suppress his grin. So João was just as duplicitous as Justin. Perhaps more so. But, as Axle had said, it didn't change anything. Not really. He put another spoon of dhal into his mouth and considered the new state of play. While he'd stopped the smile from spreading across his face, he couldn't deny that he was pleased. He felt his body loosen and rolled his shoulders to test if the strain had actually left his body. He hadn't even known he was tense!

His ease did not survive a secondary reflection. God, he thought, I'm at least as bad as Jacqui. I'm actually relieved that he's not Brazilian! I'm relieved that he's Indian. I'm as bad as the women who wouldn't date him. Scott realised that nothing would change. João was still João.

"You shouldn't have told me, Ax. I... it's none of my business. Why did he tell you?"

"I saw him at work. I mean, it's not like he confided in me. He tried to laugh it off, but his boss gave it away."

"It's not cool of him to deceive Jacqui. How long have you known? No, wait. It's not your fault. It doesn't matter when he told you."

"But, like, it's true. He said no-one would go for him on the apps until he changed the flag on his profile. That's bad, right?"

Scott faltered, trying to think through the problem. He'd developed a mental trick that allowed him to step back and assess tricky situations from on high. But here, in this moment, he felt like an animal wallowing in mud. "There's always a middle way. There must be, Ax. I probably have to reflect on it a bit, but lying to someone so they give you consent is terrible. It invalidates consent. I mean, this is what they teach in schools, right? No-one can honestly consent if they've been misled. That must be the starting point. I'm not sure, but I think we may have to tell your mother."

"You said you wouldn't."

"I said I wouldn't. I'm just trying to think this out for the both of us. Maybe you should think about it. Did he make you promise not to tell?"

"Yeah. He did."

"Well, that's worse! I can't believe he dragged you into this."

"He didn't drag me in! Well, I guess he told me not to tell. I don't know. I thought I was right in not saying anything."

"We need to step back and think. There's always a way. Let's think on it. Circling back, though, your mum and I are not getting a divorce. We're good. This whole thing might take some fine tuning, but we're all good. We might even look back on it and laugh one day. I know it's a cliché. Sorry if I was a bit snappy about it. You caught me off guard. Anyway, how are you finding the dhal? Not too tart?"

Retrenchment

"Hey, good to see you, matey," said Justin as he shuffled in his seat. "Um, what can I do you for?"

Scott hovered in the doorway. "I'm resigning. Here's the letter. Three weeks from today."

Scott had been avoiding much contact with anyone at his work for at least two weeks. He had especially kept away from the parts of the office where he was most likely to cross paths with Linnea or Justin. It hadn't been that hard, especially when neither were seeking him out. But it couldn't go on.

"Would you shut the door? Can we go somewhere and talk?"

Justin had noticed that Scott had pulled up the drawbridge. He'd heard a rumour that Scott was lining up his references and knew which staff members' emails to scan through to pick up the gossip. Still, he hadn't predicted Scott to quit.

Scott didn't move, so Justin rose, shuffled around him and eased the door shut.

Scott offered him the letter. "I'm sure of this. It's not spontaneous. I'm fine to talk here. There's nothing to say. I don't want to work here anymore. You more or less said my time was up, remember?"

"Where's your phone? Pass it here."

"It's not here. It's in my jacket, at my desk."

Justin eyed Scott's pants and made a motion for him to turn around.

Scott frowned but complied. He wasn't hiding anything, nor trying to bring Justin down with him. "Satisfied? I mean, if I were going to record our conversations, don't you think I'd be better at it than this? Give me some credit."

"Fine. Alright then. Remember that I'm not the good guy here, Scott. I'm not going to talk you out of it. But I can't allow you to burn bridges as you go."

"I don't want you to talk me out of it. I'm not here to make trouble. Just to quit. I've got a few more days of work before accumulated leave will kick in for the final fortnight. I'll need a reference though, in due course."

"Fine," said Justin, but he wasn't convinced. People who wanted to quit as quietly as possible sent an email on a Friday afternoon. "You must know management's attitude towards you. It's in my interest that you leave, you know? I'm not going to convince you to stay on."

"I know."

"What's this about, then? Can't you compartmentalise, let things scab over, move on? I thought that it was working for you."

"It's nothing to do with us. We're fine. But I do I need to move on. From here. Not from you. You told me as much yourself. We're good. You're hardly the bad guy."

Justin eyed him. He was used to lying and being lied to, but Scott seemed genuine.

"Good, mate, good," Justin said. And then, in a much lower voice, the human resources manager hung out a few sentences of what, when they next found themselves alone, he was going to do to Scott.

Scott let the words run through him but didn't react. He had, in fact, told himself he would move on from Justin, too, but that conversation could wait.

The opposite of resignation

"Jacqui. Quick word?" asked Rothman as he strode up to her desk.

"Sure, fire. I was just going to come see you, too," said Jacqui.

"Oh, right. Well, listen, I've been offered a new role as Head of Operations. It would start at the beginning of the new financial year. You know I appreciate your work here. This is a crossroads for our team. My role is open and I'd like to offer it to you. We'd advertise of course. But you'd have the inside track. I want you to know what you'd be in for, though. It's a great chance, but management can be a chore and whoever takes the role needs to want it. You know there are a lot of people round here who aren't sure of you, right? Maybe our climate work bought some goodwill and this can be your chance. For others, it got under their skin. But I'm backing you, right?"

Jacqui didn't answer.

Rothman persevered. "All I'm saying is, if you want it, you can transition into my role. You'd be supported. If you don't want it, you can stay in your current role and roll the dice as to whoever replaces me. I'd do my best to make sure that whoever it was would be in line with our work on carbon neutrality. If you were to take the role, I'd resource the position accordingly. You'd oversee the climate criminals pilot and, eventually, the whole task force. There'd be risk. There are plenty of people who are already pushing against us."

"Keeping their cars isn't enough?"

Rothman leaned forward. She would have liked to be able to slide her chair back, but he had a way of letting her know that this desk was somehow as much his as that in his own office.

"We knew that would be the case, didn't we? And there'd be reward to the role, too. You'd make a difference, a real difference. I'd use my connections to draw out some of these corrupt officers. That's what they are: corrupt. Intellectually. Sure, they're not like the cops who let friends off drink-driving charges or skim from the confiscated drug hauls. Those things are tolerable, small fry. But going against the PM's direct orders on carbon neutrality? That's gross insubordination of the highest order. Sedition. What's the other one? Treachery? No. It's treason."

"They'll drive you out, you know."

She'd dropped the jokiness. Rothman wasn't there to flirt. Perhaps he'd never been flirting and his manner was just another way that he got what he wanted.

"Maybe," said Rothman. "We've already got the intelligence service on our side. They're making a list, checking it twice. So, what do you think? Do you want to check in with your family?"

"No," she said. "Actually, I've been offered a new role myself. I'm off to one of the big three. Consulting. They just need to sign off on my references. I put you down. Hence why I was going to come see you."

"Really? Is this a bargaining thing? You want an extra 20k or something?"

"No, nothing like that. But, if you were able to put that offer in writing, it would help me in negotiating my new role," said Jacqui.

"Well, no. Like I said, the role here would be advertised. We can't just offer you a package. There are procurement rules, process, procedures."

"Fine. That's all good. I appreciate it. I do."

Chemistry

Jacqui and Scott had finished their coffees and were sharing an almond croissant. Both had spent Friday and Saturday nights at home. Jacqui had passed the halfway mark in her book on Antarctica. Axle had been at Pete's on the Friday and had gone to bed early on Saturday. It had been a refreshing change. *The Last of the Mohicans* was lined up for that evening.

"It's so loud in here," said Scott. "Is it always like this? Have you noticed? Maybe we should start heading to that other café. It's less popular, but it might be more tolerable."

Jacqui wasn't listening.

"Jacqui? Don't you think..."

Jacqui shushed him, gesturing at another table. Scott joined her in eavesdropping on a couple who sat opposite them – doddery types, quite a bit older than them, conversing over a story in *The Sunday Biz*.

He looked back to Jacqui who raised her eyebrows and nodded. This time he really listened, tuning in as best he could between the bark of the coffee grinder and the hubbub of Kelburnians. The couple were talking about an article in the newspaper. They were talking about Axle and his friends.

Scott could read the headline from a few tables over: The Undrinkable Light Beer of Bingeing. It was a story written by a droll commentator who was well known for breezy observations on the foibles of capital living.

Scott drew his phone from his pocket and went to the newspaper's website. The top stories were about sewage spills and a new mayoral candidate. He navigated to the opinion pages and there was the story. He scanned the first three paragraphs and then recited them to Jacqui.

"...but it wasn't the winner of the Wellington High Science Competition who made the most waves. One student, Reggie Henderson received a commendation from the judges for his series of experiments in adulterating light beer so that he and his friends might get drunk. While the experiments often ended in vomit and failure, the judges applauded the boy's rigorous record-keeping and commitment to hypothesis testing. One teacher at the school, who asked not to be named, said that while they do not condone their students drinking, all the experiments occurred outside of school time so the parents were the responsible, or irresponsible, parties. The principal confirmed that disciplinary action was unlikely but emphasised that the school took its responsibilities to alcohol education seriously."

Jacqui and Scott sat for a moment, pondering their next steps.

When his parents did return to the house, Axle knew they'd seen the story. He'd had a message from Pete warning him. Axle met his mother's eyes and did his best to look contrite. He couldn't quite act as sorry as he knew he ought to. These months had been the best of his life.

He eyed the floor as Jacqui listed off his deceptions and the process whereby they would decide upon a punishment.

PART 3

Family arrives

Scott was first home, wet socks and all. It had been raining that morning so he had no excuse for having not chosen better footwear. Nevertheless, what was done was done. He left his shoes by the rack at the door and threw his damp socks at the hamper on the way to the shower. He'd bought a nice bottle of Shiraz to go with dinner and there was a can of gulab jamun at the back of the pantry that he intended to finally put to use. He had wrapped Jacqui's birthday present and it sat on the kitchen table.

Jacqui was home next. She'd already completed the bulk of her contribution to the evening meal: a green bean stew that had been trembling away in a slow cooker. Her shoes had been soaked too, so she left them beside Scott's, at the door, with her trench coat dripping onto the entranceway tiles. She saw the present from her husband but ignored it. She could hear Scott in the shower and, as she tried to work out if he was just in or almost out, she stripped off her clothes and placed them with the other washing. One of Scott's damp socks had fallen into the space between the hamper and the wall so, with nothing else to do, she picked it up and deposited it in its rightful place.

Axle was last home. He'd been collaborating with a small group on a proposal for a student-led alternative to the Board of Trustees. His volunteering was a kind of penance, albeit one that would not placate the powers that be. Axle didn't shower, nor did he take his shoes off at the door. He stripped off his rain jacket and hung it beside his mother's. A little puddle was already forming on the tiles so a little more would hardly matter. Even though Axle's outer layer was dry, he'd sweated tremendously. He traipsed to his room, removed his shoes and peeled off everything but his underwear. In his bathroom, he wiped himself down with a warm flannel before slipping into fresh underwear and a pair of jeans that hadn't been washed since the previous year.

A return to communal dinners had been Axle's idea and had been one way for him to defer some of the blame for his misuse of the light beer. His parents accepted that their schedules, and even behaviour, had been a tad chaotic but they refused to enter into any ledger-tallying to make up for his lying about the light beer. Axle insisted that he'd never lied. That was true enough, but he knew he had deceived them and that the family circumstances could not be used to offset his guilt. Still, the shared dinners were reinstated and this was the third in two weeks. No apologies for being elsewhere would be given or accepted. Family was to be the priority for a while.

Axle was responsible for making the flatbread. There were four types of flour in the pantry and there was yeast in the fridge. The internet told him the secret was a tablespoon of yoghurt. Axle had bought a pottle from the organic supermarket near his school and found a simple recipe that used only these ingredients, plus water, cumin seeds and rock salt.

He was standing at the window, gazing at the evening sky, when his father entered the lounge. The dusk was deepening on the hills opposite. A strip of bright blue sky hemmed the horizon. His father stood beside Axle as another band of rain pattered against the window. The glimpse of blue sky was eclipsed as the southerly hurried the clouds northwards. When his father turned back to the kitchen, Axle followed. It was time to start the bread. Jacqui entered from the bedroom, testing the stew, then adding a pinch of salt.

"What are we going to do about this light beer fiasco?" asked Jacqui.

"There has to be some kind of repercussion, even if we're partially responsible," said Scott, before clarifying. "I didn't mean that we *are* responsible. Just that we could've eased you into alcohol in a more sensible way. Like the Europeans. A glass of wine with a meal. That's all I meant."

Axle had been paying attention to kneading the bread and would have preferred if his parents just came up with a punishment instead of making him listen to these interminable deliberations. He rinsed his hands, picking the sticky dough out from under his fingernails. When his parents weren't looking, he tasted the dough. More salt needed.

"Who'd like a glass of wine?" asked Jacqui.

"Pour me one," said Scott, leaning against the fridge and keeping out of the way of Jacqui and Axle as they prepared their parts of the meal.

"Bread is ready to go," said Axle. "And yeah, I'll try a glass of wine. Why not?"

Scott poured the wine and Jacqui poked at the dough. It was, as desired, springy to the touch. Axle had already put the skillet on high and, when his mother nodded, he placed a cube of butter onto the iron, followed by the first of the naan.

"You've used yoghurt, I see," she observed. "Listen: before we get started with the meal, one thing. João might be over, later. Likely but not certain."

Axle checked his dad's reaction. This was the first time João's name had been brought up since he told his father the truth.

"I mean, if you've already told him he can come over, then he can come over," said Scott. "I'm not going to get in the way. Hell, he can stay over. I'm easy. All I would say is that we need a better way of communicating these things. I'd like a say on it, in the future, especially on a family night. What if Justin intended to stay over, too?"

It had been many weeks since Scott had seen Justin, but he'd felt no need to communicate any of this to Jacqui.

"Yes. You're right. João has been invited this time, I'm afraid, so let's sort that out and we can work out a system afterwards."

Scott didn't say anything.

Axle finished cooking the fourth and final naan and took the plate to the table. Jacqui went to the drawer for a ladle and dumped two heaps of the green bean dish into a bowl and passed it to Scott. She did the same for Axle and, finally, herself. The table was set and they were poised to eat as they heard the front gate open.

Justin arrives

"No food for me thanks," Justin said, as he slipped off his shoes. "There's a hell of a puddle here. What? You look like you're anticipating Santa Claus? Come on! You must be Scott's wife. Pleased to meet you. Good to see you again, Axle. How are you coping with Ma and Pa? Sorry ma'am, but Scott here never mentioned your name. Didn't say it at all. Not once. Quiet one."

Jacqui glared at her husband. If it had been only the two of them, she might've been fine with Justin's banter.

"You're soaked," said Scott as he strode to the linen cupboard, retrieved a big beach towel and threw it to Justin. "By the way, you know her name is Jacqui and I've told you about her plenty of times. Anyway, what are you doing here?"

The visitor ruffled his hair, buried his face into the towel, then ran it behind his collar before throwing it back to Scott.

"I'm not staying for long. You should check your messages more, Scott. Oh, and I'm happy to drink from the bottle, but a glass would be super, too."

"Above the fridge," said Scott.

"We don't have to be all formal do we?" Justin strolled towards the kitchen with Scott, who peeled off to throw the towel into their hamper.

"Listen, Justin," Jacqui said, raising her voice so he could hear her from the kitchen, "we're having a family dinner. It's my birthday. I wonder if you might come back later on? Or Scott could meet you in town."

"Really? Your birthday. Well, many happy returns."

"My birthday is tomorrow, actually. But tonight is the celebration."

"And you'd turn me out in this weather. C'mon, can't I stay for one drink?"

"Let's have our meal and I'll head out for one drink," said Scott. "João will be here soon, anyway."

"The legendary João!" said Justin.

"Suits me," said Jacqui. Scott felt the pressure piling on him and he resented it. Was there something wrong with him telling Justin about his wife's young lover? Surely not.

"Actually, you know what?" said Scott. "It's really wet out there, and I'm just home. I'm not going back into the city. Maybe Justin can stay?"

"Hold on," said Jacqui. "Let's talk in the kitchen. Justin, help yourself to the wine. Do you want some food? You're our guest."

"Wine's good thanks. I'll just stay until the rain eases. I don't want to be a hassle."

The kitchen was usually wide open to the dining area and lounge, but Scott slid a pair of doors across to create a sequestered space. Jacqui filled the sink with water, using the noise as cover, while also preparing to soak the pots, pans and utensils. If they spoke low, they could retain some privacy.

"Truce?" asked Scott and Jacqui nodded. "Sorry about that. Him arriving like this. But, also —"

"Also, what?"

"I just don't like that João could stay over but Justin can't even sit with us through dinner," said Scott.

"But I invited him to eat with us!"

"Grudgingly."

"No!" said Jacqui then recognised Justin and Axle would have heard her from the lounge. She lowered her voice and continued, "Well, yeah. I suppose. A little. It's just how he acts. He comes in like he runs the place, like he's in charge. Imagine João doing that. You can't. He's too sweet. Justin is deliberately being a prick. Riling you up. Riling me up. What are we going to do about it?"

"But you've only just met him," said Scott. "Anyway, don't worry about him. He'll be fine. It's just how he is. Let's get tonight sorted – he can leave when he's finished his wine – and we can get back to where we were."

"I could agree to him staying if –" Jacqui stopped. She didn't want to say it. "He's just a mess, that's all. And he makes a mess of everything he touches. And you're seemingly fine with it."

"OK, fine, how about neither of them stays. It's a family night. Message João and I'll talk to Justin."

"Sure, but you talk to Justin first. Once he's gone, I'll postpone João."

It was a childish proposition – you first – but Scott agreed anyway. He didn't want Justin staying but wasn't in the mood to see Jacqui cosying up with João while he played the mature and gracious host.

Justin's laugh rang out from the dining room. Jacqui rolled her eyes. She finished washing up, dried her hands then opened the door onto the dining room.

Justin had taken the seat beside Axle and turned it to face him. Jacqui saw that a blush had crept across Axle's face. It might've been from the wine. It might've been from anything, really, but to Jacqui the situation was all pretty clear.

"My husband might not have told you much about me," she said, "But he told me a lot about you. You think you're some sort of seducer, don't you. It's none of my business usually, but under my roof, I'm not going to turn a blind eye."

Scott finished drying the small saucepan, then dumped the gulab jamun into it and placed it on the stovetop with the temperature on low.

"Well, Scott?" said Jacqui. "What do you say?"

Scott turned to see all eyes on him. He saw Axle cowed, Justin's glee and a look of venom in his wife's eyes.

"Jacqui, you've got your situation and I don't interfere with that. I'd prefer you not interfere with mine. Axle can hold his own. He's not a kid, and I don't know what you thought was going on, but I trust Axle to deal with the world as it comes to him. He's not eleven."

"He's creeping on Axle – sorry, Ax – but come on! Look at him!"

"Axle can manage himself. This isn't even about Axle. You were never alright with me and Justin. I can leave you to your illusions. You should leave me to mine."

"Illusions, please! I'm not the one scared of honesty. And let's not act like I'm a prude, just because I don't trust this guy."

Justin laughed, leaning back in his chair and enjoying the show.

"Dad," Axle pleaded.

Scott turned away from his son and faced Jacqui.

"João's actually from India, not Brazil. He's been telling you some big story, making himself out to be this exotic lover but it's a lie. And that's not even the worst part. It's on us, too, because the only reason he does it is because women on Tinder wouldn't give him a chance when he told the truth."

Jacqui didn't flinch or turn away. Scott thought he'd have to dig deeper, but then remembered how much pride Jacqui took in refusing to look flustered.

"Dad. Fuck. You promised you wouldn't say anything."

"I'm sorry, Ax. I really am. I had to do it."

"You didn't have to do it. That was the weakest thing I've ever seen, Dad. What an asshole thing to say. You're as bad as the bullies at Col."

"Sorry, Ax."

He knew he shouldn't accept his son's swearing, but Axle was right. He was a coward and had acted vindictively. But before any of them could ease the conversation towards some sort of peace, the swing and clunk of the outside gate announced another guest.

João arrives.

Justin rose to greet the guest and there was nothing any of them could do to stop him.

"João, bro, welcome. I'm Justin. I've heard a lot about you. I'm sure Jacqui has told you about me, too. Au contraire? Pull up a seat, grab some wine, all in good time. I was just about to leave, but I'm very pleased to make your acquaintance. You're as good looking as they were saying."

"Hey bro, nice to meet you," said João. "Hey guys – Axle, Scott. Hey. Shoes off, is it?" He'd brought a bottle of wine for Jacqui and a bouquet of flowers for the kitchen table.

"You the only one who didn't get wet feet on the way here? Figures that you'd walk on water," said Justin.

"Shut up, Justin," Scott said, as he filled a vase with water. Scott watched as João scanned their faces, his smile losing its ease.

"You know, Axle, your father's not to blame," Justin said. "He had no choice. Come on. What would you do? He shouldn't have to take that disrespect from your mum. You might be young, but I think you know a man must have some pride. My first wife, man, I tell you. She'd come for my pride first. Taught me a few things about women!"

Jacqui fetched a glass for João, ignoring Justin's tirade.

"What's going on?" João asked.

"Ignore him," said Jacqui.

Justin swivelled on his seat, squaring up to Axle and turning his attention away from the other members of the house. "You must have had a girlfriend by now, kid. Or a boyfriend? Whatever. You're a cute kid. I'm sure they're lining up for you. You know what I mean, right?"

"Justin," Scott warned.

"I don't know what you mean," Axle answered. "I don't have a girlfriend and I don't know."

"Listen, of all the people here, kid, I'm the one who'll be the most honest with you. No bullshit. I don't have skin in the game and I'm not lying about who I am. Okay, sometimes I bend the truth to tease your dad. But that's just fun. Like, if I say you're a cute kid and guess that you've already had your share of action, then that's an honest opinion. You ever heard the word 'twink'? Sure you ha–"

"Enough!" said Scott, standing. "Justin, fuck off. I don't know what mind games you're up to, but I'm not having it. Just fuck off. I'm over it."

Justin turned his chair back to face Scott, but didn't rise. Scott held his stance.

"I'm going to go," Axle said, pushing back his chair, "Pete's having some friends over."

"You can go to your room, but not to Pete's place," Jacqui said.

"So, I'm grounded now?"

"Temporarily," Scott said, still standing. "Until we can work out what to do. João, take my chair while I see Justin out."

João checked in with Jacqui, who nodded.

"Hey man," Justin said, looking to João, who'd just sat down, "you want to open that bottle of wine for me? A screw top, huh, not like those South American reds. You folks love your corks. Come on, drink up!"

João looked to Jacqui, who shrugged, so he obliged, pouring a glass for Justin. Justin took the bottle from him and poured one for Axle.

"Oh, so no light beer for the boy tonight, Scott?" asked Justin.

"No," Scott said. "We think a glass of wine or two with family is the mature way to go about it. Come on, Justin. It's time to go."

"To be honest," said Justin, "the whole idea of light beer is a disgrace. I think..."

"A disgrace!" Jacqui laughed. Scott shifted his weight from one foot to the other.

"I just think..." Justin said, teasing out the words, "that it is a disgrace. It is! It's cowardly, but it's a symptom of our puritanical age. Coke without the sugar. Coffee without the caffeine. Fake meat without the animal. Real meat without the fat. And beer without the alcohol. I mean it's fine for older people to water down their pleasures, but to train your son like that? It's cruel. Abuse. Look at how he knocked back that wine when given half a chance. See what you're doing to him? He's a natural. Set him free. I'll pour you another, Ax?"

"Nah, man, all good. I'm going to my room," said Axle, standing.

"No need, Ax. I'm just messing with you. Don't worry. I'm leaving. Stick around. Have another glass. Watch the night unfold."

Axle mumbled something and sat back down. He couldn't tell if he should argue or agree. Justin pushed his own chair back and stood. He gulped his wine, blew a kiss to Scott, winked at Jacqui and strode to the door.

It could have been a charismatic exit if Justin had been able to walk right out. As it was, he wrestled his shoes back onto his feet offering a string of grunts and curses.

As a gust of cold air blew in through the door, the others kept their silence. In his own sweet time, Justin disappeared into the night.

"He'll be fine," said Scott. "The rain's stopped. Good riddance."

Justin leaves

Scott poured himself a fresh glass of wine. The exorcism was over. He looked to João, who nodded back at him. He checked in with his son, who played with the stem of his glass. Everyone had eaten their meal except for him. He took a sip of wine and ate.

"Quick word?" said Jacqui as her husband sponged up the last of his meal with the naan.

They went to the kitchen, not bothering to draw the doors closed this time. Scott stirred the gulab jamun then turned it off. He'd forgotten it was on the stovetop but the liquid hadn't evaporated off.

"João can stay over, then?"

"You still want him to stay, given everything?"

"He told me the India stuff. Weeks ago. The whole story," said Jacqui. "It's fucked up. It's sad. But it's complex."

"And you're alright with that," said Scott, realising that she was.

"Not alright, but he did tell me. Proactively. He was really embarrassed."

"But did he only tell you because Axle found out?"

"Maybe. I didn't ask. It doesn't matter. I don't know."

"Right," said Scott.

"So, he can stay?"

"Yeah. Up to you. I'll sleep in the spare room, even. It's your birthday. You get what you want. No problem. I shouldn't have said anything."

"Oh, I don't mind. I mean, I mind being lied to. But what do they say? Mitigating factors. Whatever. I'm more concerned about Ax, anyway."

"We ground him? Or no?"

"I don't know."

"We said we'd never. It's so reductive."

Scott dipped a teaspoon into the gulab jamun syrup. It was the right temperature.

"Agreed. Another bottle?" Jacqui asked. He nodded and they made their way back to their seats in the lounge."

There was a blip of silence as they returned.

"Axle has just been telling me about his friends' science experiment. It's quite clever, no?"

"Your accent, João. You've still got a Brazilian accent," said Jacqui.

"What? Me? No?"

Scott felt pity for João and what was to come. He knew how good Jacqui was at tightening the screws. He'd felt it before. Many times. She had a way of speaking calmly and easily, luring you into a conversation that appeared to have no stakes. And then – bam! – you were confessing all the ways that you'd wronged her.

"Yeah," Jacqui said. "You're putting on an accent. I wasn't sure, before. I could have sworn. Now that I listen, I can hear that you do sound like a South American."

"I did live in Brazil, you know, Jacqui? I think Axle was right to tell you. It's good, Axle, brave. Honest. Loyal. A good son."

"Oh, so Axle told you that he told Scott and Scott told me? Interesting," said Jacqui. "And enough with the *Zhack-ki*, okay? You hear that accent, Axle? That accent is deeply insincere."

"But you've got to admit, it's unfair of us to treat him differently solely because of where he's from," Axle said. "It's sort of racist."

"Is this what you two have been chatting about, then? Setting me up as the bad guy?" she asked.

Scott picked up his wine and turned to the main window in the lounge. There was no point sitting at the table while all of this played out. He saw that the worst of the weather had passed, thought about telling everyone, but then thought better of interjecting. The evening had become still and clear, but they could still feel the damp in the air. The leaves on the surrounding trees were lush and heavy. It was almost completely dark.

"Jacqui come on," João said. "Ax was only pointing out a fact. Nothing about it is right. Don't pretend that you would have swiped right on me if you knew I was Indian."

"That's not true. I don't use those apps and I wouldn't. I meet men in the normal way. Through friends, or in a bar."

"Fine. But if Kaye had said, 'there's this Indian guy I want to introduce you to,' what would you have done?"

"I'm not saying I'm perfect, João – is that even your name?"

"Yes. It is actually my name. I've told you that already."

"I can't say what I would have done. Maybe I'd have been like all the other women, yeah, maybe. I don't know. Listen, it's fine. We all got we wanted. I won't pretend otherwise. And maybe I'm responsible too. Or irresponsible. Or no-one is, and no hearts were broken and maybe we can go on as before?"

"Why don't we trial some new ground rules for a few months. A reset?" said João. "What do you think Axle?"

Axle shrugged.

"Just sleep on it," said Scott. "Give it time. Think it over."

"Great," said Jacqui. "Fine. I'm going to bed, then. I want to sleep alone, tonight. A birthday treat. Scott, I love you. Can you sleep downstairs?"

"Happy to," said Scott, who stopped himself and repeated himself, "really, I am happy to."

"And thanks for standing up to Justin. I'll open your present tomorrow. João, thank you for the wine and flowers. You're welcome to stay over since I said you could, but perhaps on the couch or wherever."

"I think I'll probably go," said João.

"I understand. One last thing," said Jacqui. "Has Kaye been in touch?"

"Yeah. She's coming back at the end of the year."

"And are you going to see her?"

"I said I would."

"Did she say anything about me?"

"She said not to tell you that she called me."

"And you weren't going to tell me? No. You know what? Forget it. I'm going to bed."

Jacqui leaves

Axle looked up at his dad as Jacqui left the room. No-one spoke until the bedroom door shut with a mild thud.

"Shit," said Scott, rising and dashing back into the kitchen. "I forgot about the dessert, again."

"Sorry about telling Dad," said Axle.

"Apology accepted. It's fine. You know I told your mum, too, right?"

"I picked that up," said Axle.

Scott returned with three bowls and took a seat. He'd left one bowl in the kitchen in case Jacqui came back to claim her dessert.

"Sorry. It's cooled down a bit."

Axle dug in, but João didn't pick up his spoon.

"We don't need to keep going over this," said Scott. "Let's reset. Let bygones be bygones. Is that what that phrase means? Anyway, I feel like we're at a kind of peace. An awkward peace, but one with some good faith."

João nodded, paused and then dipped his spoon into the dessert.

"Since we're all agreed that we're at peace – but I'm still grounded – I'm off to bed," said Axle. "Wait, I'm just checking: you're sure I can't head to Pete's?"

Scott glared at him. It was a look of love, but one that feigned exasperation.

"Fine," said Axle. He quickly finished his dessert, leaving his empty bowl at the table, before making his way towards his room.

Axle leaves

The sound of his son preparing for bed soothed Scott. When the whirr of the electric toothbrush started, he imagined the minty grit of toothpaste in his son's mouth. He poured the leftover wine from Axle's glass into his own. He caught João glancing at him with an expression that sat between pity and piety.

"My generation feels a responsibility to finish a drink if we've had one poured for us," Scott explained. "We don't waste alcohol."

"It's like finishing all the food on your plate?" asked João. He gestured to the one remaining naan and Scott signalled it was his to eat if he would like.

"Yes, but different. With food, it's out of respect to the chef. It's the same in India I guess?"

"In Diu, yeah, traditionally. Respect to mother for cooking, and to father for providing. I don't know about the other parts. In the south, in the north. Muslims? Dravidians? I don't know. It could be different. Though it's probably not."

"Alcohol, though," Scott said, "I don't think that's about respect to the maker or provider. We finish our glass because... Maybe it's that my generation doesn't like to waste things?"

"But there's so much waste over here."

"I'm not saying we're consistent. Theory and practice and all that. But maybe it's because drinking is such an easy thing to do. Even spirits. It's not like finishing off a meal with all that chewing and swallowing. With a glass of wine, beer even, you can just open your mouth and down the gullet it goes. Drink it all in a gulp and deal with any consequences later."

The two men sat at the dining table, eyeing their glasses in lieu of eyeing each other. Scott peered out the window but could hardly see past the reflection of the lounge. He opened his phone, connected it to the wireless speakers and put on music to match the weather and time of day.

"What would you do about our situation, then?"

João's expression didn't change. Scott realised he could have been talking of three or four topics that would qualify as a situation.

"With Axle and his friends' drinking?" asked Scott. "There's alcohol in India, right? And in Brazil. You're a man of the world. What would you do?"

"What I would do is simple. Maybe it would work. Maybe not. You want to hear?"

"Go ahead," said Scott, finishing his glass and topping it up without thinking. The pours were not getting any smaller.

"First: respect alcohol. That's the first point. There is a power in alcohol that none of us can understand. Words don't do it justice. A man once said, 'The conscious water saw its Lord and blushed,' and that is good. So we must be reverent. And how do we pass on respect for what we revere? We introduce those things to people at a young age and we make them a part of life. We have a glass of wine or two with dinner."

"Ah, so we're not doing so bad, then," Scott laughed. "But you do sound so certain! Like a scholar. Sorry, I'm interrupting. Go on. Second point?"

"Second, you need to make this stuff as normal as possible. For beer, show him the recipe. Sugar, malt, hops, tap water. A little bit like Axle was doing with his friends. Yes, Jacqui shared the article with me. She was a little proud, I think. You know what I mean, you do it with your cooking. Jacqui has told me that, too. Absolute nutrition. No mystery. Vegetables and rice, very little sugar, salt and oil. Some beans. These things can be traced straight to someone's garden. The trick is to be slow, take your time, feel the whole, living thing."

Scott poured himself another glass of wine, tilting the bottle in João's direction. He didn't think the younger man would accept, but he nodded and Scott topped up his glass.

"I'm serious. If you want your son to treat alcohol with respect, you need to make him think of it more like a good meal than junk food. Teach him to make it himself. To wait for it."

"Home brewing, then? The idea being that if it takes six weeks for him to get access to the alcohol then he'll respect it more?"

"Maybe. To start, it probably won't taste good enough for him to get too drunk off it. After a few failures there will be a success. And from that, he will likely get drunk. He'll understand more about it though."

"Isn't that more or less what we *have* been doing? Getting him the light beer? I mean, I accept that light beer is very easy. See: I'm not trying to be difficult but I just don't see how it would make a difference. It's only that I feel there's something big I'm missing?"

"No, no. You understand. It's not a solution for his drinking. You don't have much control on that. It's wider. This is more about what you can do for your son in all respects. There's no way to step outside that relationship. He thinks you're a god."

"I can tell you that he doesn't."

"Not a god, then, but you know. More than human. You know what I mean."

"Maybe. I'm not sure. Sometimes I walk into these liquor barns – you know the ones – and shrink at the power of it all. It's horrific. All that power. Not just one genie in a bottle. Thousands. I think of the chaos that'll get released when that alcohol is drunk, and I just want to blow the place up, go in swinging with a golf club."

João topped up their glasses. The bottle was empty. Scott was drunk and he'd stopped trying to truly understand what João was getting at, but it sounded right and he wanted to hear more and to have João listen to him, too.

"So, then, new topic. What would you say to me, then? About Jacqui, about the rest of my life. Love... all of that?"

João leaves

João and Scott continued like this until the clock showed two and the last bottle of wine was empty. That made five bottles. No-one was keeping count. The two men parted ways with a handshake and a hug. Scott brought a blanket and pillow to the couch and took his leave downstairs.

Scott lay on his back and stared at the ceiling. He thought back to his time with Justin and of the collection of their clothes that had fallen to the floor. He considered sneaking upstairs to slip into bed with Jacqui. But he didn't want to wake her and, since it was well past midnight, it was her birthday. He would respect her wishes.

For her part, Jacqui was still awake. She'd tried to go to sleep, but the noise in the lounge had frustrated those efforts. At first, she was amused that Scott was entertaining João. She recalled the way João had conversed with Rothman and she wondered if the same gallantry had developed between him and Scott. But then, when the conversation continued and the men's laughter increased, her curiosity turned to bemusement and, finally, agitation. She couldn't sleep. She picked up the Antarctic book and dedicated herself to it. She galloped through the years of men being explorers and then through the cold war years. Sooner than she would have wished, she turned a page to find the story was over and only the endnotes, references and index remained. She wished the book had better indicated that it was coming to an end. At that point, she set the book aside, climbed from the bed, and pulled on a pair of track pants. She was going to join the men in the lounge. But, as she eased the bedroom door open, she heard her husband offer the couch to João and wish him a good night. She'd missed her chance. It was better for her that she returned to bed.

Under his covers, Axle's phone lit up. He pulled the charger from it and checked the time. Well after midnight. There was a notification from Tanasi.

Sorry that his stupid science
experiment got you in trouble.

All good.
He couldn't have known.

I broke up with him.
Or it was mutual.
It doesn't matter.

You there?

Yeah. I'm here.

I just wanted to say.
Pleasant dreams.

He plugged the phone back in, turned it upside down and drew the covers up around him. He felt a little rush of electricity over his body, from his chest, up his spine and into his head. He pictured her face, sounded out her name. Tanasi. He closed his eyes. He was the first to sleep.

João – a stranger in this house, really, despite it all – stepped out of his jeans and reclined on the couch. He closed his eyes and thought about his place in the world. His advice to Scott had been well intentioned but had he, himself, been living by it? What kept him in balance? He was not one for nostalgia but thoughts of himself at Axle's age came back to him.

João didn't know what the time was when he finally decided that sleep would not come and it was pointless to stay. He rose, pulled on his jeans, then socks, and crept to the door. He made only the faintest of sounds, and the house around him made no sound. He pulled on his shoes, gently eased the door away from its frame, walked outside and – just as gently – put the door back in its place.

The air was still wet, but the rains had stopped. The cool southerly had swung around to a warm breeze from the north. He walked away from the house, the snib on the gate clanging as he left.

João paused on the path, recalling his last conversation with Scott and knowing this would be the final time he would see the family. He climbed to Upland Rd, dodging the dampness of the overgrown agapanthuses. The orange light of the city swirled against the clouds above him but this was no early morning apparition. The swirl came from a set of lights atop roadworks trucks. The street had been closed off and the trucks were flanked by orange cones prohibiting cars from taking their usual streetside park beneath the elms or outside the school.

The people laying the new seal paid no attention to João as he wandered towards them. Perhaps they knew not to disturb ghosts of the night. The smell of fresh bitumen assailed him, while the warmth from the newly laid tar made him feel like he might be walking across a lava field. As he walked up to the workers and then past them, he strode into the middle of the road and closed his eyes. He imagined lava fields like this, with molten rock beneath the thin crust of the road's surface. The surface was vast and the journey precarious. His life hung in the balance. At any moment, a plume of fire could shoot out of the ground, or a new flow of lava could pour down from the hill above. He was neither scared nor reluctant. It was his road to walk.

João opened his eyes and stopped. His spine ached at the base of his neck. He was right to have left the couch. Ahead of him were more road cone sentinels, and a sign directing traffic up Plunket Street. Beyond this, were other early morning dwellers, a truck delivering milk, a man smoking while leaning against a taxi, a pair of young women in tight plastic skirts staggering towards him. Someone had tagged "climate justice now!" on the side of the milk van and, when he walked past the taxi driver, the man tried to solicit a fare, but broke off mid-sentence with a sigh. João hurried on until all that was left of Upland Rd was the downhill to the city and sea. From his vantage, he saw the lowlands with their flashing oranges and reflector tape. He saw the ones who worked below the surface, plugging pipes that had sat beneath for a century, unmolested until they'd given up. He saw the other people who worked on the surface, using the fire hydrant access points to hose the overflown shit into the drains that led to the harbour. Other workers still – not in orange, nor red, nor white – took samples from the harbour and measured them against viable standards. He pictured the Mayor and the Council and all the words and infrastructure that allegedly held the city in place.

João bent down, removed his shoes, peeled off his socks and started on his way. He knew a shortcut home, down a pathway to the edge of Aro, skipping into the city.

Acknowledgements

Down from Upland was first conceived and written under the title, *The Undrinkable Light Beer of Bingeing* and I'd like to think some of the spirit of that title lives on in the book.

I want to thank early readers Brannavan Gnanalingam, Stephen Parry, Hannah August, Sarah Webster, Josh Wright and Thomasin Sleigh for your insights and counsel. Thanks also to Pip Adam for writing a letter recommending the book and to Alan Ibell for allowing the use of "Ascendants" on the cover. Paul Neason touched up our layout and I thank him for his kind guidance. Thanks also go to Johanna for proofing, to Brydan for refreshing our promo strategies and to Matt H for organising things when Bran and I can't.

I want to thank the readers of *Rat King Landlord* who encouraged me to write a sequel (which I haven't) and who, I hope, will be satisfied with this demure novel on the follies of moderation and communicative reason.

My thanks to the rest of the Lawrence & Gibson collective for their co-operative energies and to the Rebel Press collective and related publishers for being a home from which this, and other books, emerge. Thanks to those who helped Rebel Press buy a flash new printer and to John for making the guillotine slice smoothly.

Thanks to the lovely folks in the wider literary sector, especially the media folk and festival programmers who ensure audiences are appraised of our books.

Thanks to my colleagues at New Zealand Red Cross and the Centre for Asia Pacific Refugee Studies at the University of Auckland for artful collaboration on issues of justice and freedom.

Warm appreciations to Creative New Zealand for a publishing grant that allowed this book, and others, to start life with a push start.

On top of those already mentioned, my personal thanks to Chris, Hannah, Dylan, Jack, Sasha, Anna, Kirsten, Max, Emily, Ibrahim, Golriz, Cally, Pera and Willie, Ben, Hannah, Karam, Tariq, Eva, Rachel, Ash, Sarah, Anna, Ollie, Dick, Heleyni, Jesse, Sara, Matt, Jessie, Erin, Kelly, Wayne, Behrouz, Charlotte, Erena, Balamohan and Sophie. Close contacts at Maida Vale, Shannon Street, Rochester and at Athfield's. Family up north and down south. Apologies to anyone I may have left off this list. I'm genuinely exhausted right now. We'll thank you at the launch.

Finally, I want to gesture to Lachlan, Rhys, Hayden and Cody who made the last years of high school much better than they might have been as we crafted a sense of gleeful, alcohol-fuelled experimentation that I drew on for much of the scenes involving Axle and his friends. Respect, also, to the sober ones and those who have had their disagreements (and more) with alcohol and other drugs.

"On her first day the sky had a salmon tint to it; after the rain, and before the cloud entirely cleared, as if it had been put into a washing machine with roses. Someone was probably really annoyed at the way they had run. Aljce parked in the asphalt car park outside the Therapy Hub. She was looking forward to her new job. It would be an exciting adventure with new challenges."

Aljce in Therapy Land is the first novel from Alice Tawhai. She is best known for her short story collections *Dark Jelly*, *Luminous* and *Festival of Miracles* (all released through Huia). The story traverses workplace bullying, online relationships and stoned friendships, with a good measure of Wonderland added in. It was longlisted for the 2022 Jann Medlicott Acorn Foundation Prize for Fiction at the Ockham New Zealand Book Awards.

www.lawrenceandgibson.co.nz

Slow Down, You're Here

Brannavan Gnanalingam

Kavita is stuck in a dead-end marriage. A parent of two small kids, she is the family's main breadwinner. An old flame unexpectedly offers her a week away in Waiheke. If she were to go, she's not sure when - or if - she'd come back.

"A quietly virtuosic demonstration of shifting tones within one story." Paul Little, *North & South*

"It's an inferno alright. A cracking good one. Many a regular human has speculated on just how Gnanalingam does it. *Sprigs*, his acclaimed fifth novel, only came out, what, yesterday? But hold on to your babies, folks, because he's done it again." Claire Mabey, *The Spinoff*

Brannavan Gnanalingam is a novelist and lawyer based in Wellington. His last three novels have all been longlisted for the Jann Medlicott Acorn Foundation Prize for Fiction at the Ockham New Zealand Book Awards, including the shortlisted *Sprigs* and *Sodden Downstream*.

www.lawrenceandgibson.co.nz

Colossal rats invade from the town belt! Your rent is up but everyone is calling it a summer of love. Vivid posters incite residents to an evening of mayhem. For many years rats have contented themselves with scraps. But as summer heats up and the cost of living skyrockets, we can no longer ignore that our friends are seeking their own rung on the property ladder.

Rat King Landlord was Murdoch Stephens' first novel under his own name. He has previously published numerous books with Lawrence & Gibson as Richard Meros, including *On the conditions and possibilities of Helen Clark taking me as her Young Lover* ("The underground publishing hit of the decade" *NZ Listener*). He is also the author of the non-fiction *Doing Our Bit: the Campaign to Double the Refugee Quota* (BWB Texts) based on the campaign he founded in 2013.

www.lawrenceandgibson.co.nz